The Acclaimed Warlock Series
by Christopher Stasheff

"FRESH...WELL-WRITTEN AND ENTERTAINING!"
—W. D. Stevens, *Fantasy Review*

"ENCHANTING ADVENTURE...ONE STARTS TO GET THE FEELING OF WHAT IT'S LIKE TO BE A CHILD WITH MAGICAL POWERS."
—*Fanzine*

"IT'S REFRESHING TO SEE A FANTASY HERO AIDED BY HIS WIFE AND CHILDREN!"
—Rick Osborne, *Fantasy Review*

The series includes:
ESCAPE VELOCITY

THE WARLOCK IN SPITE OF HIMSELF

KING KOBOLD REVIVED

THE WARLOCK UNLOCKED

THE WARLOCK ENRAGED

THE WARLOCK WANDERING

THE WARLOCK IS MISSING

THE WARLOCK HERETICAL

THE WARLOCK'S COMPANION

THE WARLOCK INSANE

THE WARLOCK ROCK

WARLOCK AND SON

D0596328

THE WARLOCK IS MISSING

CHRISTOPHER STASHEFF

ACE BOOKS, NEW YORK

This book is an Ace original edition, and has never been previously published.

THE WARLOCK IS MISSING

An Ace Book / published by arrangement with the author

PRINTING HISTORY
Ace edition / September 1986

ISBN: 0-441-84826-5

ACE®
Ace Books are published by The Berkley Publishing Group, 200 Madison Avenue, New York, New York 10016.
ACE and the "A" design are trademarks belonging to Charter Communications, Inc.

PRINTED IN THE UNITED STATES OF AMERICA

15   14   13   12   11   10   9   8   7   6

To
Isobel-Marie
for Her Unicorn
and
with thanks to
the New Jersey Science Fiction Society

1

Once upon a time, there were three little warlocks and a witch, and they lost their mommy and daddy.

Well, they didn't lose them, really. Their parents went out for the night, and left them with an elf for a babysitter. The elf's name was Puck (it was really Robin Goodfellow, but most people preferred his nickname), and he was very mischievous. He was so mischievous that the children made sure they did whatever he told them to, even though they could all work magic of their own. They even went to bed on time.

But they didn't go to sleep. The boys lay awake talking to each other in whispers, and the girl came in to join them—she had a bedroom of her own, but it wasn't nearly as much fun as her brothers'. There weren't any other children in it.

"They should have been home ere now," Magnus whispered. He was the eldest—twelve years old.

"Nay, surely 'tis not so late," Cordelia protested. She was nine—nearly as old as Magnus, as she reminded him at least twice a day.

"'Tis late enow." Geoffrey was gazing out the window at the stars. "The Plow is over Cuchullain's Hill." He was only seven, but that was old enough to realize that the whole sky seems to turn like a great wheel during the night, and to remember where the star-pictures called "constellations" have moved to, every hour.

Cordelia frowned. "Where could they have gone?"

Magnus shrugged. "Mayhap a band of trolls leaped upon them from hiding."

"Poor trolls," Geoffrey sighed.

"Thou dost but regret that thou wast not with them," Cordelia accused.

"In some part," Geoffrey admitted. "Yet thou must needs own that any band of trolls would come off much the worst, were they to go up against our parents."

Their mother, Gwendylon Gallowglass, was a witch, though a very pretty one; and their father, Rod Gallowglass, was a warlock, which is what you call a man who has powers like a witch's.

"Mayhap the King and Queen have summoned them," Gregory pointed out. He was the youngest, only five, but he already knew that the King and Queen of their country sometimes called on the children's parents to help them, when their kingdom of Gramarye was in trouble.

"Aye!" Cordelia sat bolt-upright, her eyes gleaming. "Mayhap the Abbot and his monks have called up the barons 'gainst the King and Queen again!"

"Or an evil sorcerer may once more have risen 'gainst them." Gregory's eyes lit.

"Or mayhap an army of monsters hath come out of the forests!" Geoffrey grinned. He liked armies. Monsters, too.

"Or mayhap ghosts have come haunting the castle," Magnus cried.

"Or mayhap," rumbled a deep voice from the doorway, "the witch and the warlock are so pleased by themselves, with no children to pester them, that they have stayed longer than they had planned, amidst the flowers and the cool forest air— and mayhap four naughty children have kept themselves waking when they should have fallen asleep!"

The boys dived under their covers, and Cordelia dived under Magnus's bed.

Their foot-and-a-half babysitter strode into the room. "Shame upon thee, then! Can thy parents not enjoy a single evening to themselves, but thou must needs bedevil them with thy guessing, even though they be not here?"

"We were not thinking *at* them, Puck," Geoffrey protested. All four of the children were mind-readers, who could also put their own thoughts into other people's minds.

"Nay," said Puck, "but thou wast biding in wakefulness, belike to spring out upon them when they did return."

"We would do no such thing," Magnus said indignantly. After all, he'd only been toying with the idea.

"Be certain thou wilt not," Puck assured him. "Now lie still and close thine eyes—and thy mouths also! Or I shall close them for thee!"

The boys instantly squeezed their eyes shut. They remembered the last time Geoffrey had talked back to Puck. It had taken Mama an hour to figure out how to get the padlock off his lips.

"And thou, damsel! To thy chamber!" Puck stabbed his finger toward the doorway.

The room was silent for a moment; then Cordelia rolled out from under Magnus's bed and sprang to her feet. "Thou spoilsport, Robin!" And she flounced out of the room.

Puck gazed after her as though he were considering how she'd look with goggle eyes and webbed feet; but he must have decided against it, for he turned back to rumble, "Sleep! Or the hobgoblin will catch thee!"

"What," said Magnus, "is the hobgoblin?"

"I am," Puck snapped. "Now sleep!" And he slammed the door.

The boys were still as mice for three minutes.

Then Geoffrey whispered, "Dost thou think he might truly..."

The door crashed open, and Puck boomed, "Sleep!"

They slept.

When they came down to breakfast the next morning, they found a very worried-looking Puck sitting by the hearth, knuckling his chin. They gathered around him, wide-eyed and silent. Finally, Magnus asked, "Have they not come home, then?"

Puck dismissed the notion with a gesture. "'Tis naught. Belike they'll step in the door ere the sun's up."

Gregory darted a quick glance at the window. "'Tis risen, Puck—and thou knowest not where they be."

"Not know!?!!" Puck sat up straight, glaring in indignation. "Whence cometh such a thought?"

Gregory shook his head. "An thou didst know, thy face would not show such concern."

"Thou seest too quickly for my liking."

"Or mine," Gregory agreed, "for if thou knowest not where they be, they are gone."

"What?" "Nay!" "What sayest thou!" his brothers and sister cried.

But Gregory only shook his head. "If the Wee Folk know not where our parents be, they be not within this Land of Gramarye."

"Why, how dost thou riddle that?" Puck studied the boy's face.

Gregory shrugged. "'Tis plainly seen—for what one of the Wee Folk know, all will know presently. And naught doth happen that they know not of, for there are pixies, elves, and fairies throughout the length and breadth of this kingdom, so that there lies not a square yard of ground in all our Isle of Gramarye that the Wee Folk see not. Thus if thou dost not know where our parents be, they be not in this land."

"But they cannot be gone!" Cordelia cried. "How should we manage without them?"

"How should the kingdom manage?" Puck breathed, for Gramarye had many enemies that only the High Warlock and his wife kept at bay.

"And how—how canst thou say it?" Geoffrey threw up his hands in exasperation. "How canst thou stand there with so bland a face, cheerfully consigning thy mother and father to who knows what fate?"

"Nay!" Big brother Magnus instantly clapped an arm around Gregory and pressed him against his side. "Be not so cruel to thine own brother! Belike he's as frighted as thou . . ."

"I am never frighted!"

"Alarmed, then," Magnus said between his teeth. "As alarmed as thou, yet brave enough not to show it."

"Yet I am not alarmed, neither." Gregory looked up at his brother. "Nor am I frighted—for they have been gone aforetime, have they not? And ever they've returned."

They all stilled, staring at him. Then Magnus said carefully, "Thou dost remember that?"

"Thou wast but a babe!" Cordelia burst out. "Aged scarce half a year! Nay, hardly do I recall that, myself!"

"Nor do I." Gregory shook his head, wide-eyed. "I have only some odd feeling that 'tis so."

"A memory, but one that lies so deeply he doth ken it not," Puck explained. "Yet 'tis so, lad—thy parents did vanish, and thy brothers and sister with them."

What he did not say was that it had been baby Gregory who had anchored his family to Gramarye. They had been whisked away to another world, a land of magic, and had only been able to return because Gregory's infant mind, longing for his mother, had reached out through the emptiness between the worlds to pull them back—with a power amazing in any person, let alone a baby.

"They did vanish, and they did return." Gregory smiled. He didn't smile often. His brothers and sister found themselves smiling too, even though they were nowhere nearly as certain as he was. In fact, when they stopped to think about it, a feeling of dread began to seep through them.

Geoffrey couldn't allow that. "Out upon them!" he cried. "Seek and find!"

Magnus and Cordelia cheered, and dashed for the door.

"Now I cry HOLD!" Puck roared.

They froze, with Magnus's hand on the latch. "But Puck —an our parents be strayed, 'tis our duty to seek them!"

"'Tis thy duty to do as they have bade thee!" The elf seemed to flicker like a candle flame, and was suddenly standing with his back against the door, fists on his hips, glaring at them. "They have charged thee to stay, and obey my commands—so stay thou shalt, and stay I shall, until their return!"

Storm clouds began to gather in the boys' faces.

Cordelia tried reason. "They did not know they would vanish, Puck. Assuredly, then, they would have wished us to seek them."

"Assuredly, if their enemies have become strong enough to capture them, they would wish thee safe at home! And safe thou shalt be, guarded by legions of elves!"

"Legions?" Gregory stared, wide-eyed.

Then he dashed to the window, to peer out. Geoffrey was right behind him—"legions" meant an army. Cordelia and Magnus wavered, then ran for the window too.

They stared out at an empty garden and a meadow beyond it, with the forest rising up at its far edge.

"There's naught there!" Geoffrey cried in disappointment.

"Nay, there is," Puck assured them. "Thou mayest not see them, but there's not a foot of that meadow or garden that hath not its elf with his sling, or a fairy with her dart. *Thou* couldst wander all day, and see never a one of them—but let a stranger approach, and he'll stumble and fall, never to rise again."

Magnus turned slowly, his face set and expressionless. "Are they to keep us penned within, also?"

Puck answered with a sour smile. "Credit me with some sense, warlock-ling! I know thy sister can fly away on her broomstick, and that any of thou lads can fly without one—or disappear, and reappear miles away. Nay, I'd not seek to pen thee here by force."

"Yet thou wilt seek to hold us," Cordelia said quietly.

Puck nodded. "I will hold thee by thy love of thy parents —for look you, what was their last command to thee?"

The children were silent, scowling at the floor and scuffing their toes.

"What did they *say?*" Puck demanded.

"That we should stay," Cordelia admitted, as though the words were dragged out of her, "and obey thee."

And they did obey him, all that day. Two wizened little women, scarcely a foot high, popped up to make breakfast, and two more to make dinner. It took three to make supper, though.

And all the while, the children did their best to find things to do. They tried a game of hide and seek, but their hearts just weren't in it; Magnus just barely managed to make himself look like a little apple tree, and Gregory did so poor a job of casting his glamour that Cordelia lifted her head, saw the large toadstool next to her, and scowled. "Thou art not to hide 'round my base, Gregory! 'Tis thou must be 'it' now!"

Freeze-tag was worse; they couldn't summon up the energy to freeze a beetle. And when they tried to play catch, Magnus's and Cordelia's minds kept wandering, so the ball would fall to the ground in the middle of a throw.

Finally, in desperation, Puck sat them down and gave them lessons. This was bad enough while they were angry and grumbling; but it became worse when they became puzzled.

"But, Robin—Papa says there are ninety-two elements that endure," Cordelia said.

Gregory nodded. "And some of those are so rare, they are never seen."

"Thy father!" Puck wrinkled his nose in disgust. "He, with his outlandish notions of what is real and what dreamlike! Children, reach about thee, and feel what is there! Canst thou see this 'uranium' that he speaketh of, or this 'aluminum'? Nay! But thou canst feel the earth 'neath thy fingers, and the air blown against thy cheek as a wind! I tell thee, there be but four elements, as there have ever been—earth, water, air, and fire!"

"Yet what is rock, then?"

"Only earth, packed tightly."

"And what's a tree?"

"Why, a thing compounded out of earth and water!"

"And iron?"

Puck shuddered; iron was poison to elves. "Let us speak rather of copper. Where dost thou find it? Why, where rocks are put into fire! What should it be, then, but a thing made up of earth and fire?"

And so it went. Puck had very definite views about everything in nature, and the children began to become interested, in spite of themselves.

"Now, there do be three trees only that do signify," Puck lectured, "Oak, Ash, and Thorn."

Gregory frowned. "What of the pine?"

"Fit only to be brought within doors, for the Yuletide."

"What of the holly and the ivy?"

"The one's a bush, the other a vine. I speak of trees!"

"What of the briar, and the rose?"

What could Puck do then but sigh, and tell them all the tale, the sad, winding story of Fair Margaret and Sweet William, of their meeting and courtship, of his leaving her to wed another woman, and Sweet Margaret's death, and Sweet William's, and the briar and the rose sprouting from their graves, to climb to the top of the church steeple and twine in a true lover's knot.

Cordelia sat enthralled throughout it, but the boys did begin to seem a little restless; so of course, for them, Puck had to tell the tale of the child Merlin, and his capture by the evil King Vortigern, of the tower that would not stand and the two dragons that slept under it. From there, one tale led to another, of course—of the boy Arthur, and his growing to become a king who brought peace and plenty to a strife-torn England; of Lancelot, his bravest knight, and his saving of the sweet Elaine; of their son Galahad, and his quest for the Holy Grail; and of Arthur's nephew Gawain, and the Green Knight.

"And what of his brothers?" Geoffrey demanded. "What of Agravaine, and Gareth and Gaheris?"

"Ah, but if thou hast heard of them aforetime," Puck sighed, "wherefore shouldst thou need to hear of them again?"

"Because the tale is always filled with wonder and magic!"

"But most so when *thou* dost tell it, Robin." Cordelia already knew the virtues of a compliment.

So did Puck, but he puffed out his chest and grinned anyway. "Ah, but I've had such practice at the telling of them—hundreds of years! Yet the hour groweth late, and I think I smell a supper cooking."

Four little heads snapped up; four small noses sniffed the

evening air. Then four voices yelped, and the boys disappeared in miniature thunderclaps. Cordelia leaped on her broomstick, and sped like an arrow toward the front door, crying, " 'Tis not fair! Thou must not commence without me!"

Puck heaved a long, shaky sigh. "Eh! I've kept them busy for this one day, at least. Yet how shall I manage for the *morrow?*"

But the next day took care of itself; for Cordelia awoke before the sun was up, and sprang to her window to look for her parents—and, by the cool, moist gray light that comes before dawn, she saw, in their garden, a unicorn.

She was tall and slender, milk-white, with a golden mane and a gilded horn; and as a cry of delight welled up within Cordelia, the unicorn lifted her head and looked right into Cordelia's eyes. The girl froze in wonder.

Then the unicorn turned away, lowering her head to graze among Mama's flowers, and Cordelia rushed to pull on a dress, hose, and slippers, and ran out into the garden, still lacing her bodice.

She skidded to a halt, realizing again that she might scare the unicorn away; but she had nothing to fear. The unicorn stood quietly, watching her, chewing on a mouthful of sweet clover, and Cordelia caught her breath, enchanted by its beauty.

Then the unicorn lowered her head to the clover, and Cordelia felt saddened, because she could no longer see the great, lovely eyes. She plumped down in the grass, sitting on her heels, and pulled a patch of sweet dill from the herb-bed. She held it out in her open palm, calling softly, "Come. Oh, come, I beg thee, most beauteous one—for I long to stroke thy velvet cheek, and caress thy silken mane!"

The unicorn turned, lifting her head, and looked right into Cordelia's eyes again. The girl watched, scarcely daring to breathe, as the unicorn came toward her slowly, one delicate step at a time, until she stood right in front of Cordelia, and slowly lowered her muzzle to accept the dill. A thrill shot through Cordelia as the unicorn's soft, gentle nose tickled her palm, and she hurried to pull some more dill with her left hand. The unicorn took that, too, staring into Cordelia's eyes. Greatly daring, she reached out slowly to rest her hand upon the muzzle. The unicorn moved her head, letting Cordelia's hand rub against her cheek, and the girl stroked the velvet smoothness, breathing in delight, "Oh! Thou art so beautiful!"

The unicorn bowed her head, accepting the tribute and pawing the turf. Cordelia reached out her other hand to touch the golden mane.

The unicorn's head snapped up, and Cordelia snatched her hand back, afraid she had offended. Then she saw that the unicorn wasn't moving away, but was staring toward the house. Following the direction of her gaze, she saw her brothers, standing together just outside the back door, wide-eyed in wonder.

Cordelia couldn't speak aloud, for fear of frightening the unicorn; so she pressed her lips tight in anger and thought at her brothers, *Thou great oafs! Begone, ere thou dost scare her away!*

She doth not seem afrighted, Magnus thought back at Cordelia, *nor ought she; we come only to watch.*

But Geoffrey's thought came right after: *Ah! How fine a thing 'twould be, to ride so fine a mount!* And he stepped forward, raising a hand.

NAY! Cordelia's thought fairly shrieked. *Thou wilt afright her!*

And, true enough, the unicorn moved back a pace. Geoffrey froze.

A frown puckered little Gregory's brow. *Was it truly Geoffrey caused her to move? Let me see.* And he took a step.

Thou little lummox! Cordelia fumed. *Wilt thou leave her to me!*

The unicorn moved another step away.

Why, she is not thine! Geoffrey thought, in indignation. *Thou canst not bid us not to touch her!*

Yet the unicorn *can.* Magnus pressed a hand against Geoffrey's chest to hold him back. *Cordelia's right in this—we do afright the beast.*

But Gregory shook his head, and whispered aloud, "She is not frighted."

The unicorn's gaze riveted on the youngest.

"See." Gregory spoke a little louder. "She doth hear me, yet doth not flee."

"Then she will let us come nigh her!" Geoffrey took another step.

Nay! Cordelia thought furiously; and sure enough, the unicorn stepped away again.

Magnus pushed Geoffrey back, and the younger boy

scowled, sulking. "I thought Gregory did say she did not fear us."

"Nor doth she." The youngest still sat on his heels in the grass, gazing at the unicorn. "Still, she will abide us no closer than we are now."

"Yet she did come nigh Cordelia!"

Gregory nodded. "And will again, I doubt not. Attempt it, sister."

Cordelia stared at him as though he were crazy. Then she frowned, musing, and turned back to the unicorn. Slowly, she stepped toward it.

The unicorn stood still, as though it were waiting.

Thrilled, Cordelia took another step, then another and another.

Still the unicorn waited, unmoving.

Finally, Cordelia's outstretched hand touched the unicorn's neck, and she stepped close, reaching up to stroke. "Oh, thou hast let me come nigh thee!"

"'Tis not..." Geoffrey started to yell; but Magnus clamped a hand over his mouth—with the palm cupped, so his brother couldn't bite it. Geoffrey glared at him, thinking furiously, *'Tis not fair! Wherefore ought it to allow* her *to approach, and not us?*

"'Tis the way of unicorns," Gregory answered. "I mind me, for I read it in a book of a time."

Geoffrey glared at him. Gregory had been reading for two years now, and it drove Geoffrey crazy.

"They will allow maids to approach," Gregory explained, "yet not lads."

Geoffrey turned away, fuming.

The unicorn lay down, tucking his legs beneath her body.

Cordelia stared in surprise. Then a radiant smile spread over her face and, very carefully, she leaned forward, resting her weight on the unicorn's back.

"Now 'tis *thou* who wilt afright her!" Geoffrey hissed; but Cordelia turned slowly till she was sitting sideways on the unicorn.

Magnus stiffened. "Cordelia! I prithee, come away! For of a sudden, I do sense danger!"

"Pooh!" she scoffed. "Thou art but jealous!"

"Nay!" Magnus protested. "'Tis more than that! I . . ."

So smoothly that she seemed to float, the unicorn stood up again. Cordelia gasped with joy.

"Cordelia, thou art but mean!" Geoffrey cried in outrage. "Thou art selfish, aye, and spiteful!"

"'Tis the unicorn's choice, not mine," she returned. "Am I to blame if she doth find thee vile?"

"Cordelia, I prithee!" Magnus insisted, really alarmed. "Where might she take thee?"

"Why, wheresoe'er she will," Cordelia answered; and sure enough, the unicorn turned away toward the forest.

The shouting brought Puck out, rubbing sleep from his eyes and scowling. "What coil is this?"

"A monster doth abduct our sister!" Magnus cried.

The unicorn trotted away.

Puck stared after it. "A monster? Where?"

"There!" Geoffrey shouted, and he ran after the unicorn. "Thou one-horned thief! Come back with my sister!"

"Nay, Geoffrey! Fly!" Magnus leaped into the air.

Geoffrey looked up at him, startled. Then he grinned, and leaped ten feet up. "What ails me, brother? I had forgot!"

Gregory sped toward his two brothers like a stone from a slingshot. Together, they darted after the unicorn.

With a crack like a gunshot, Puck appeared right in front of them, hovering in midair. "Halt, younglings! Where dost *thou* think to go?"

"Why, after the beast who doth bear off our sister!" Magnus said. "Do not seek to bar us, Robin! She's endangered!"

"Endangered! Nay, speak sense! Ne'er hath a unicorn offered harm to a maiden!"

"If 'tis not from the beast itself, 'tis from something it doth bear her to! I tell thee, Puck, I feel dread in every bone!"

Puck hesitated. He had some idea of Magnus's powers, but nothing definite; not even the boy's own parents knew the limits of his abilities. He could do things that no Gramarye warlock had ever been able to do—nor any witch either, for that matter. Why might he not also be able to see the future? Puck was sure the boy's father had one of his nonsensical words for the power—as though the talent would not be there if there were no word for it!

But whatever danger there was, Puck was quite sure he could handle it—unless it were something that needed a score of elves. And if it did, why, he had the score at hand. He weighed that chance of manageable danger against the exasperation of trying to keep four young magic-workers occupied for another day, and decided that the danger was definitely the lesser risk. "Well enough, then, thou mayest pursue. For if there's any slightest danger..."

But he was talking to empty air. While he had hesitated, the three young warlocks had disappeared with a thunderclap.

"Owls and batwings!" Puck cried in exasperation, and darted off after the unicorn.

2

Through the forest went the unicorn, so smoothly that she seemed to glide. Dabs of sunlight lay here and there about, making the green of the leaves seem darker, but filling the woods with brightness. Cordelia rode blithely through the cool shade, singing with joy, happily ignoring her brothers, who flitted through the trees to either side, calling for her to stop.

Puck had vanished.

Then Cordelia rode out of the trees and into a village.

It was very small, perhaps a dozen houses, set against the foot of a rocky slope, with open meadow between itself and the forest. Cordelia called out happily, expecting people to look up in amazement when they saw her astride her unicorn.

Only silence answered.

Cordelia lost her smile. She stared ahead, realizing that she could see no one in the village, not a soul.

Gregory swooped toward her. The unicorn shied, and he swerved away, calling, "Cordelia, none live in that village— and there hath been fire! Turn back!"

"I cannot," Cordelia answered. "'Tis the unicorn who doth go where she wist, not I who guide her." Though, truth to tell, she suspected that her mount would have turned aside, if Cordelia had asked it of her.

Now that they were closer, she could see the remains of the fire Gregory had spoken of. The walls of the cottages were scorched, their thatched roofs burned away, leaving only charred timbers. A huge black blemish hid the village common; what was left of its green field was brown and brittle grass. Doors swung ajar; bowls and tools lay scattered where they had fallen.

The deserted village lay silent; the only sound was the sigh of the wind. A shutter clattered against a window, then sagged open again. In the forest behind them, birds sang—but none here.

Magnus hovered near a roof-beam, reaching out to touch it. He snatched his hand away with an oath. "'Tis yet hot, and embers glow. This fire burned not long agone."

Geoffrey nodded, landing near the square, looking about him. "The doors may swing in the wind, but none have torn from their hinges—nor are the wooden bowls and tool-handles weathered."

"They have left with no plan aforetime." Gregory stared about him.

The unicorn halted, nose pointed toward the mountainside.

"'Tis here that she hath meant to come, I think." Cordelia's voice was low. "And she did intend to bring us here."

"'Tis reason enough to go, and quickly," Gregory whispered.

"Nay!" Magnus's heels jolted against the charred earth as he landed. "I would we had not come—but now that we have, we must discover what hath happed in this place. There may be folk in need of such aid as we can offer."

"Nay!" Puck popped up from a burned-out bush. "Thou must needs go back, and quickly! For the elves of this village have told me what hath happed this night past!"

"Then say!" "What was't?" "Tell, Robin!" The boys clustered around him.

"A dragon."

The boys only stared. Cordelia watched, wide-eyed, from the back of her unicorn.

Puck nodded. "A great, vile monster it was, fifty feet from nose to tail-tip, with fangs of steel and fiery breath!" He whirled, pointing to the mountainside. "Seest thou where it did crawl away?"

The children looked and, for the first time, noticed a broad trail of scorched earth that led away from the village and up the rocky slope, winding away out of sight around the curve of the hill.

"And it lurks up there still?" Geoffrey whispered.

Puck shrugged. "Who may say? Never have the Wee Folk seen the monster aforetime. Mayhap 'tis gone again."

"Or mayhap it doth lurk about the countryside," said Geoffrey, "awaiting the unwary passerby."

Huge feet pounded the dusty lane behind them, and a massive body clashed against a burned-out wall.

The children spun about, hearts hammering; the unicorn

whirled to face whatever came, and Puck leaped out in front of them all, arms poised to hurl his most dire spell.

An enormous black horse came around a cottage and out into the village square.

The children stared, frozen.

Then they whooped with relief and ran to leap onto the animal, throwing their arms around its neck and drumming their heels against its sides. "Fess!" "How good art thou to come!" "We should ha' known thou wouldst follow!"

Fess was their father's horse, and a very strange and wonderful horse he was. Papa said he was made of steel, and that the horsehair covering him was only put on with something like glue. Papa said he was a "robot," but the children weren't sure what that meant. They knew it was something magical, though, because Fess could do things that no ordinary horse could—and one of them was talking. Only to Papa, usually —but he could let Mama and the children hear him if he wanted to. Inside their minds.

"You should have known I would not let you wander without me, children," he scolded. "And you were very naughty to stray off by yourselves."

"But we are not alone," Gregory assured him. "Puck is here."

"And this!" Cordelia whirled away, suddenly remembering her unicorn. She threw her arms about the beast's neck, as though she were afraid it would get away. "I have a new friend, Fess!"

The big black horse stared at the unicorn for a moment. Then his knees began to tremble. "But . . . unicorns do not . . . exist. . . ." Suddenly, his head dropped like a stone, and his legs locked stiff. His head swung gently between his fetlocks.

"We should have warned him," Gregory said.

"We should indeed." Magnus heaved a sigh. "Ever doth he have such a seizure, when he doth encounter something that he thinks cannot be real."

Puck nodded. "So he did when first he did espy an elf. Yet I should think he would have become accustomed to the sight of strange new beings."

"Papa said 'tis one of the nicest things about Fess," Cordelia explained, "that he never doth grow used to strange new sights."

Magnus groped beneath Fess's saddle horn for the big lump

in his backbone. He found it and pressed hard. Something clicked, and Fess slowly raised his head. "I . . . had a . . . seizure . . . did I not?"

"Thou didst," Magnus replied, "because thou didst see a unicorn."

Slowly, Fess turned toward the snow-white animal. "Unicorns . . . are mythical . . ."

"Mayhap *she* would think the same of iron horses," Cordelia said, irritated.

The unicorn *was* eyeing Fess warily, and her nostrils were flaring.

"I can comprehend her feelings," Fess murmured.

Geoffrey exchanged a glance with Magnus. "Ought we to tell him?"

"You surely must!" Fess's head swiveled, the great eyes staring at him. "What should I know?"

"We are not sure thou shouldst." Magnus avoided Fess's eyes. "It might cause thee to have another seizure."

Fess was still a moment, then said, "I have braced my system for my senses tell me things that I know cannot be true. Since I am prepared, I will not have a seizure. Tell me, please."

Magnus exchanged one last glance with Geoffrey, then gestured about them. "Dost thou see signs of fire?"

"Of course. This village has suffered a major conflagration. No doubt that is why its people have fled."

"But it has burned out." Gregory tugged at Fess's mane in a bid for attention. "Would not they have come back?"

Fess was still a moment, then nodded. "One would think so, yes. Why do you think they have not?"

Gregory exchanged glances with Magnus, then said, " 'Tis because of what did cause this fire."

"And what was that?" Fess's tone hardened.

The boys locked gazes with one another, and Magnus said, "There is no easy way to say it." He turned to Fess. "It was a dragon."

Fess stood very still. They all watched, waiting in apprehension.

Finally, the robot said, "I have accepted the idea. I do not understand how a dragon may exist, but I recognize the possibility."

The four children heaved a huge sigh of relief.

Puck frowned up at the horse. "Tell us, then, O Fount of

Wisdom—how shall four children and an elf do battle with a dragon?"

"Do not forget the unicorn." Fess turned to look at Cordelia's mount. "It is a dragon's natural enemy, according to tradition."

Gregory stared. "Thou dost not mean to say that, because the dragon came, the unicorn appeared to battle it!"

Fess was silent for a moment, then slowly nodded. "It is possible. Given the buried powers of the people of Gramarye and the potentialities of the environment—yes. It could have happened as you say."

"But the unicorn could not oppose the dragon by herself!" Cordelia cried. "Surely she is too delicate!"

"Do not underestimate her," Fess advised. "The legends say the unicorn had great strength."

"Yet there's truth in what Cordelia doth say." Geoffrey frowned. "This unicorn knew she stood in need of aid to fight so fearsome a monster—and therefore sought us out."

"But how could she have known of us, if she is but newly come?" Cordelia demanded.

They looked at each other, puzzled. As for Puck and Fess, if they suspected the answer, they kept it to themselves.

Then Magnus shrugged. "However 'twas, she knew of us. Can we not then lend her the aid that she doth seek?"

"We can," Puck said slowly, "but I've some doubt as to our powers. Mayhap all the elves in Gramarye could overwhelm the dragon—but there would be grievous losses. I misdoubt me an we poor few could bring it to defeat—and I'm loathe to try. If one of thou wast hurt, children, thy mother and father would ne'er forgive me. There might yet be elves in Gramarye, but the Puck would not be amongst them!"

Geoffrey scowled. "Surely thou art not afeard!"

"Nay, but I've some small amount of sense."

"He speaks wisely," Fess agreed. "We are too few to overcome such a monster by brute force—and you, children, might well be killed in the attempt. If we are to assist the unicorn and fight the dragon, it must be by trickery."

Cordelia, Magnus, and Geoffrey just stared at each other—but Gregory plumped down cross-legged and closed his eyes.

Geoffrey frowned. "What doth he? 'Tis no time to . . ."

"Hush!" Magnus held up a hand, palm outward. "Let him be!"

Gregory opened his eyes. "'Tis his flame. An we put out his fire, he will sleep for an hundred years or more—until one doth give him flame again."

Geoffrey stared.

Magnus asked, carefully, "Whence cometh this knowledge?"

"Why, from Vidor."

"Vidor!" Cordelia stepped over to him, fists on her hips. "Thine imaginary friend? Are we to go to battle with naught but the advice of a dream?"

"He is no dream!" Gregory's face puckered in a scowl. "Vidor is real!"

"Then how is't none but thee ever doth see him?" Geoffrey gibed.

"Why, for that he's not here."

Geoffrey threw up his hands. "He is not here. Ever dost thou tell us he is real—yet he is not here!"

"I've never *said* he's here!" Gregory insisted. "He cannot be—he's in Tir Chlis!"

His brothers and sister were instantly silent, staring at him. Tir Chlis was the magical land they had all been kidnapped to when Gregory was a baby.

"There was a babe," Magnus said softly, "the son of Lord Kern, the High Warlock of that land."

"The man who looked so like our Papa," Cordelia agreed, "and whose baby son was the image of our Gregory."

"He yet is," Gregory said helpfully. "He looked into a mirror for me, and I looked out through his eyes. I might have been gazing at myself."

"When Mama was in Tir Chlis, she could hear Gregory's mind." Magnus was watching his littlest brother. "She could hear him when she held Lord Kern's babe."

"Aye," Cordelia breathed, "because Gregory's mind did reach across the emptiness between our world and Tir Chlis, to blend with the babe's."

"It is all impossible," Fess sighed, "but since you children, and your parents, have experienced it, I cannot but acknowledge that it may have happened."

"And if it did, then why should Gregory not have continual conference with this Lord Kern's son?" Puck's gaze didn't waver from Gregory's face. "How sayest thou, O Beast of Cold Iron? Is there no absurd word for this?"

"There is, though it's not absurd," Fess said stiffly. "Lord

Kern's son is Gregory's analog, in an alternate universe."

"And could he indeed advise our Gregory as to dragons—this 'analog'?"

"His name is *Vidor!*" Gregory cried.

"Yes. Vidor is your analog in Tir Chlis." Fess nodded. "And he could give you information about dragons—if there are dragons in Tir Chlis."

"Oh, there are! Their knights have had to fight them for *ever* so long!"

The others exchanged glances again. "Ought we to believe it?" Geoffrey asked.

"Certes thou shouldst! Vidor would not fib to me!"

"'Tis difficult to do so, when another hears thy thoughts," Magnus agreed, "and I see no harm in making the attempt."

"No *harm!*" bawled his baby sitter. "When thou and thy brothers and sister could but serve as kindling for his flame? When this dragon may but roast thee first, and taste thee later? No *harm!!?!*"

"Nay," said Magnus, "for how doth one put out a dragon's flame?"

They all looked at one another, at a loss.

Then Fess said, "With water."

"Aye, certes!" Cordelia beamed. "Thou lads can all make things to disappear, and appear again in different places! Thou canst wisk small boulders inside trees—for I've seen thee do it, for no better reason than to watch them fly apart with great explosions!"

"Thou hast *what?*" Puck cried, scandalized. Trees were very special to elves.

"'Twas but an idle prank." Magnus couldn't meet Puck's gaze. "A foolish notion, and deeply do I regret it." And *how* he regretted it—when the treetop fell, it had almost crushed him. "But boulders will not damp a dragon's flame."

"Nay, but water will, as Fess doth say." Gregory's eyes lit with enthusiasm. "And if we can whisk boulders about, we can do the same with gobs of water!"

Magnus and Geoffrey looked at each other. Magnus lifted his eyebrows. Geoffrey shrugged, and closed his eyes, tilting his head back.

There was a loud CRACK! and a three-foot shimmering ball appeared right above Cordelia's head. An instant later, it fell apart with a huge splash, drenching her from head to toe.

"Oh! Thou *curmudgeon!*" she cried, and a glob of soot

flew from the nearest burned-out house to strike Geoffrey right in the face. "Thou shrew!" he shouted, and leaped at Cordelia.

But Magnus jumped in between them, slamming his body against Geoffrey's. The younger boy tumbled to the ground. "Nay!" Big Brother said. " 'Tis the dragon we must fight, not one another!"

"But she hath soiled my doublet past believing! Mama will have my hide!"

"Fear not," Magnus assured him, "I'll wash it for thee," and with a CRACK! another globe of water appeared over Geoffrey and, with a SPLOOSH! surged down over him. He floundered to his feet, sputtering in rage, while Cordelia laughed in delight. Geoffrey glared at Magnus, but Big Brother said, "Nay, hold! Ere thou dost bethink thee of any more mischief, consider—thy tunic's cleaned, and thou hast still a dragon to fight."

Geoffrey calmed instantly, and even began to smile again. The thought of a good fight always cheered him up.

They drifted up the rocky hillside, following the dragon's trail. Scorched earth and cracked rocks showed where the monster had passed.

"Is he still so angered, that he must needs blast at all that doth come within his path?" Geoffrey wondered.

Magnus chewed at his lip. "Thou dost bethink thee that he must needs breathe fire out of anger."

"Why, certes," Geoffrey said in surprise. "I would."

"Thou art not a dragon."

Cordelia started to say something, but she saw Puck glare at her, and closed her mouth.

"Mayhap a dragon cannot breathe outward *without* breathing flame," Gregory guessed.

"And mayhap he doth it for joy." Cordelia's broomstick seemed to dance in an upward current of air.

"For myself," Puck called up from ground level, "I wonder less wherefore this dragon doth breathe fire, than why thou four must needs hunt it. Dost thou feel not the slightest fear?"

"None," Geoffrey said, a little too quickly.

"Only enough to lend excitement," Cordelia called.

Magnus shook his head. " 'Tis folly. Be mindful, this beast could roast us in an instant."

Gregory nodded. "*I* fear. Yet not greatly, Puck—for an the beast doth threaten, I can soar upwards. Or even disappear, back to the village."

"There's some truth in that," the elf admitted. "Yet mind thee not to come too close, or he will fry thee ere thou canst flit."

Scales rattled against rock.

"'Ware!" Puck cried. "The beast doth come!"

The children shot upward as though they'd been thrown from a catapult

Around a wall of rock it came, its body as big as a cottage, its neck long and tapering, its head as high as a rooftop. A row of pointed plates came down the top of its neck and along its backbone to the tip of its tail, where it ended in a huge arrowhead. It was green with yellow streaks here and there, and had eyes the size of dinner plates. Its muzzle was long and wide, with flaring nostrils. A forked tongue flicked out of its mouth, tasting the air.

Fess began to tremble.

"Nay!" Geoffrey shouted. "Thou hast known of this, Fess!"

"You have told me," the robot agreed, "yet encountering the reality strains my conceptual framework. . . ."

"It may have been made by magic like unto Father's," Gregory called.

Fess calmed. "It could be a robot, as I myself am. True."

A streak of silver flashed past Fess. The unicorn reared in front of him, dancing off toward the side of the path, drawing the dragon's attention away from the horse. She pawed the air, aiming her horn toward the monster.

The dragon roared. A tongue of flame blasted out ten feet in front of it. It waddled toward the unicorn with astonishing speed.

"Nay!" Cordelia shrieked, and her broomstick shot downward in a power dive. "Get thee away from my darling, thou monster!"

"Cordelia, up!" Puck shouted in panic. "He will sear thee!"

The dragon looked up, took a deep breath, and roared. Flame lashed out fifteen feet; but Cordelia pulled out of her dive and swooped upward, with a good twenty feet to spare.

"Cordelia!" Gregory cried. "Thy broomstick!"

Cordelia turned, startled. The straws behind her had burst

into flame. But even as she stared, a ball of water materialized around the fire with a whip-crack sound. It rained downward, leaving smoking straw.

It also splashed on the dragon's muzzle, hissing up into steam. The beast roared with pain and blasted flame at Cordelia again.

"Why, thou horrid beast!" she cried in indignation, and a boulder shot up from the ground to crash into the dragon's jaw. It bellowed in anger, then suddenly clamped its jaws shut as its whole body rocked, as though from the blow of an invisible fist. The strangest look of puzzlement came over its face, just before its body rocked again. Then its cheeks swelled, its chin tucked in, and it let loose a huge belch of hissing steam. It swallowed, then tried a tentative roar. The sound came, but no flame. It frowned, and roared again—and again, and again. A little steam came out, but not so much as a spark.

Magnus scowled at it, thinking toward it as hard as he could. *Sleep*. His brothers and sister joined their thoughts to his. *So sleepy...Need shelter...Cave...Go back...*

The dragon blinked, staring about, stupefied. Slowly, it turned around and began to climb the hillside again. It disappeared around the cliff-face.

The children drifted upward, following. Fess and the unicorn climbed, too, but a bit more cautiously.

They found it again just as it dragged itself into a gaping hole near the top of the hill. They came lower warily to peer into the darkness, and could just barely make out the huge scaly form as it curved back on itself, coiling up to rest its chin on its tail. The huge eyelids blinked, then closed. It gave a sigh of contentment. The children watched, waiting, as its breathing deepened and steadied. Finally, it snored.

" 'Tis even as thou didst say," Geoffrey said to Gregory.

"Certes," Gregory said indignantly. "Vidor would not fib to us."

"Some unwary soul might wander in there," Magnus said thoughtfully.

"Indeed," Puck said, from among the rocks. "And evil souls might seek it out, to light its fire once again."

"Not truly!" Cordelia cried in dismay. "Surely people are not so horrid!"

"I doubt me not an Puck doth know whereof he doth speak," Magnus said grimly.

Geoffrey grinned. "We would not wish our poor, weary dragon to be rudely wakened, would we?"

"Indeed we would not," Magnus said, with decision. "Up, my hearties! Get thee clear!"

Geoffrey scowled, but he bobbed upward, rising as fast as a March kite, and Gregory followed.

Magnus and Cordelia drifted upward, too, and away from the cliff. Together, they concentrated on a huge boulder high above the cave. It stirred, then moved a little bit forward, then a little bit backward, then a little bit forward again, then backward, beginning to rock like a cradle. It rocked harder, and harder and harder—until, all at once, it rocked just a little too far, seeming to balance on the edge of the cliff for a moment, then slowly, majestically, bowed forward and fell, crashing and booming down the hillside, knocking loose a horde of smaller boulders behind it. Down and down they stormed, more and more, until a full avalanche crashed into the ledge, to bury the entrance to the dragon's cave under a fifty-foot pile of rock.

"He will sleep now," Gregory said softly, "forever, I think."

"Or unless someone is foolish enough to seek to wake him," Puck said, frowning. "For mind you, news of this will pass from village to village right quickly, and the tale will grow greater with each telling. Within a fortnight, I doubt not, folk will speak of a tall and noble knight who did this deed, not four children; and by year's end, 'twill be a legend full-blown. Mothers will tell it to their babes at nightfall to lull them to sleep—and when those babes grow up, like as not one of them will find a way to burrow into this cave, to discover whether or not there's truth to the tale."

The children stared, eyes huge. "Such an one would not be so foolish as to seek to light the dragon's fire again, would he?" Magnus asked.

But Geoffrey nodded with certainty. "Oh, aye. For naught but to be able to say he had done it—aye. I can credit it."

"That *thou* canst, I am sure," Cordelia snorted. "Yet could any *but* Geoffrey be so foolish, Puck?"

The elf only shook his head and sighed, "Lord, what fools these mortals be," and led the children away.

Cordelia was riding the unicorn again as they came down to the burned-out village. Puck stopped and called out in a curious, warbling tone. The hillside lay quiet a moment; then a little man dressed all in brown, with a face tanned dark by sun and wind, popped up from between two small boulders. "What dost thou wish, Merry Wanderer?"

"Bear the word," Puck commanded. "The dragon sleeps behind a wall of stone."

"We have seen," the brownie chortled. "We rejoice. A thousand thanks rain down on thee, Robin Goodfellow! And these children, whom thou hast brought to our aid!"

Cordelia blushed, and bowed her head graciously. Magnus and Geoffrey bowed; but Gregory only stared.

The little man frowned at him. "Why, how is this? Hast thou never seen a brownie ere now?"

Slowly, Gregory shook his head, eyes round as shillings.

The brownie lifted his head, and smiled gently. "Well, small wonder. Few are the mortals who ever do see any of the Wee Folk—and they're never heeded. Their mothers and fathers laugh at them, or think them crazed—as do their playmates. And never doth one see us, once he's grown."

"Save these," Puck qualified, "and their parents."

"Aye," the brownie admitted, "yet they're not so mortal as most. There's something of the elf about them."

Puck glanced nervously up at the children, then back at the brownie. "Aye, they're magic folk, indeed, as thou hast seen." The brownie started to say something, but Puck overrode him. "Now do thou bear the word! And let thy villagers begin to think 'tis safe to come back and rebuild their homes—so long as they do keep fools from that hillside."

The brownie nodded. "A good thought. They'll have their homes again, and we'll have guards."

"Even as thou sayest," Puck agreed. "Now go!"

The brownie grinned, and disappeared.

Gregory still stared at the place where he'd been.

"Aye—enjoy the sight of them, whilst thou may," Puck advised him, "for they be shy folk, these brownies, and will most assuredly not show themselves to thee when thou art grown." He turned to Cordelia. "Where doth thy mount wish to take thee now?"

Cordelia shook her head. "Nowhere, Robin. She doth attend us in docility."

Puck frowned. "'Tis not the way of unicorns, for all I've heard of them."

"Have *you* never seen one before?" Fess asked quickly.

"Once," Puck admitted, "but 'twas two hundred years agone. As I've said, they do be shy."

"Then perhaps he wishes to repay your kindness, by serving Cordelia awhile longer," Fess suggested.

Puck nodded. "That hath the ring of rightness to it—and her aid will be welcomed, I assure thee." Aid in what, Puck didn't say. He only sighed, and turned away. "Come, children. Thou hast had thine adventure for the day. 'Tis time to turn thy steps homeward."

"But, Puck," Geoffrey protested, "'tis noon—and I am hungered."

Puck stopped. For the count of ten, he stood very still.

Then he turned back with a sigh. "Well, 'twill occupy some time. But I warn thee, if thou dost wish to eat, thou must needs catch thy dinner."

3

What with gathering, preparing, cooking, and eating, lunch took two hours. For some reason, Puck didn't object. He didn't even try to hurry them.

Finally, he ordered them to put out the fire and start for home. When the ashes were a sodden mass, he pronounced them safe, and started back into the forest. The unicorn followed, with Cordelia singing and Fess bringing up the rear. The boys darted ahead, playing tree-tag.

Gregory ducked behind an oak with a giggle of delight—that turned into a cry of dismay as a crackly voice howled, "Owwww! Me head! Me shoulder! Ye vasty clumsy oaf, can ye not see where one hangs in distress?"

Magnus and Geoffrey popped out of hiding and exchanged startled glances—but Cordelia glowered and shot off toward her little brother's voice on her broomstick. The boys leaped after her.

"I—I am sorry," Gregory stammered. "I had not meant to injure thee."

The voice softened amazingly. "Why, 'tis naught but a bairn! There now, laddie, be of good cheer. 'Tis the way of lads to be careless and blundering, surely. Eh, but ye must not let the nasty old elf afright ye!"

Puck popped up out of the underbrush right in front of Cordelia and the boys, scowling up at the oak tree, arms akimbo. "Why, thou knob, thou burl! How hast *thou* grown out of that limb?"

The elf whirled to glare at him—and went on whirling, with a yelp of dismay. He dangled from the lowest branch of the oak by a silver chain. One end was wrapped around his middle; the other was tied to the tree.

"Must thou forever be asking, sprite?" he squalled. "Is't not enough for ye, to see that one of yer kind stands in need of yer aid? Nay, be done with yer askin', and pry me loose from this devil's contrivance!"

A slow grin spread over Puck's face. "Nay, I think not. Thou dost well adorn this old tree."

The elf sputtered and fumed at him. He was shorter than Puck, only a foot high—or long, in his present position—and was clutching a green top hat, to keep it on his head. His coat was green, too—a swallow-tailed cutaway—and so were his knee breeches. But his weskit was saffron, and his stockings were white. His shoes were black, with gleaming buckles. He wore a brown forked beard and a scowl. "I might ha' known," he grated. "What else ought I expect from the Puck?"

"Ah," Puck cried in mock surprise, "dost thou know me, then?"

"What one of the Wee Folk would not know ye, ye addle-pated, idling jester? Surely none who labor could help but know of him who only passes time in mischief!"

Gregory frowned. "But the Wee Folk do not labor—save the gnomes, who mine, and the dwarves, who craft—yet thou art neither."

"See ye not his clothes?" the top-hatted elf pointed at Puck. "See ye not his shoes? Dost'a think Robin Goodfellow would craft his own?"

Cordelia caught her breath and clapped her hands. "I know thee now! Thou art a fairies' shoemaker!"

The elf swept off his hat, clapping it to his stomach, and bowed his head. "The same, sweet lass!"

"Why dost thou wear green and saffron?" Geoffrey asked.

"Why, for that he's Irish," Puck said, with a lopsided grin. "Yet Erin's Wee Folk ever wore their whiskers in fringes round their chins, and ne'er did wear moustaches. Wherefore is thy beard so long?"

"And forked?" Magnus added.

"Why, 'tis because my forebears came from the Holy Land in bygone ages."

"From Judea?" Gregory asked, wide-eyed.

The elf nodded.

"Then," cried Cordelia, "thou art . . ."

"A leprecohen." The elf inclined his head again. "Kelly McGoldbagel stands ready t' serve ye."

"Nay; he doth hang." Puck squinted up at the silver chain. "How didst thou come to so sad a pass, elf?"

Kelly's face reddened. "'Tis a foul brute of a Sassenach landlord hath done me thus, belike with the aid of an Ulster witch! For how else would he ha' known that naught but a silver chain could hold a leprecohen?"

"And to hold him in it the whiles he did unearth thy crock of gold?" Puck guessed.

"'Tis a foul thief!" Kelly bawled. "'Tis a highway robber who doth not hearken to the words an elf doth say!"

"Or who doth attend them too shrewdly, belike," Puck snorted. "Nay, thy kindred are famed in the Faery Kingdom for the oaths they break in spirit, the whiles they heed their letter!"

"Oaths that are forced!" Kelly howled. "Oaths extorted, under pain of prison! How binding could such be?"

"As binding as a silver chain," Magnus pointed out. "Should we not pluck thee from this branch ere we talk longer?"

"Aye, and greatly would I thank yer worship!" Kelly nodded so fiercely that he began a slow rotation again. "Oy vay! I beg thee, good laddie, bring me down!"

Magnus floated up and untied the chain from the limb.

"Here now, gently! Carefully!" Kelly chewed at his beard. "Have a care when ye loose the knot—I've more weight than ye'd suspect!"

"Why, then, I shall support thee," Cordelia declared.

"What, *ye?* Why, how couldst thou, lass? Thou'rt not even near . . . *Whuh!*"

Magnus pulled the last strand of chain, and the knot fell open. Kelly plummeted, with a shout of terror—all of about an inch. "What! But . . . How . . . Eh! But I'm drifting!"

"Down to the ground," Cordelia assured him. "It but took me a moment to gauge thy weight."

"Eh! But a nasty turn ye gave me!" Kelly grumbled. "Why could ye not but say . . . Um. Aye. Thou didst."

Cordelia nodded brightly. "Now dost thou believe me?"

"Aye." Kelly peered up at her from under shaggy eyebrows, while his head swung up slowly and his feet swung down to touch the turf. "But would ye be tellin' me how ye come to be able to . . . Oh. Ye're a witch-lass, are ye not, now?"

"Now, or at any time," Cordelia agreed. "And I assure thee, I've borne many loads more weighty than thou."

"I'm believing you," the elf muttered. Then he saw the white head and silver horn behind her, and his eyes rounded. "Eh! But what wondrous beastie is this?"

"'Tis a unicorn," Cordelia answered.

Kelly spared her a glance of scorn. "And never would I have been guessing it! Eh, but surely!" His gaze fastened to the creature again, rapt with wonder. "Why, 'tis years since I've seen one! Hundreds of years!"

"Two hundreds?" Gregory guessed; but Kelly seemed not to hear him.

He stepped over to the unicorn, reaching up to touch her knee lightly, then probing with a bony finger. "'Tis real enough, truly! Eh! Magic one!"

The unicorn lowered her head, letting Kelly touch her nose.

"Now may all spirits of wood and dell defend ye!" the elf breathed. Finally, he turned back to Cordelia. "But how comes this magic creature to accompany ye?"

"She came to seek us out," Cordelia explained, "for that she'd found a dragon, and needed our aid to subdue it."

"To subdue . . . ? And ye . . . ?" The elf's voice came out as a squeak. He cleared his throat, glanced at Puck, then back at the children. "Am I to understand ye did it? Conquered a dragon, I mean. Did ye?"

"Aye, but it did take all of our efforts."

"Oh, did it now!" And Kelly turned away, shaking his head and muttering, "Children! Babes, they are! And a dragon? Naught but babes!"

Then he whirled toward Puck, forefinger stabbing out. "Why, ye scurvy knave! Ye bloody boar of a Sassenach! Ye Tory scoundrel! Would ye, then, let mere babes stand against the foulest of monsters?"

"I would not, but they did insist on giving thee rescue." Puck's eyes narrowed. "Wouldst thou believe I might truly allow these children to come to harm?"

"Believe it? Aye—and proclaim it! Why, ye fevered son of a horse-trader, what e'er possessed thee to hazard these wee, poor babes to such peril?"

"But," Geoffrey said, "we are not . . ."

". . . staying," Puck snapped, cutting him off. "Children, come! Thy good deed is done, and he whom thou hast aided doth denounce us! Turn, and away!" He spun, and strode toward the underbrush.

The children stared at him, taken aback. Then, "Robin! Wait!" Gregory cried, and leaped after him.

"Fare thee well, elf." Cordelia leaped on her broom and sped off after Puck.

"What! Will ye follow blindly where the Sprite of Mischief leads?" Kelly cried. Then his face firmed, and he reached up to yank his top hat more firmly down onto his head. "Nay, I'll not have it!" And he strode off after the children.

Catching up to them, he cried, "Fear not, children! The leprecohen will not abandon ye to the hard heart of the hobgoblin! I shall accompany ye!"

Puck turned on him, face thunderous. "None have asked it of thee, elf! Now I bid thee—bide!"

"And desert them to the mercies of the Sassenach?" Kelly settled himself, glowering. "Nay!"

"Why, thou nail, thou burr, thou thorn! What use canst thou be? How much more wilt thou swell up their hazard?"

"Hazard?" Kelly fairly screeched. "Why, what could be safer than a child with a leprecohen to guard it?"

"A man with his head in a noose, or a lord with his neck stretched across the headsman's block!" Puck took a deep breath. "Why, what could be less use, or more hazardous company, than a leprechaun who doth allow his crock of gold to be stolen?"

Kelly's head snapped back as though he'd been slapped. Then his face reddened, his head drew down between his shoulders, and he reached up to push his hat over to a rakish angle. "Now ye've said it, now ye have said it! Now must I prove the lie ye have given—and I will, by staying with ye till the death!"

"Thy death, or theirs?" Puck said acidly.

"Yers, if Heaven smiles!" Kelly turned to the children. "Fear not—I'll never abandon ye to the dangers of his company!"

"But there *is* no danger in his company!" Gregory cried, and Cordelia said, "None could be safer than in the care of the Puck, good elf."

"Puck or not, his protection's uncertain," Kelly maintained. "Nay, I'll accompany ye, if for naught but to ward ye from *him!*"

Gregory shook his head in confusion. "Wherefore dost thou mistrust him so?"

"Why, because he is English!" Kelly cried, and turned away to the green of the forest.

4

"Yon, children." Puck pointed to the right-hand path, where the trail forked.

"Nay! 'Tis fraught with peril!" Kelly jabbed a finger at the left-hand path. *"Yon* is where ye should wend!"

Puck rounded on the leprecohen. "'Ware, elf! Constrain me not to flatten thee!"

"And what would ye be doing then?" Kelly said, glaring up at the bigger elf. "Smite me? Starve me? Banish me beyond the Pale? 'Twas ever the way of the tyrant!"

"Tyrant or not, thou'lt wear webbed feet and hop, an thou dost defy me more!"

"Puck," Cordelia pleaded, "do not . . ."

"Nay, lass! The elf is not welcome—yet an he will not help, he must not hinder!"

"Do yer worst!" Kelly cried. "'Twas ever the way of your kind!"

Puck's eyes narrowed, and a fly buzzed by. Kelly's head snapped up, staring; then his hand shot out to snatch the insect out of the air. With a glad cry, he popped it toward his mouth —then froze, staring at his closed fist in horror. Slowly, he looked up at Puck.

The Puck grinned wickedly.

Kelly gulped, and plucked up his courage to glare again in defiance—but it wasn't convincing.

"Dost thou have a sudden hunger for flies, then?" Puck crooned. "Nay, fear not—the rest of thy body will change then, to fit it. Do thy shoes pinch? 'Tis naught of concern— only thy feet, spreading into frog's paddles."

With a howl, Kelly threw the fly from him, spreading his fingers and staring at his hand as though to reassure himself it wasn't growing webbing.

"Puck, thou must not!" Cordelia cried.

"Wouldst thou be a bully then?" Geoffrey demanded.

"Aye, assuredly he would," Kelly muttered. "'Twas ever his way."

31

Puck's eyes narrowed.

Fess lowered his head to Kelly's level. "I would counsel caution as the better part of valor. Remember that the Puck delights in mischief."

Kelly nearly jumped out of his skin. He leaped about, staring up at the great black horse. "Begorra! Is it a talking horse, then?"

"A pouka." Puck eyed Fess askance. "A spirit horse—though 'tis a spirit of a different sort. It is made of cold iron, elf."

"Nay, surely it cannot be!" Kelly stared up at Fess, paling. "Poor, wee tykes! What greater peril could four children be in?"

"Why, he is our friend!" Gregory shot upward to wrap his arms around Fess's neck. "Our father's closest, and ours!"

Kelly didn't answer; he only cast an apprehensive glance at Puck.

The bigger elf smiled, with malice. "And wouldst thou worry about my poor self, then?"

"Nay, surely not!" Kelly drew himself up, color returning. "With so fell a beast by? And having wormed its way into their affections? Lead onward, elf! 'Tis the two of us must shield them, now!"

Puck grinned, and sauntered away down the right-hand path.

The path widened out into a little clearing, dappled with sunlight in shifting patterns as the shadows of the leaves moved gently in the breeze. The floor of the clearing was strewn with fallen leaves and underbrush, and three stumps, where woodcutters had felled oak trees.

An old woman poked about in the underbrush, muttering to herself. She wore a shabby brown dress and a shawl, with a gray kerchief tied around her head.

The unicorn came to a halt. Magnus hopped down off Fess's back and stepped forward. "What have we here, Robin?"

"A hermit matron, belike," the elf answered.

"I doubt not 'tis a poor beldame who found her friends had died, and none still living in her village gave her welcome," Kelly said. "Thus came she here, to live alone. There are many such."

The old woman looked up at the sound of voices, frowning. "Who comes?"

Magnus waited for Puck to answer, but he didn't hear a word.

"'Tis four bairns!" the crone snapped. "What dost thou here? Begone, now! Shoo!"

Magnus looked down at Puck for advice, but the elf was gone. He looked around, surprised, to find that Kelly had disappeared, too.

Cordelia leaned over to murmur in Magnus's ear, "They do not wish grown-ups to see them."

"Wilt thou not mind thine elders?" the old woman cried. "Begone, I say!" She snatched up a stick and threw it at them.

The unicorn shied, but Magnus reached out and caught the stick, frowning. "We've done naught that ye should scold us so." Then he remembered his manners. "Good day, good-wife."

"'Goodwife,' is it?" the old woman spat. "Nay, never was I wife, nor would be! How is it even bairns do think a woman must needs marry? Nay, not old Phagia! I had no need of men—nor of any person! And of children least of all! Begone, I say!"

"If I've offended, I regret," Magnus said.

"Do not say so," Geoffrey snapped. "Ye've done naught to give offense!"

"Aye." Cordelia said, puzzled. "Wherefore should she hate us so, at first sight?"

"Dost'a not hear me?" the old woman screeched. "Go!" And she began to wade through the underbrush toward them, catching up sticks to throw.

Without even thinking, Cordelia stared at a stick. It leaped up into the air and flew away.

Phagia watched it go, eyes widening. But they narrowed as she looked down at the children. "So 'tis witch-brats come upon me, eh? Well, I've tricks of my own at hand!"

Suddenly, sticks burst from the floor of the clearing all around the children and shot toward them.

"Catch!" Magnus cried, and the sticks sailed on up over the treetops as all four children thought at them at the same time.

Phagia turned ashen. "What manner of warlock-lings are these, that do catch things with their thoughts? Only witches may do so!"

"Nevertheless, that power's ours, come to us from our father," Magnus explained.

"And wilt thou, then, bedevil a poor old woman with this power of thy sire's?" Phagia spat. "Nay, then! Contend with this!"

Nuts suddenly rained down on them, as though a thousand manic squirrels had jumped in for target practice.

"Ouch! Oh!" Cordelia wrapped her arms around her head and ducked. Her brothers howled with dismay; the nuts hit *hard*.

"We must meet this all as one!" Magnus cried. "Together, now! *Up!*"

The other children squeezed their eyes shut and joined their thoughts to his, and the rain of nuts backed upward, away, leaving a dome of clear air about them, as though the small missiles were bouncing off a huge, invisible umbrella.

"Wilt thou then band against me?" Phagia snarled. "Nay, I must teach thee manners! Avaunt!"

Flames leaped up about the children, roaring toward them, leaving a wake of char behind.

"Be mindful!" Magnus shouted. "Fire's but the heat of molecules in motion! Slow them, still them! Make them cool!"

All four children stared at the flames, thinking tranquil thoughts, slowing movement, spreading it over a much wider area, transferring energy throughout the floor of the clearing. The day seemed to grow a little warmer, but the fire died.

Phagia stared at the smouldering char, appalled.

Magnus heard Geoffrey's thoughts: *Brother, leave her or subdue her. An we do neither, she shall attack again.*

Magnus nodded. *We might then injure her as we fought back—and Mama and Papa would be angered.*

Nor should we leave her free to follow, Geoffrey added.

Magnus agreed. "Let us do what we must."

Phagia's head snapped up, fear suddenly contorting her features. She lifted a clawlike hand—but Cordelia stared at the crone's feet, and they shot out from under her, whipping up level with her shoulders. She screeched; then her face hardened with determination and her feet slowly moved downward.

Cordelia bit her lip, face tightening with strain, and the witch's feet moved upward again. She howled with rage, and they steadied.

Magnus glanced at a vine that had wrapped itself up high, around a tree. It uncoiled, whirling backwards around and around the trunk, then groping out toward Phagia. Geoffrey frowned at it, and the vine broke off near its root, then whipped about the witch five times, pinning her arms to her sides. Phagia shrieked with horror, then clamped her jaw shut and heaved at the vine with all the strength of an adult mind. Sweat beaded Geoffrey's forehead as he fought to keep the vine in place—but as he did, Gregory reached out with mental fingers to whip the ends into a square knot. Phagia screeched, but Geoffrey relaxed with a smile. "Well done, tadpole."

"'Tis well thou didst teach me that knot last Friday," lisped little brother.

"A pox upon thee!" old Phagia raved. "Thou knaves, thou curmudgeons! Hast thou naught else to do, but thou must needs torment a poor old beldame?"

"We did naught to trouble thee," Geoffrey contradicted.

"Nor would we have, hadst thou not turned upon us." Cordelia spoke more gently, trying to balance Geoffrey's contrariness.

"Turned upon thee! Eh! Innocent children, thou knowest not what those words do mean! Turn upon thee! Nay! But wait till thou hast had all the folk of a village come to chase thee, hounding thee from out thine home to harry thee throughout the countryside! Wait till they have caught thee, and bound thee to a ducking-stool, to sink thee in deep water, deprive thee of thy breath! Wait till thou dost feel thy lungs clamoring for air, till thou canst no longer bear it and must breathe, yet know thou'lt suck water in if thou dost—then they hale thee up into the air, at the last second, screaming, 'Vile witch, confess!' And thou dost not, for whosoe'er it was that did the wrong they've found, it was not thou! Yet they will blame thee, aye! Doth a cow's udder run dry? 'Twas thou who caused it! Did a sheep then sicken? 'Twas thou who cursed it! Did a child fall from out a hayloft? 'Twas thou who tripped him! It must be thou, it needs be thou—for naught but thou art a witch!"

"But we have not, we shall not!" Cordelia cried, pale and trembling. "We never would!"

"Tell that to these gentle souls who have lashed thee to the ducking-stool, and now plunge thee deep again! And if thou dost hold fast, and never dost confess to deeds thou hast not done, they'll take thee off to torture thee, with fire and steel, till the pain, the agony, and the sight of thine own blood do so afright thee that thou dost cry at last, ' 'Twas I! 'Twas naught but I! Say what thou wilt have me say, and I will speak it! Only leave off thy hurting of me!' "

Ashen-faced, Cordelia had clapped her hands over Gregory's ears, but he waved her away impatiently. "I'll but hear her thoughts as she doth speak them!" He looked up at Magnus. "Can it truly be as she doth say?"

His brother nodded, face set and grim. "Mama and Papa have told us that the witches are ill-treated. Yet they've only hinted at such horrors!"

"Thy bold bluff peasants will do more than hint," Phagia assured him. "At the last, they'll lash thy torn and bleeding carcass to a stake, and pile fagots about thy feet, bundles of sticks as high as thy legs, and thrust a torch within them! Then wilt thou truly scream, as flames mount up to sear thee!" And she turned away, sobbing.

Cordelia faced her brothers, trembling with emotion. "Small wonder that Papa and Mama are so angered with folk who speak against witches!"

Magnus nodded, his face set like rock.

Gregory stepped forward shyly, and knelt by Phagia. "Is this why thou didst seek to chase us? Because thou didst fear we would summon folk to hurt thee?"

Phagia's head turned about, eyes staring at him. "Nay, little lad! Poor little lad! 'Tis from another cause—the one that made me hide myself away, where none would find me!"

Gregory frowned. "What cause is that?"

"Not the hurt that they did me," Phagia explained, "or that I did them; but hurt that was done to them because of me."

Gregory shook his head, not understanding.

"Done because of thee?" Magnus came up. "Who did it, then?"

"Lontar." She shuddered at the sound of the name. "Even in his youth, he had determined to work evil in every way he could. He courted me; 'Why should not two witch-folk wed?' quoth he. 'How much stronger will their wizardly get be!' Yet I knew him for what he was; his evilness fairly oozed from him; he reeked of it. 'No,' I said, and 'No,' again, and yet again; but he would not heed, till at last he sought to pursue me through my cottage door, and I slammed it into his face. He fell down, stunned, whiles I bolted the door and collapsed against it, shaking. When he came to his senses, he could but rave—for warlocks cannot make locks move of themselves, praise Heaven!"

Gregory shared a quick glance with his two older brothers.

"What might he do then, but rail about my door? Yet that he did—and most puissantly. He laid a curse upon me, that anyone I might befriend would die, and in a fashion most horrible. I did credit him not; but within a fortnight, everyone I'd counted as a friend lay dead, and in a manner most repulsive. They lay . . . No!" She squeezed her eyes shut, clamping down on the thought before it could form fully in her mind. "I shall not speak of it to children!"

But enough of it came through to make the children glad she'd buried it—a brief, disgusting mental image of limbs, separate and partly flayed, bare bones sticking out. Even Geoffrey shuddered, and Cordelia gave a little cry before she pressed her hands against her mouth. Gregory let out one bleat of fright and dove into Cordelia's skirts. She hugged him, staring at the witch, who lay sobbing, struggling within herself. They could see her back and shoulders stiffen. "Nay! I will not! Children, thou hast mis-served me quite, stirring that foul memory up from the depths of my mind, where I had buried it!"

"We are most truly sorry," Cordelia murmured, and exchanged glances with her brothers. They pooled thoughts quickly, in a way that Mama had taught them; it kept anyone from outside the family from hearing them.

She could not be truly wicked.

Nay, not if she doth seek to hide this sight of horror from our minds.

In truth, she could not.

Aloud, Cordelia said, "Is that why thou didst seek to send us from thee?"

Phagia nodded. "And 'tis why I came here to the forest. For seest thou, children, when I saw folk who'd been my friends from childhood lying dead in so repulsive a manner, I turned away, and resolved that never would I have a friend again. Deep into the forest I fled, and in its gloom I built mine hut—and oh, children, I assure thee, 'twas hard, so hard! I was a lass in the first bloom of womanhood, when folk most dearly need others, and I ached for company, and for young men's arms! Yet I did not weaken in my resolve; I stayed within my thicket—and oft did I bethink to seek mine end!"

"To slay thyself?" Cordelia gasped.

"Even so." Phagia nodded. "Yet I withstood temptation, and did live. Thus have I done for fifty years; here still I dwell, and my food is roots and berries, wild thyme, wild greens, and what little else that I may hunt or gather. Ever and anon comes one who would befriend me; yet have I spurned them, even as I sought to drive thee from me."

"Fear not," Magnus assured her, "we will be thy friends, aye, but only for some hours few. What harm could come to us in time so brief?"

"An we unbind thee," Cordelia asked, "wilt thou undertake not to harm us?"

Phagia swallowed her sobs and nodded.

Gregory stared at the knot of vine. Slowly, it untied itself.

Staring at it, Phagia sat up slowly.

The vine rose up, swaying, unwinding from about her.

"I thank thee," she breathed. "Yet heed the voice of wisdom, children. Flee! Get thee hence from me!"

"We shall bide only a short while," Magnus assured her.

"Fear not; we now are warned." Geoffrey grinned. "Let any dare seek to harm us!"

Phagia smiled in spite of her dread. "Four such doughty children must needs be proof against such evil." She shook her head in amazement. "Yet be mindful, thou art but bairns. How wilt thou fare against the power of a wizard grown?"

The children exchanged another glance. It wasn't necessary to remind each other not to tell her about the Witch of the Red Hill, or about the old sorcerer under the mountain. They all knew better than to let any grown-up learn about them. They'd never believe the children anyway—and if Mama and Papa ever found out, they'd be very upset.

"I think we may withstand such threats," Magnus said carefully.

"Nay, better." Geoffrey grinned like a wolf cub. "An we discover that foul wizard, let him guard himself!"

"Thou hast too much pride," Phagia chided. She stood up slowly, painfully, and brushed the dead leaves off her skirt. "Eh! But my bones ache with age! . . . Be not too unafraid, children. Beware—thou art but bairns."

"And we are hungry." Gregory tugged at her skirt. "Canst spare us morsels?"

Phagia looked down at him, and her face softened.

Then, with a wordless cry, she threw her arms wide. "What

matter? Mayhap 'tis even as thou dost say—mayhap thou art proof against the horror! Nay, let me for an hour or two enjoy thy company! Come, children—let's find food!'"

The children raised a cheer and followed her off through the woods as she hobbled away toward her hut.

But in the shadow of the leaves behind a root, two small figures exchanged glances, and shook their heads.

"She is truly a nice old dame." Gregory snuggled down under the blanket and closed his eyes.

"Ouch! Haul thine elbow from out my ribs!" Geoffrey snapped.

"I did not mean to." Gregory inched away from him.

"Then tell him thou art sorry," Magnus commanded from his other side.

"Sorry," Gregory sniffed.

The room was silent.

"Geoffrey. . ." Magnus said, with grim warning.

"Oh, well enough! 'Tis all right, Gregory," Geoffrey growled.

"She truly seemed to take delight in our guesting," Cordelia murmured from the narrow bed on the other side of the spare room.

"Aye, once she was satisfied she'd warned us, and done all she could to scare us away," Gregory agreed.

"'Twas a good supper," Magnus sighed. "What meat was that the pie contained?"

"None," Cordelia said, with the complete certainty of the beginning cook. "'Twas naught but nuts and tubers, so cleverly combined the taste was like to fowl."

"Not foul at all." Gregory lifted his head, frowning. "'Twas good."

"Nay, wart," Magnus said fondly, "she means the bird, not the bad."

"She's nice to guest us," Geoffrey sighed, "though I'd have liefer slept outdoors."

"Then go," Cordelia snorted. "I doubt not Robin and Kelly will guard thy slumber."

"Where have they gone?" Gregory pouted. "Want my elves!"

"They're nearby, I doubt not," Magnus reassured him. "They rarely wish grown-ups to see them."

"Kelly especially," Cordelia agreed. "Look what chanced

with him when last a grown one met him!"

"And what he lost," Magnus agreed. "Eh, Gregory?... Gregory!"

His little brother sighed deeply.

"He sleeps," Cordelia whispered. "A long day hath it been, for so small a fellow."

"And the bed is soft," Geoffrey agreed. "I could almost . . ." He broke off for a huge yawn.

Magnus smiled and held his peace, waiting. So did Cordelia.

Geoffrey finished the yawn with a smile and burrowed his head into the pillow. Two heartbeats later, he breathed lightly, evenly.

"Good night, sister," Magnus whispered.

"Good night," she answered.

The room was still.

Magnus jarred awake at a sharp pain in his nose. He could not breathe! He opened his mouth to yell, but something rough jammed into it—woolen cloth! He leaped out of bed, or tried to, but his arms and legs pressed against something holding them down. Rope! He was bound and gagged!

Phagia's face loomed over him in the moonlight, mouth hooked upward in glee. She gave off a high, thin giggle, nodding—but there was something odd about her eyes, as though they weren't quite focused, seeing Magnus but not really registering him.

"Art chilled?" she cackled. "Fear not; thou'lt be warm soon enough." And she turned away and went out the door, giggling still.

Rigid with fear, Magnus lay still and reached out with his mind, listening for his brothers' and sister's thoughts. The room seemed to darken even more, and the clattering old Phagia was making in the next room dulled. Just barely, he could make out their thoughts, too fuzzily to tell what they were thinking, but enough to know they were there. He forced his head up and looked about. Dimly, by moonlight, he could just make them out—bound and gagged, even as he was.

He lay back, feeling sweat start to bead his forehead, and fought for calm. Really, there was nothing to worry about. What if she had bound him? He'd just think at the knots and untie them!

But the rope wouldn't move.

Magnus closed his eyes and concentrated furiously on the knot. He felt it twitch, barely, but that was all. He gave up and sagged back on the bed, feeling the sweat of fear trickle down his cheek. What horrible spell had Phagia worked on him? And on his brothers and sisters, too, no doubt!

Then he remembered the supper—the vegetable stew that had tasted so wonderful, and that his sister had assured them had contained no meat. What *had* it contained, though? What herb had Phagia discovered in her fifty years in the forest, that could dull the senses of a warlock and rob him of his powers?

Phagia was singing, some odd, irregular tune that slid up and down from one off-key note to another. Pots and pans rattled, and he heard a long creak of an unoiled hinge. He remembered the sound from supper—it was the oven door. He heard the scratch of flint and steel, heard the gentle gusting of the bellows, heard Phagia's giggle. "Warm, yes. Nice and warm, for the poor chilled children. And sauce. Young ones never like any meat, if it hath not a good sauce." And she broke off into the weird humming again, as liquid poured and a wooden spoon knocked against the side of a pot.

Her sarcasm chilled Magnus, the words and tone of a kind old granny contrasted with what she meant to do. He understood the evil sorcerer's curse suddenly and clearly—exactly what disgusting form of death Phagia's friends had met!

Cordelia. Gregory. He couldn't let them be killed, shoved into an oven for an old witch's gluttony!

Or an ancient sorcerer's revenge. It was Gregory's thought, so faint Magnus could barely understand it—and, in a sudden wave of understanding, he realized the youngest was right. *She knoweth not what she doth,* he thought as hard as he could.

Aye, certes, came Cordelia's faint thought. *That glazed look in her eye—her soul's asleep!*

Only her body wakes, Gregory agreed.

'Twill suffice to make mutton of us, Geoffrey thought—harshly, to mask his fear. *What can we do?*

A shadow blocked the light from the kitchen, and Phagia came back in, crooning, "Ah, the poor wee lad! So chilled in his bed! Nay, he must be warmed ere the others." And she went across the room, to scoop Gregory up in her arms.

Sheer terror cut through the fog of drug, and Gregory howled through his gag as his mind shouted, *Magnus! Cordelia! Geoffrey! Aid me!*

Fear and rage galvanized his brothers and sister, and they thought blows against the old witch—but the drug dimmed their powers; Phagia only wavered as she stood up and turned, cradling Gregory in her arms. "Dizziness! Oh!" She stood still for a moment, eyes squeezed shut. Then they opened, and she smiled. "'Tis past. Now, lad—let us prepare dinner." And she hobbled toward the kitchen.

Magnus thought mayhem at her again, but she tripped on something more substantial—and, just as she tripped, something small and dark shot through the air and slammed into her shoulder blades. With a scream, she toppled . . .

And Gregory sailed out of her arms, straight toward the open oven.

His thoughts screamed as he stared at the oven in terror.

As one, his brothers and sister reached out with their minds to pull at him.

He slowed, coming gradually to a halt, mere inches from the oven door.

Magnus breathed a sigh of relief, then thought, *Down, now, and slowly.*

Gently, carefully, they lowered the little boy to the floor.

In the bedroom doorway, Phagia struggled to lever herself up off the floor. A small shadow loomed up by her head, slamming downward with a miniature hammer. It connected with a dull *CLUNK!* and Phagia slumped, with a tired sigh.

The small shadow chuckled, then looked up at Magnus. It was Kelly—and he sprang up to Magnus's bed and yanked the gag out of the boy's mouth. "Well, lad! Ye're safe, then—but 'twas a near one."

"Too near by half," Magnus agreed. "My deepest thanks, Kelly." He turned to the larger shadow. "And thou, Robin. Great thanks for fair rescue!"

"Great welcome," the elf replied, but his face was severe. "What could I have said to thy parents, had I brought thee home roasted? Yet, now!" He glowered at Magnus, then turned his head to glare at Cordelia and Geoffrey as the gags pulled themselves out of the children's mouths. "What would have happed to thee, hadst thou not had thine elf nearby?"

"Death," Cordelia answered, round-eyed.

"True death." Puck nodded. "Not children's play, from which thou couldst arise and walk. Now, when next thine elf bids thee retreat from danger, what wilt thou do?" And he turned his glare on Geoffrey.

"We will heed thee." The middle boy gazed back at Puck with the weight of realization. "I will own, now—there be perils that be too great for children—even we four!"

"We will obey thee," Magnus agreed. "We will heed even thy doubts, Robin."

Puck glowered at them—but he couldn't maintain it; his seriousness frayed, and mischief gleamed through.

The children saw, and relaxed with a shaky sigh. "Eh, Puck!" Magnus cried, "we feared thou wert *truly* enraged with us!"

"Which did no harm, I warrant." Puck turned and went over to Cordelia. "What is this stuff that muffled thy thoughts, child? Doth it wear thin?"

"Let me try." She stared at the rope that bound her wrists. The ends twitched, then began to draw back out of the knot— but slowly, so slowly! "We do recover."

"Not quickly enow." Puck seized the rope and whisked the knot loose. "Unbind them, Tacky!"

"I'll thank ye to remember yer manners, Barkface," the leprecohen retorted. "If ye ever learned any, that is," but he poked long fingers into Geoffrey's bonds and untied him in a trice.

Magnus wrenched his hands loose and seized his dagger. He cut through the rope that bound his ankles and leaped up to go to his little brother—and stumbled, nearly falling; but he caught the door frame in time. He yowled at the pain of the tingling in his ankles.

"Aye, the blood is angry at having been dammed from its normal course," Puck agreed. "Patience; it will return."

"There's scant time for patience." Magnus hobbled over to Gregory. "She may wake at any moment."

"No fear," Kelly assured him. "I've still a hammer."

But Magnus had untied Gregory, and the little boy flung his arms around his big brother's neck. "There, there, lad," Magnus crooned. "'Twas horrid, but 'tis done."

"Hammer or not, 'twould be well to be gone," Puck said. "I hate all housen in clear weather—and this one reeks of evil. Come, children!"

He turned away to the door, and Geoffrey and Cordelia followed him with a very good will. But Magnus sent Gregory after them with a pat on the bottom, then turned back toward Phagia, frowning.

Puck turned back too, nettled. "Nay, lad! Come away!"

"She's but stunned," Magnus answered. "I bethink me we need her to be senseless for a longer time."

Cordelia looked up, alarmed. "What dost thou, brother?"

But the eldest was staring at the witch.

"What doth he?" Geoffrey demanded.

Gregory touched his shoulder. "Peace. He pushes thoughts of sleep into her mind."

Geoffrey's face hardened with envy. Magnus had been able to project his thoughts for a year now, but Geoffrey still couldn't. He had better sense than to make a jealous fuss at a moment like this, though.

The witch's eyes suddenly snapped open in surprise. Then they blinked, several times. She stiffened in alarm, realizing what was happening to her—but Gregory and Geoffrey caught hold of Magnus's hands, channeling their own strength into him; and slowly, Phagia's eyes closed. Her body relaxed, and her bony chest rose and fell with the slow rhythm of sleep.

"Well done, my brothers," Cordelia murmured.

"Softly," Magnus cautioned. "Her sleep is not yet deep."

"Come, now," Puck urged. "It doth behoove us to leave, and let her sleep."

"All away, then." Magnus stepped back to wave the others past him. "Whiles we may, without unpleasantness." He looked up suddenly, then whirled back to the bedroom. "Gregory!"

The youngest hovered above old Phagia, sitting cross-legged in midair, frowning down at the sleeping witch's face. "Big brother . . . there's something odd within her mind . . ."

Puck and Cordelia looked back over their shoulders, and both his brothers stilled. "Odd?" Magnus breathed. "What oddity is that?"

"Nay, I catch his meaning!" Cordelia leaped back to the old witch. "'Tis some manner of compulsion, buried!"

"Cordelia!" Magnus cried in alarm.

Phagia stirred in her sleep, muttering.

Magnus instantly lowered his voice. "Beware!" he called in hushed tones. "Have thy broomstick by thee!"

"Oh, fuss not so!" Cordelia hissed back. "There's no danger—and were there, thou couldst lift me away right quickly. Now—leave me be a moment, the whiles I peek within her mind." And she knelt stock-still, staring down into the sleeping woman's face.

"Thou wilt heed thine elf this time!" Puck said by her shoulder. "Away, child! There is danger, deep in people's minds!"

"I misdoubt me an 'tis so deep as all that," Cordelia murmured. "Dost'a not recall, Puck, that Northern sorcerer who didst cast compulsions on all soldiers who came against him? Mama taught me then, how to break such spells."

"Well . . . mayhap, then . . ." Puck frowned and watched.

Cordelia gazed at the sleeping witch. Her brothers gathered around, watching silently. After awhile, she shuddered. "'Tis vile! That foul sorcerer must needs have a gutter for a mind!"

"What did he?" Magnus asked softly.

"He tied friendship through her childhood urges in her nether parts to her need to eat—they merge at our ages. And those she loved—her mother and father—had denied her sweets when she wanted them, as all parents must, if they do not wish their children to fall ill—and she'd grown angry at that denial, as all children do. Since she loved them, that anger turns against all who befriend her, and she eats to gain revenge on her mama and papa."

"Doth she know any of this?" Geoffrey cried in indignation.

"Shhh!" Cordelia cautioned, and Phagia stirred in her sleep.

Magnus clapped a hand over Geoffrey's mouth.

"She knoweth naught," Cordelia whispered, "even as we thought. He cast a spell into her mind, in that way Papa calls 'hypnosis.' When she waked from the trance he made, she remembered naught—but in her sleep, the spell comes on her again, whene'er she's near a friend. Her deeds tonight were like to sleepwalking."

"Canst thou break the spell?" Magnus asked.

"Aye. 'Tis deeper than the sorcerer Alfar's, but not so deep that I cannot find its roots. Come, nubbin, lend me power." She caught Gregory's hand and gazed at Phagia. Gregory frowned, too, in intense concentration.

Geoffrey and Magnus were silent, watching. Puck's face was screwed up with worry, and he stood tense, ready to leap to aid if he was needed.

Phagia stirred in her sleep, muttering a stream of words that the boys couldn't quite understand. Her body twitched a few times, stiffened, then suddenly relaxed. She breathed a deep sigh.

So did Cordelia, leaning back and going limp. "'Twas a sore trial, that."

"There was danger!" Puck accused.

Cordelia shook her head. "Only in that I might tire—but Gregory's strength was enough to lean on. And he sensed weakened points that I could break. 'Tis done; she'll not seek to bake another. She'll wake well rested, and with a greater sense of well-being than e'er she's had." She dropped her face into her hands, shuddering. "But, oh! That any could be so evil as to wreak such havoc in a person's mind, as that fell Lontar did!"

"Doth he still live?" Geoffrey's face had hardened.

Cordelia shrugged, but Kelly said, "He may. Word of such an one doth run through fairy gossip, now and again. Yet none know where he dwelleth."

"Well, we are warned." Magnus turned to Puck. "An we come near him, Robin, we'll be fully on our guard. This magus, at least, is naught to trifle with."

"And merits death." Geoffrey's eyes glowed. "An we encounter him, brother, take no chance. We'll smite him down, ere he can know we're by."

"Nay, surely thou wilt not!" Puck glared up at the boy, his fists on his hips. "Thou wilt not encounter him, be certain! For thou wilt now march home right quickly! Out the door! Off down the path! At once!"

Geoffrey glowered down at him in rebellion.

Magnus touched his shoulder. "Be mindful . . . webbed feet . . ."

Geoffrey looked up, appalled. Then he sighed and capitulated. "'Tis even as thou sayest, Puck. *Anything* thou sayest."

"Home," Gregory chirped.

5

They hurried on down the path, unnerved and shaken. Gregory glowered his darkest. "How could a man be so vile, Puck? 'Twould have been foul enow to weigh his greater strength against a woman; she had scant enough hope of fighting him even had she known she was beset—but to cast so horrid a spell on her, unawares!"

"'Tis, foul, I know," the elf agreed. "And men have done worse, lad."

"But to rend her whole life thus!" Cordelia cried.

Puck shrugged. "What cared he? So long as he felt the satisfaction of revenge—of what concern was her life to him?"

"'Tis the most vile of Sassenaches," Kelly muttered, face thunderous. "An we can find him, we must slay him!"

Gregory shuddered.

"That may not be true," Fess said quickly. "The wrong he has done, will not necessarily be righted by the equal wrong of his murder."

"Mayhap not—but it will surely prevent him from harming any others!"

"How now, brother," sneered Geoffrey, "thinkest thou to imprison a warlock?"

Magnus turned to scowl at his impertinent younger brother. "Wherefore not?"

"Why, for that he'll disappear clean from any cell thou mayest find for him!"

Gregory's eyes lost focus. "Mayhap there is a way..."

Geoffrey eyed him warily. "Dost think to craft a gaol that will hold a magic-worker? 'Ware, brother—ere thou dost find thyself imprisoned within it!"

"An he doth, he'll discover a way to come out," Magnus assured him, "yet no other would. An we can catch this vile sorcerer, I doubt not we can hold him."

"And how shalt thou catch him?" Cordelia scoffed.

"Why, thus!" Magnus cried, and he swatted at Geoffrey. "Tag!"

Geoffrey rounded on him, incensed, but Magnus disappeared with a bang—a double bang, for Geoffrey disappeared right after him. From a thicket a hundred feet away, his voice cried, "Tag!" followed by the sound of a small explosion, then another in an oak tree a few yards away; its top swayed with sudden weight. But a small boom echoed it, and the treetop lashed wildly as Magnus's voice shouted, "Thou art 'it'!" Geoffrey howled in anger, but Magnus answered with a laugh that cut off with another small explosion, followed immediately by another bang as Geoffrey disappeared after him.

Kelly leaped for the nearest oak root. "What manner of weird game is *this?*"

"'Tis young warlocks' play," Puck answered. "Dost know of mortal children's 'tag'?"

"Wherein one must flee while another seeks to touch him? Aye."

"'Tis much the same, save that the one who is 'it' must read in the other's mind, the instant ere he doth disappear, some passing hint of the place he doth flee to. Then the lad who is 'it' doth disappear also, and doth attempt to reappear in the same place as the one he pursueth, that he may tag him."

"And they who are not 'it' must needs try to hide their thoughts, so that he cannot follow them," Cordelia added, glaring toward the treetop.

Kelly frowned. "And if the one who is 'it' finds no hint of where the other is going? Or if he reads the hint wrongly?"

"Then must he cast about, mind open to all impressions, seeking his quarry's thoughts."

Magnus reappeared with a thunder-crack right behind Gregory, eyes alight with glee, crying, "Hide me!" and ducking down behind his little brother.

"Thou great oaf, I can see thee most clearly!" Cordelia cried; but Gregory squeezed his eyes shut, concentrating furiously, thinking of apples and oranges, of a large bowl of luscious fruit, of their tantalizing aromas.

Air boomed, and Geoffrey shouted, "Tag!" as he swatted Magnus's shoulder, then pivoted to Gregory. "I had lost him; he 'scaped without a trace of a thought of where he was bound. Yet when I listened for sign of his presence, all I could find was a picture of luscious fruits in thy mind—and, methought, 'There's no reason for Gregory to be so suddenly entranced with food.' Therefore did I know thou didst seek to hide knowledge of him—wherefore, he must needs be near thee."

"Thou dost talk overlong." Magnus slapped his shoulder and disappeared, crying, "'Ta . . .!"

"It will not serve," Geoffrey hollered. "Thou must needs remain long enough to finish the word!" But he was talking to empty air. With a hiss of impatience, he turned to tap Gregory. "Thou, too, art in this game! Tag!"

He disappeared with a firecracker's bang, and Gregory disappeared after him with a whoop of joy.

Cordelia stamped her foot. "Oh! How naughty of them! They know Papa was wroth with them for playing this game, how afeard he was that two of them might appear at once in the same place together, and both be slain!"

"Aye," Puck agreed, "till thy mother did explain to him how some instinct within a warlock's mind ever seeks ahead of himself, to be sure he will not appear inside a tree or rock —and that it must needs work so with this game of tag, sin that the one lad is always ahead of the other, by no matter how slight an interval."

"Oh, aye! Yet Papa did say that such a knack must have grown because little warlocks whose minds did not work in that fashion, must needs have died young!"

"Yet he could see thy brothers all lived," Puck reminded her, "and was therefore persuaded that their minds did have such guarding within." Privately, he thought Magnus had found an admirable way to shake his brothers and sister out of the effects of their harrowing night—and didn't doubt for an instant that the eldest had intended just that.

"Naetheless! Mama hath forbade them to play this game, when I've naught to do by myself!" Fuming with jealousy, Cordelia glared off toward the series of small explosions like a string of firecrackers. "Oh! Vile lads, to play so without me!"

"Yet what withholds ye?" Kelly demanded. "Go! After them! Horse and hattock! Ho, and away!"

"I cannot," Cordelia answered, seething.

Kelly frowned. "Wherefore not? Can ye not read minds as well as they?"

"Aye," Cordelia answered, "mayhap better—but I cannot teleport."

"No witch can." Puck frowned at Kelly. "'Tis a warlock's

power only. Dost not know so simple a fact?"

"Nay." Kelly reddened. "Nor do I now, since word of it has come only from an Englishman. Is 't true then, lass?"

Cordelia nodded, face thunderous.

"How do ye know it, then?"

"Papa hath told me, as Mama hath also. Nay, further—so hath every other witch and warlock that I've met."

"Ah, well, then," Kelly sighed, "if all do say so, it must needs be true."

Puck scowled at him. "Mind thy sarcasm!" But Cordelia didn't notice; she was too busy trying to follow the peripatetic tag game by telepathy, as the whole acre of woodland resounded with pops, bangs, and cries of "Tag!" "Nay, 'tis thou art 'it'!" "Base!" "There is no base!"

Air boomed, and Magnus stood before them, darting glances around the trail. "Where is he? Hath he not returned to thee, sister?"

"Nay, he hath not! Which 'he'?"

Geoffrey was there beside them with a bang, swatting at Magnus. "Tag!"

"Oh, be still!" Big Brother snapped, before Geoffrey could disappear. "I've lost track of Gregory."

Geoffrey shrugged. "'Tis his purpose, in this game. Rejoice that he doth it so well."

"I do not." Responsibility made Magnus peevish. "There's too great a chance of one so small being hurted. Listen for him, brother. If I can have but a single happy thought from him, I'll pretend I've heard it not, and take up our game again—but I must know he's safe!"

"Oh, Magnus!" Cordelia cried, exasperated. "He's no longer a babe! Gregory doth know what danger is!"

"Even so," Geoffrey agreed. "'Tis silly of thee to worry."

But for once, Magnus's concern was warranted.

Gregory popped into sight in the middle of a thicket some distance away, and found himself staring up at a half-dozen men in dirty, ragged livery, rusty steel caps, and three-day beards. They stared at each other, stupefied.

Then Gregory felt a surge of panic—but before he could think himself back to Magnus, two of the men lunged and seized his arms, and he froze in fright, staring up at them.

"Hugh!" cried one. "What in the name of all that's foul is *this?*"

"Ah, that? Why, 'tis a lad, Bertram—naught but a lad. Dost'a not see?"

"Oh. Well, uh, I can see 'tis a lad, Hugh—yet what doth it here?"

"Well asked." Hugh frowned down at Gregory. "And how came it amongst us so suddenly, and with so great a noise? What dost thou, boy?"

Well, after all, he was only six years old—and being Gregory, he couldn't think of anything but the truth. "Why, I do but play!"

"Play?" The men eyed him warily. "What manner of game is this?"

" 'Tis flit-tag."

" 'Flit-tag'?" Suspicion sharpened.

"Aye, one doth flit from place to place—and the other must seek in his mind to discover where he hath fled."

"In his mind?" Wariness was edged with fear, and the hands clenched more tightly on his arms. Gregory winced, but they paid him no heed.

"He is a witch-child!"

"Aye—yet which child?" Hugh fixed Gregory with a glare. "What is thy name?"

"Gr-Gregory. G-Gallowglass."

Bertram, Hugh, and their mates locked gazes. Together, they all nodded. " 'Tis the one we've been sent for."

Fear stabbed through Gregory, horror welling in behind it. What had he done?

Then he caught something odd, and the horror receded. He frowned. "Thy garb is motley. How canst thou be sent?"

Six gazes whipped back to him. "What?"

"Thy garb," Gregory repeated. "Thou dost not wear livery. Thou dost wear each colors that differ one from another. Thou art not, then, all of one lord's company; therefore no lord can have sent thee."

The men exchanged glances again. " 'Tis even as we've said," one snarled. " 'Tis a witch-brat."

"Aye! Let us slay him and be done with it!"

"Slay?" Gregory gasped, and his mind screamed, *Magnus! Cordelia! Geoffrey! Aid me!* "Why! Wherefore wouldst thou slay me? I have done thee no harm!"

"I would not be sure o' that, sin that thou art a witch's brat," Bertram snarled. "If thou hast such power as thou dost show, how canst thou *not* harm me?"

Gregory stared, made speechless by absurdity—and in his mind, Magnus's voice soothed, *Courage, brother.*

Oh, Gregory . . .!

Bide, Cordelia! Gregory, we dare not leap upon them, lest they strike at thee.

Yet if they do strike, thou must flit! Geoffrey added. *If thou dost bear two great hulking brutes with thee, fear not! We shall deal with them!*

If thou canst, Magnus agreed. *Yet we'll seek to come upon thee, if we may; 'tis more sure. Do thou keep them occupied in talk, the whiles we do stalk them.*

Gregory swallowed heavily, reassured, but still frightened. "Is that wherefore thou wouldst slay me?"

"Nay," Hugh growled. "For that, 'tis a matter of money, lad—pure silver. Living comes hard, to we who have fled to the greenwood. We must take food, or coin, where it comes."

They are soldiers who have deserted their lords! Geoffrey's thought was scandalized and enraged. *'Ware, lad! For an they did flee their posts, belike 'twas for that they'd committed heinous crimes!*

Thou dost not aid, Magnus thought, exasperated. *Gregory, lad! They do wish to talk! Ask, accuse! But keep them in speech!*

Keep them in speech! How? But Gregory plucked up his courage, and tried. "How—how will slaying me, gain thee silver? I have none!"

"A thought," growled another soldier, and he patted Gregory quickly down both sides, then shook his head. "'Tis as he doth say—he hath no purse."

"Surely not, Clodog!" said Hugh in disgust. "'Tis but a lad, when all's said and done."

"'Tis a fee," Bertram explained. "They have hired us to slay thee—and thy sister and brothers."

Gregory felt a cold chill spread out from his spine. "Yet— how canst thou know who to slay?"

"Why, the High Warlock's children!" Hugh replied. "How could we mistake thee? All in Gramarye do know of thee— three warlock-lads and a witchling!"

Gregory tried to ignore the mental squawks of rage. "Who —who could have hired thee? Who doth hate us so?"

"Any of thy father's enemies, I warrant," Bertram snorted.

Hugh shrugged. "Who can say who they were? We know only that three slight, meager men with burning eyes did come

to us, give us silver, and promise us more if we slew thee."
He shook his head sadly. "'Tis a pity—thou dost seem a good
enough lad."

"An he were not a warlock," Clodog growled.

"Still, we have need of the silver," Bertram grunted, and
he whipped a dagger up.

"Nay, hold!" Gregory stared at the naked blade, terrified.
"An they will pay thee silver to slay us, Papa will pay thee
more to spare us!"

The dagger hovered, but hesitated. "More?"

"Gold!" Gregory cried in desperation.

"Yet who will pay it?" Hugh scoffed. "Thy father is vanished! So the meager men did say—and so say all we have
heard by the roadside!"

"The King!" Gregory gasped. "King Tuan will ransom us!"

The thugs exchanged glances again. "Belike he will," Bertram said slowly. "'Tis known how the King doth treasure his
warlocks."

"I mislike the thought." Another bandit darted glances
about the thicket, as though expecting to see King's men pushing through the brambles.

"Eh, he'll not come himself," Hugh growled. "Dost thou
think a king to be a page? Nay, belike he'll send a knight."

"With men-at-arms!"

"We'll bid him not to."

Gregory sighed with relief, going limp. Then he saw the
glint in Hugh's eye and tensed again.

"Wherefore ought we to take gold for one, when we may
have gold for four?" Hugh purred.

Gregory watched him, feeling like a sparrow beset by a
snake.

The dagger whipped about and down, its point pricking
Gregory's throat. He gasped in horror and froze.

"Call thy brother," Hugh breathed.

Gregory stared at him, wide-eyed. *Magnus! He doth wish
thee to come, too! Do not—'tis danger!*

Mayhap, Magnus thought slowly, *yet not for us.*

The dagger twisted, pricking deeper. "There is blood on
thy throat," Hugh growled. "Summon him!"

Air boomed. Even though they'd known it was coming, the
thugs flinched away. Geoffrey stood beside his little brother,
his lip twisted with contempt. "He hath summoned. What wilt
thou have of me?"

Hugh reddened, and stepped forward again. "What! Is there no more than this?"

Geoffrey set his jaw, eyes narrowing. "Aye, there do be more Gallowglass children. Art truly so foolish as to wish us all here?"

Huge hands seized him, and Hugh snarled, "'Tis thou who art foolish. Summon thy brother!"

"Be not so hasty," Geoffrey sneered. "I do marvel thou hast the courage for it, sin that thou wast so craven as to flee thy lord!"

The back of Hugh's hand cracked into his cheek. "Mind thy tongue, when thou dost speak to thy betters! Now summon thy brother!"

"On thy head be it, then," Geoffrey gasped, and thought, *Come, brother! The lambs are led to the pen!*

Magnus was there, in a crack of thunder. He nodded to Hugh with grave courtesy. "My sibs tell me thou dost wish speech with us."

The soldiers stared, frozen.

Magnus nodded, with sympathy. "Aye, 'tis unnerving. My father hath said he shall never become accustomed to such flittings in and out."

Bertram swore, and set the edge of his dagger against Magnus's throat.

"Hold!" Hugh barked. "We lack yet one!"

"What—my sister? Wouldst thou slay lasses also?"

"Do not seek to school me." Hugh's eyes narrowed. "What I must needs do for a living, I must needs do."

"Thou mayest yet live without slaying children."

Hugh turned and spat. "Hiding in thickets? Sleeping on bracken? Eating roots and berries and, with good fortune, the meat of a badger? 'Tis not what I would call living! For that, I need gold."

"Which thou wilt gain by my blood?"

"Aye, and thy liver and lights, if need be!" Hugh roared. "Now summon thy sister!"

Magnus sighed, and closed his eyes.

Save thine effort. Rage imbued Cordelia's thoughts. *I flit to thee already!*

And Robin?

He hath gone before, with Kelly! Fess stands ready, too, if needed, but I shall leave my sweet unicorn behind.

"She comes," Magnus reported, "yet more slowly; lasses cannot appear and disappear."

"We'll be done with thee, then," Hugh snarled, and nodded to Bertram. The brute grinned and yanked the dagger back for a stab.

Gregory bleated and twisted; his brothers shouted as his body whiplashed, slamming the thugs who held him against the ground. Bertram's dagger stabbed into bare dirt.

Then a tearing scream pierced their ears, and a missile shot down from the sky to slam into Bertram, knocking him backwards. "Foul beast!" the ten-year-old witch cried. "Wouldst thou then slay babes?"

The other thugs roared and leaped for her—and lurched against something unseen, something that yanked them up to dangle, feet a foot off the ground, as their faces grew purple and they thrashed about in panic—but the only sound that emerged from their throats was a muted gargling.

Hugh stared up at them, pop-eyed; then he whirled and slammed a vicious backhand blow into Magnus's face, knocking him back and away. He yanked Gregory up against him, holding the boy in front of his chest and backing away, his own dagger in his hand. "Stay away! Do not seek to take me—or I'll slit his throat!"

Geoffrey's eyes narrowed, and a rock shot up off the forest floor to crack into Hugh's skull. His arm loosened as his eyes rolled up, and he slumped to the ground.

"Gregory! Art thou hurted?" Cordelia dove for her baby brother, cradling him in her arms; but he stared past her shoulder at the men dangling from the trees, fear and horror in his face. "Cordelia! What hath happed to them?"

Into the ring of hanging thugs strode an eighteen-inch elf, face white with rage. "Hear! Oh men of no heart—as I know thou canst for a minute more, ere thy breath ceases. 'Tis the Puck who doth stand before thee, and elves who ride the high branches above thee, with nooses braided of hundreds of strands of spiders' silk that thou canst see not!"

"Eh! Fell captain!" cried a voice from the leaves, and the children turned to see Kelly strutting on a limb by a small brown person who knelt, guarding an invisible twine. "Shall we harvest this rotting fruit, then?"

"Puck, do not slay them!" Cordelia cried. "They be evil men, yet surely not so evil as that!"

"Be not so certain." Geoffrey stood glaring up, pale and trembling. "They have fled from their brothers in arms. Surely such could do anything, no matter how foul."

But the thrashing was weakening, stilling, and the staring eyes dulled.

Puck nodded at Kelly. "Cut them down."

The Irishman nodded at the brownies, and the thugs fell with a crash. Foot-high elves popped up next to them, slashing with tiny knives, and the deserters' chests rose, slowly.

"They live." Puck spat. "Though I regret it. Still, I would not afright thee too greatly."

"I thank thee," Cordelia breathed, and Gregory, huddled next to her, nodded.

The elf stumped over to the unconscious Hugh, eyes hidden in a scowl. "He doth lie senseless, children, yet I've no doubt thou canst peer within his mind. Do thou find the pictures of the men who have bribed these villains to slay thee."

The children crowded around, and Cordelia frowned down at Hugh's face. They waited, poised; the image appeared in her mind, and the others saw it, then sat back with a sigh.

"'Tis the slight ones," Magnus said, "the old ones with scant hair and burning eyes."

Gregory nodded. "They who seek to abolish all governance."

"As indeed they must be," Geoffrey said, "and have gone far already in so doing." He shuddered. "Only think! That governance could be so far decayed as for soldiers to desert their stations!"

6

They set off into the moonlit wood, Puck leading the way with Cordelia right behind him on her unicorn. Kelly brought up the rear, on its rump. "Wherefore," said he, "should I then walk?"

"And thou hast the gall to excoriate *me* for lack of industry," Puck snorted.

But half an hour into the woods, the unicorn suddenly stopped, lifting her head and looking off toward the east.

Geoffrey frowned. "What ails her?"

"I think that she doth hear summat that we cannot." Puck cupped his ear, listening. Then he shook his head. "An she doth, it escapes me quite. What sayest thou, Horseface?"

"A moment, while I boost amplification." Fess lifted his head, ears turned in the direction the unicorn was pointing. "I do hear cries. They are very high-pitched, and faint with distance."

"'High-pitched'?" Puck scowled. "And of interest to a unicorn? That hath the sound of Wee Folk in need of aid. Come, children! Let us seek!"

The children didn't need persuading.

They wound through the woods for half an hour, with Puck dodging around the roots of shrubs and through gaps in the underbrush, and Fess following him, to beat down a path. Behind him came the unicorn, with her nostrils flaring, and white showing all around her eyes.

Finally, the children could hear the cries too. They were very high, as Fess had said, and sounded very distressed. As they came closer, the children could understand the words: "A rescue! A rescue!" "Help us! Aid, good folk!"

"There is, at least, no present danger," Cordelia said. "There's unhappiness in those words, but no *great* fear."

"Then let us find them ere it comes," Magnus said.

" 'Tis here!" Puck cried.

The children stopped, startled, for the voices had still been so faint that they had thought them some distance away. But Puck dove into the underbrush almost under Fess's nose and started pulling back branches. The unicorn let out a musical neigh and pushed forward, pawing at the bushes and fallen leaves. Between them, they uncovered a small iron cage, with two foot-high people in it. They were clothed in green, the one decorated with flowers, the other with red, yellow, and orange leaves. They looked up with children's faces, and cried with delight when they saw the unicorn.

" 'Tis one of the Silver People!"

"Greeting, Velvet One! What good chance brings thee?"

The unicorn whickered softly, butting her nose against the cage.

"She wants them out." Cordelia knelt by the cage, and the two fairies fell silent, staring up at her, wide-eyed. "Oh, fear me not! I wish thee no hurt!"

" 'Tis but a lass," the flowered one said to her sister, in a high, clear voice.

"Aye! A bairn would not wish us ill!" The leafy one turned back to Cordelia. "I am Fall, and here is my sister, Summer."

Summer dropped a curtsy. She was chubby and ruby-cheeked, with a smile that seemed as though it could never fade.

"I am Cordelia." The girl bobbed her head in lieu of a curtsy, since she was already kneeling. "What is this horrid contrivance that houses thee?"

"Why, 'tis a rabbit's trap." Puck sauntered up. "How now, sprites! What coneys art thou, to be caught in so rude a snare?"

"As much as thou art a lob, to stand there and jibe without loosing us," Fall retorted. She was slender and supple, with short-cropped brown hair.

"A hare was caught within," Summer explained. "We could hear its frantic thumpings, and we took sticks to pry the door up and free it."

"Most kindly done." Puck grinned. "And did it lock thee in, for thanks?"

"Nearly," Fall confessed. "We held up the door, and the hopper thumped on out—but as it fled, one great hind foot caught me in the middle, and sent me sprawling. My sister could not keep the door up alone."

"It crashed down on me, most shrewdly," Summer sighed, "and we were trapped within."

"But what manner of trap is this, that can hold a fairy?" Cordelia asked.

"One of Cold Iron," Puck snorted. "What fools were they, to risk such capture!"

"And what a knob art thou, to stand and mock us!" Fall jammed her tiny fists on her hips, glaring at him.

"Truly, Puck!" Cordelia reproached him. "'Tis most unkind of thee! Hast thou no care for others' feelings?"

"Why, none! Or canst thou truly believe that they'd be thereby injured?"

"Nay, certes they would! Unkind words too oft give hurt!"

"Nay, not to them. Say, ask!"

Cordelia turned a questioning glance on the two fairies.

A slow, grudging grin grew on Fall's face. "I cannot deny it. His teasing doth not trouble me."

"Nor I," her sister smiled, "so long as we may chide him in return."

"As bad as children," Cordelia proclaimed with every ounce of her ten-year-old dignity.

"And as careless of time as a grown-up." Geoffrey frowned, glancing about him. "Whosoe'er set this trap, will shortly come to search it. Ought we not to set them free?"

"Aye, at once!" Cordelia fumbled with the trap. "Yet how doth it open?"

"Ye've but to lift," Geoffrey snorted. He knelt down, pressed a catch, and lifted the door. The two fairies darted out and swirled up into the air on gossamer wings, caroling with joy. "Free! Free!" "Ah, the blessed air!"

"And the cursed Cold Iron." Puck glowered at the trap. "How comes this, elf? Must the folk of thy woods forever be using traps of steel?"

"Nay, or the Wee Folk would torment them sore." Kelly stumped up beside him, glowering at the cage. "Our trappers here use wooden boxes when they wish to take their prey alive, or, if they do not, then snares of cord that slay in a moment."

"Then there's a hunter newly come unto thy woods," Puck said grimly, "or an old one who's taken up new ways." He turned to Summer and Fall. "Ward thee, fairies—for I misdoubt me an some souls do be preaching disregard of Wee Folk unto all the parish."

"And disregard of animals' suffering," Kelly agreed. "Beware—mayhap more traps of iron dot yer forest."

"An they do, they'll be quickly buried," Fall promised.

"Never fear—we'll broadcast word," Summer affirmed. "And we thank thee, mortals." She dropped a curtsy to Geoffrey and Cordelia. "We owe thee favor now."

Cordelia exchanged an excited glance with Geoffrey. To have fairies owing them favors!

"If ever thou hast need," Fall agreed, "only call, anywhere throughout this Isle of Gramarye, and Wee Folk will fly to aid thee."

"That doth not mean their aid will suffice." Puck fixed the children with a gimlet glare. "Thou shouldst not therefore court danger."

"Be sure, we'll not," Cordelia said, round-eyed.

Puck didn't say a word; he only bent a stern glance on Geoffrey.

The boy glared back at him, then looked away, then back again. "Oh, as thou wilt have it! Nor will I court danger, neither!"

"'Tis well." Puck nodded, satisfied, and turned back to Summer and Fall. "But we will seek. Some mortal doth speak for Cold Iron in the elves' demesne—and that we'll not abide. Nay, we must seek him out, and school him. Children, come!"

He turned, striding off through the forest.

The children stared at his upright, determined back in total surprise. Then Geoffrey grinned and started after the elf.

Magnus looked down at Gregory, then grinned and hoisted the little boy to ride before him. Gregory squealed with delight and thumped his heels against Fess's sides. The great black beast seemed to sigh.

Cordelia followed all of them on her unicorn, singing softly, "A-hunting we will go, a-hunting we will go . . ."

7

As they traveled along the forest path, Geoffrey glowered behind at Cordelia, swaying gently on the unicorn's back and singing happily as she plaited a wreath of flowers. The two fairies rode with her, chatting. But Magnus kept an eye on his younger brother, and was well aware that his scowl was deepening and his mood darkening. After a little while, he turned to Puck. "It hath been some few hours that we've been afoot, Robin. I do grow a-hungered."

Geoffrey looked up sharply. "Aye! Food, good Puck! I shall find it, and gladly! Let us rest and dine!"

Fess glanced up at the leafy canopy and calculated the time from the light. "The sun will rise soon. Stop and rest—and find whatever is about that may be edible."

Geoffrey whooped and disappeared into the leaves. They rustled for a second or two; then none but the songbirds knew he existed—and even they might not have been sure.

Cordelia slid down from the unicorn's back. "Eh! What berries may I find nearby, good Summer?"

"Raspberries, mayhap. Come, and I shall show thee!"

Gregory sat down, leaned back against a tree. In three breaths, his eyes closed and his head nodded forward.

Puck smiled. "I had thought as much. 'Twas little sleep thou hadst this night past."

"Naetheless, Geoffrey will not wish to nap," Magnus warned.

Puck shrugged impatiently. "He never doth; he fears some part of life will pass him by, the whiles he sleeps. Even so, he hath need of slumber."

"Aye—he doth grow sullen. I think that he doth aim this secret anger at Cordelia's unicorn."

Fess agreed. "Yes. Because it allows her to ride, but will not let him near."

"That could breed trouble," Magnus mused.

Puck shot him a keen glance. "Thou wilt be a wise captain some day, youngling. 'Tis even as thou sayest—thou must needs find some way to quench his envy, or he'll wreak havoc."

"'Tis as I've thought," Magnus admitted, "yet I can see no way to it. The unicorn will not abide him near. What can I do?"

"Thou hast not seen it, then?" Puck grinned. "Seek within the terms of the situation, lad. The unicorn will not allow him near—yet doth it bear him ill?"

"Nay," Magnus said slowly, "not while he doth keep his distance."

Puck nodded, waiting.

"So," Magnus mused, "I must find some way for the beast to pay him heed, though he cometh not nigh."

Puck broke into a broad grin. "Thou hast the right of it. Now thou hast but to find the way."

Magnus found it as they finished breakfast.

As they ate, he sat there, looking about him, trying to find something to pull Geoffrey out of his black jealousy. The younger boy was a bit better, now that Cordelia had climbed down off her high horse long enough to gather a quart of berries and join them for roast partridge; but Magnus knew it would be just as bad, just as quickly, when she mounted again, and Geoffrey had to watch her riding. He could fly, of course, or ride Fess, but that was boring now. Riding a unicorn was something new.

Magnus eyed the unicorn, standing thirty-feet away, nibbling at some leaves. Then, as he turned back to his brothers and sister, his gaze fell on the wreaths Cordelia had plaited, resting on her head and on those of the fairies. The idea hit, and Magnus slowly grinned. "Cordelia—wilt thou lend me thy wreath?"

The girl looked up warily. "What wouldst thou do with it?"

"Naught but to play a game."

Cordelia eyed him, not trusting the simplicity of his claim —but she couldn't see anything wrong with it, so she held out the stack of wreaths with a glare.

Magnus caught them up and, with a gleeful whoop, flipped one sailing toward the unicorn.

She looked up, startled, poised to flee—and saw the wreath skimming through the air toward her. She whinnied, ducked to aim her horn, and caught the flower loop with a toss of her head.

"Nay!" Cordelia cried, leaping to her feet. " 'Tis not fair!"

But Magnus was flipping wreaths to Geoffrey and Gregory, and the unicorn was swinging her head around in a circle, making the wreath spin around her horn, then suddenly ducked, and the flower ring sped back toward Magnus. He caught it with a yelp of delight. "I had not thought she could toss back to me!"

"Play with me, too!" Gregory cried, and spun his wreath through the air toward the unicorn.

"Nay, 'tis *my* turn!" Geoffrey insisted, and his wreath went flying, too.

Gregory's ring flew wide; he was a little short on motor development, but the unicorn dashed to the left and caught it anyway. Then, with a leap, she was back where she had been, to catch Geoffrey's wreath and rear up, pawing the air with a triumphant whinny.

"No! Nay, now! Give back my wreaths!" Cordelia shouted.

"Peace, lass," Puck counseled. "They do but play, and will give thee back thy wreaths when they are done."

"But they will have torn them to shreds!"

"And if they do, what of it? Thou mayest weave more quite easily."

"Oh, thou dost not comprehend, Robin! Ooh! They make me so angered!"

"Aye, certes," Puck said softly. "Why, 'tis thy unicorn, is't not?"

"Aye! How dare they play with her!"

"Why dost thou not join also?" Puck asked. "If she can play with three, she can most certainly play with four."

"But they have no right to play with her at all! She is *mine!*"

"Nay, now. There, I say nay." Puck shook his head. "She is a wild and free thing, child, and though she may befriend thee, that doth not give thee ownership over her. Never think it, for if she doth feel constrained, she will flee from thee."

Cordelia was silent, glaring at her brothers, growing angrier and angrier at their whoops of glee.

"She doth prance to catch each ring," Summer piped up, "and her eyes sparkle. She whinnies with delight. Nay, if I mistake me not, this unicorn doth rejoice to play at ring-toss thus—so long as thy brothers keep their distance."

Cordelia's glower lessened a bit.

"You," Fess pointed out, "are the only one who can go close to the beast. Why not, therefore, let your brothers have what little pleasure she'll permit them?"

"'Twould be most generous of thee to allow it," Summer agreed.

Cordelia's glower was almost gone now.

"Show them thou dost grudge them not their sport," Fall urged.

"Why, how may I do that?"

"Play," the fairy answered.

Cordelia stood, wavering.

"What!" Kelly cried. "Will ye have them gaming with yer unicorn, while ye yerself do not?"

Cordelia's lips firmed with decision. She caught up a handful of flowers.

"I have one plaited for thee." Summer thrust a wreath into her hand.

"I thank thee, good Summer!" Cordelia dashed forward, tossing her ring backhanded toward the unicorn. The silver animal saw, and caught it with a neigh of delight, then sent it spinning back.

Summer heaved a sigh of relief.

"Aye," Puck agreed. "'Twas a near thing, that—but we have them all a-play together."

"And the lass will not turn away from the unicorn in angered jealousy." Fall beamed.

"A steaming kettle of nonsense," Kelly muttered. "Wherefore must these mortals be so obstinate?" Nonetheless, he, like the other three, gazed at the playing children with a smile of satisfaction. In fact, they were so taken with the sight that they didn't notice the four brawny men slipping from tree trunk to tree trunk all around the clearing, coming closer and closer to the children.

They drifted up as silently as the wind in the brush, till they stood just behind the first rank of trees—burly men in livery, with steel caps and ring-mail jerkins, watching the children, poised to spring.

Cordelia decided to assert her position as resident unicornfriend, and skipped up toward her, holding up her ring of flowers. "Here, O Silver One! I shall not hurl this, but give it thee!"

The nearest man leaped out, sprinting toward her.

Just then, Geoffrey tossed a wreath a little too far to the side. The ungenerous might have thought he intended to hit Cordelia with it.

But the unicorn didn't. It spun and leaped, tossing its head to catch the ring on its horn.

The soldier gave a shout of triumph as he pounced on Cordelia.

The unicorn's horn slashed through his jerkin. Blood welled out of his arm. The man shrank back with a bleat of terror, pale and trembling at such a close brush with death.

"Footpad!" Geoffrey howled in anger. "A vile villain come to seize our sister! Brothers, rend him!"

But the trees and bushes all around them erupted, armed men boiling out of them with blood-curdling battle cries, leaping toward the children and catching them up with yells of triumph. Gregory squalled, and Cordelia shrieked with rage. But Geoffrey clamped his jaw shut, narrowed his eyes for better aim, and sent his wreath sailing right into the face of Cordelia's captor.

The soldier was startled; his hold loosened, and Cordelia twisted free.

Magnus's wreath skimmed into the face of Gregory's captor. It was a rose wreath, with thorns. The man bellowed in pain, and dropped Gregory, who shot up like a rocket and disappeared into the leaves above. Geoffrey's captor saw and blanched, just before Cordelia's wreath struck him on the brow. Geoffrey shot away from him to land beside Cordelia. "Thou hadst no need to aid! I would have had him kneeling in an instant!"

"Ever the mannerly gentleman, thou," she scoffed.

The last soldier tightened his hold on Magnus. "Thy wreaths shall avail thee naught—I shall not loose my hold!"

Magnus glanced down at the man's feet. A creeper nearby unwound itself from the base of a sapling and writhed over to the soldier, winding up around his mailed leg, then yanking hard. He shouted a startled oath, lurching back, then caught his balance—but for a moment, his hands loosened, and Magnus sprang free.

The first soldier shouted in anger and leaped at Cordelia again.

The unicorn sprang forward, head down, horn stabbing. The man leaped aside with a shout of fear, and the silver horn scored a trail of blood across his cheek. He dodged back, drawing his sword; but the unicorn danced before him, parrying his lunges and thrusting at him, driving him back.

"Wouldst thou hurt her then?" Cordelia cried. "Vile wretch! Have at thee!" His sword wrenched itself out of his hand and flipped about to dance in front of his face. He paled and backed away, until he bumped into a tree trunk and could go no further. Nearby, three more soldiers fell under the hooves of the great black horse.

Another soldier bellowed and lunged at Geoffrey. The lad disappeared with a bang and reappeared a second later behind the soldier, jamming a knee against the back of his neck and an arm across his throat. The soldier turned purple, gargling and clawing at Geoffrey's arm, then yanked and bowed, sending the boy tumbling through the air. He didn't land, of course—he only soared up higher, yanking a rotten fruit from a tree and hurling it down at the soldier as he cried, "Cordelia! Mount and ride! We may not retreat whiles thou dost remain!"

"Wherefore retreat?" she retorted. "Let us stay and knock them senseless!"

"For once, he hath the right of it." Puck stood by her knee. "Thou mayest prevail—or they may take thee unawares, one by one, and capture thee all. Flee, damsel! Or dost thou wait to see one hurl a spear through thy unicorn?"

Cordelia gasped in horror and whirled to leap onto the unicorn's back. "Quickly, my sweet! Leave these swinish men far behind!"

The unicorn reared, whinnying, then leaped out and sprang into a gallop, dodging away between the trees so lithely that she seemed to dart through their trunks.

"One hath escaped, Auncient!" a soldier cried.

"We shall follow and find!" the biggest soldier answered. "Seize these!"

"'Tis not likely," Geoffrey retorted, and more rotten fruit came plunging off the tree. The soldiers leaped aside, but the fruits veered to follow them, and landed in their faces with a gooey sound.

"Be off, while they're blinded!" Puck cried. "Retreat, lads! Avoid!"

"Wherefore?" Geoffrey's eyes glittered with excitement as he landed; his whole body was tensed for battle. "Dost truly think they can stand against us?"

"Mayhap! Thou mayest lapse, thou mayest grow careless!"

"Yet we are not like to! Nay! Let us stay, and stretch them senseless on the greensward!"

"There is no need," Magnus pointed out, "and 'tis witless to hurt them when we need not."

Geoffrey hesitated.

"We shall brawl at thy side, when we must," Gregory piped, "as we have done already. Yet now, brother, I prithee —let us be gone, sin that we can!"

"Away!" Puck commanded. "Till we discover who hath sent them! Why seize the sheep, when thou mayest have the shepherd?"

The soldiers finished wiping the goo off their faces and strode forward.

"So be it, then," Geoffrey said with disgust. "We go!" He relaxed, straightening up, and disappeared with a bang. A double explosion echoed his, and the soldiers found themselves staring at one another over an empty clearing.

Gregory turned the spit slowly, eyes huge and mouth watering as he watched the roasting partridges growing brown.

"What word, Puck?" The firelight reflected off Magnus's face as he watched a tiny elf muttering into Puck's ear. The sprite darted away, and Puck sat up straight, nodding. "'Tis even as we thought."

Geoffrey nodded with satisfaction. "Their livery was in good repair, and their weapons bright. These were no renegades, but men-at-arms of some lord."

"And, their mission failed, they returned to their master," Magnus finished.

Puck nodded. "So indeed they did—but knew not that elfin eyes watched their every step." He grinned, preening. "I thought that I did know that livery."

"What is it then?"

"The lord's arms confirm it," Puck bragged. "He is Count Drosz, a nobleman of Hapsburg."

"Of Hapsburg?" Geoffrey frowned. "What doth he in Tudor?"

"Small good, belike," Cordelia opined.

"What dost thou think, Robin?" Magnus asked. "Doth he come to join Earl Tudor in some form of mischief?"

"Nay!" Geoffrey's eyes lit with excitement. "Belike he doth seek to join battle with Glynn, the lord of this county! Oh, Robin! A melee! Please, oh! I must follow, to watch!"

"Nay!" Puck recoiled, startled and horrified. "A lad of eight, near a battle? 'Tis too great a chance thou might be hurted!"

"Assuredly they'd not harm a child!"

Puck started to answer, then caught himself, and said only, "Thou knowest little of the ways of soldiers in wartime, lad. Nay. What should I say to thy father and mother, if thou didst come to harm?"

"But . . .!"

"Nay!" Puck snapped. "Let thy father escort thee near battle-lines if he will, when that he doth return! Let his conscience bear the chance of thine hurt, if he will—but I will not risk it, whiles thou art in my care! Thou art not my son, after all."

"Praise Heaven," Geoffrey muttered as Puck turned stamping away into the forest.

The elf turned back, frowning at the children. "Now come, follow me!"

"But," Gregory pointed out, "the soldiers have gone in the other direction."

"Thou hast noticed," Puck said dryly. "Come."

8

A little after sunrise, they came out of the forest into a meadow dotted with wildflowers. "How pretty!" Cordelia exclaimed; then, "Yon is a footpath!"

Off to their right, a dusty track wound down the slope toward the fields below.

"And people beyond it." Magnus squinted from his vantage point on Fess's back. "Eh, but they're awake betimes!"

"Country people rise before the sun," Fess informed them. "May I suggest the unicorn seek a more discreet route?"

"But why?" Cordelia cried.

Puck shook his head. "I must own the iron beast hath the right of it. Bethink thee, child, what mortal men, full grown, would seek to do with such a creature."

Cordelia stared, her eyes widening. "Surely thou dost not mean they would wish to enslave her!"

"Aye, certes they would—and would try to steal her from one another." Geoffrey smiled with tolerance for his sister's innocence. "And the creature might be slain in the fighting."

Cordelia leaped down from the unicorn's back as though it were a hot griddle. "Oh, I could not bear it!" She caught the great silver head between her hands and stroked the muzzle. "I could not bear to have thee hurted! Nay, my love, my jewel! Go thou, and hide thee! Be assured, we'll meet again when we come back to this forest."

But the unicorn tossed her head as though scorning danger.

"Nay, I beg of thee!" Cordelia pleaded. "Hide thee! Thou knowest not how vile some men may be!"

Puck smiled, with a cynicism that softened into fondness.

The unicorn gazed into Cordelia's eyes. Then she tossed her head, turning, and trotted back into the forest.

"Will I see her again, thinkest thou, Puck?"

"Who may say?" Puck said softly. "Such creatures are wild and free; no man may summon them, nor no young lass, neither. They come when they wish." He turned to smile up at

Cordelia. "Yet I think this one will wish it."

He turned away. "Now, come! Let's trace this track that thou hast found!"

They went down a slope glorious with blossoms. As they neared the bottom, they passed a stile, a set of stairs that went up one side of a wall and came down the other, so that people could cross, but cattle could not. A pretty peasant girl was leaning against the stile with a mocking smile, gazing up through half-lowered eyelashes at a young farmhand who stood, rigid with anger, fists clenched so tightly his knuckles were white.

"Nay, then, Corin," the peasant girl purred. "How durst thou think that I might spare a glance for one who's craven?"

Magnus and Geoffrey stopped to stare at the girl. "Why, she is beautiful," Magnus breathed.

Geoffrey swallowed heavily.

Cordelia looked at them as though they'd taken leave of their senses. So, for that matter, did Gregory.

"Craven?" Corin exploded. "Nay! I'm as brave as any man! Show me any foe, and I will fight him!"

"Foe?" she scoffed. "Nay, walk into the greenwood! Go into the hills! Stride down any highway! Thy foes will leap to meet thee—bandits, thieves, and outlaws! 'Tis come to be so bad as that! Any man who's restless, or hath an ounce of mettle, doth break the law, and runneth off to hide and thieve —and leaveth wife and children to the care of those dull males who have no daring!"

Puck had hidden in the heather near Magnus's foot, but the children could hear him growl, "Assuredly, 'tis never so bad as that!"

"'Tis not a word of truth!" Corin bawled. "'Tis not needful for a man to work evil, only because he's a man! Nay, there's strength required to stay and ward, and care for those ye love!"

"Love?" the girl sneered. "I spit on that which you call love! Oh, caring there may be—but there's naught of thrill nor joy within it!"

Corin stepped toward her, hands outstretched, palms up. "If thou didst love me, thou wouldst see the error of thy words."

"An I did love thee," she spat, "I would needs be as dull as thou! Nay, how could I love a man who'd leave his wife and bairns in threat of pillaging?"

"I would never do so!" Corin cried.

"Yet thou dost! Thou dost permit these bandits to roam wild throughout the hills! Thou dost give leave to highwaymen to rob and beat whomsoe'er they please! Nay, no woman's safe to walk abroad now by herself! Within these two days gone, three lasses that I know have suffered, and a dozen men have run off to the hills. *True* men." Her eyes glittered as she looked directly into his. "Not mere boys."

"In only two days' time?" Puck snorted. "Such could never hap so quickly."

But Fess's voice sounded inside their heads: *It could, if the High Warlock's enemies were fully prepared to accomplish such disorder, and were only waiting for his disappearance to unleash their agents.*

Corin had reddened. "Thou dost wrong me, sweet Phebe! What could I do to halt them? At the least, I stay to guard the village!"

"And assuredly, thou wilt repel them when they come against us," she said with sarcasm.

"What else might I do?" he cried.

"Why, join the Shire-Reeve and march behind his banner! Go to fight for him, and capture or put down these outlaws who would prey on us! That is what thou mayest do—and might have, these three days past! Yet I misdoubt me an thou wilt, for there'd be danger! Only real men, who can conquer fear, will fight for him!"

Corin's face firmed with resolution. He straightened, squaring his shoulders. "Thou dost wrong me, Phebe. I will go unto him straightaway—and thou shalt see how little I do fear!"

"Brave lad!" she cried, and leaped forward to seize his face and give him such a kiss as he had likely never had—a kiss both long and lasting; and, when she stepped back, he gasped for air, and seemed quite dazed.

"Go now," she cooed, "and show me what a man may earn!"

He nodded, not quite focusing, and turned away to drift on up the pasture lane between plowed fields, off toward the highway.

Phebe watched him go—and as she did, her face hardened, and her eyes glittered with contempt.

"And such, I doubt not, hath she done to half the lads of the village," Puck muttered, unseen. "Kelly, go! Find near elves, and tell them to ask for news: Hath banditry truly begun so horribly in only two days' time? And discover, too, if other maids have done as she hath."

"I go," the leprecohen's voice crackled. "Begorra! If such as she taunts men to this Shire-Reeve's army, we'll know what to do with him!"

But Magnus was drifting toward Phebe, and Geoffrey was following as though an invisible string drew him.

Magnus cleared his throat. "Your pardon, but we have heard what thou hast said. Tell, we pray, who is this Shire-Reeve thou speakest of?"

Phebe whirled about in surprise, then smiled, amused. "Why, child! Knowest thou not what a reeve is?"

"Aye," said Magnus, "'tis the man who doth tend to all the King's business in a district. A shire-reeve is one who doth take the King's taxes and levy low justice for a whole shire; and he must put down bandits if the barons do not."

"There! Thou didst know it, straightway," Phebe laughed. "Yet our Shire-Reeve is somewhat more—for look you, he is Reeve of Runnymede; and he hath seen that even in the King's own shire, Their Majesties cannot keep down bandits and highwaymen. Nay, even more—they cannot keep their kingdom in peace and order! Ever must the King's army be marching and countermarching, trampling through the hard-grown crops and levying stores of provender that we peasant folk put by for winter, to be putting down rebellions, and those who would unseat Their Majesties from their thrones. In but the last two days the Counts of Llewellyn and Glynn have taken it into their heads to take more land into their counties —and have not thought it needful to ask a by-your-leave of Their Majesties! So they do call up all their knights, who call their peasants away from their fields, and this with the summer haying hard by, to go make war upon each other! And what do Their Majesties do, what?"

"I know not." Geoffrey gazed up at her, entranced. "What do they?"

"Why, naught, little one," she said, with a silvery laugh. "They do naught! And our good Shire-Reeve hath grown weary of such lawlessness. Nay, he hath risen up in righteous wrath, and hath declared that the King hath failed to govern. And, saith he, an the King will not wield the law to keep the peace, our Reeve will, himself! 'Tis for this he doth gather lads for his armed band—that he may, by force of arms, put down these bandits, and make the roads once again so safe that a woman may walk them alone. Already hath he sallied 'gainst an outlaw band and broken them—and daily do more young lads flock to his banner!"

"Small wonder," Cordelia muttered, "an they do encounter lasses like to thee!"

"Why 'tis glorious!" Geoffrey shouted. "Let us join with this Shire-Reeve! Let us, too, go forth to do battle with evil-doers and outlaws! Let it be said of us that we, too, did aid in restoring the peace!"

"I had not known it had fallen so badly," Cordelia said dryly.

"Only since Mama and Papa went away," Gregory reminded.

Magnus's gaze stayed glued to Phebe's face, but he gave his head a little shake and blinked. "Nay, tell me—what difference is there between what this Shire-Reeve doth and what the counts do? Is he not also making war, and disturbing the peace?"

Phebe frowned. "Oh, nay! He doth restore the peace!"

"By making battle?" Gregory asked.

Phebe's face darkened.

"I cannot help but think that he doth behave as badly as the counts," Magnus agreed. "Tell—doth he, too, not seek to increase the territory he doth govern? Doth he, too, not attempt to bring more villages under his sway?"

"He doth push farther and farther afield 'gainst the bandits, that's true," Phebe said, frowning. "Is this conquest?"

"Certes," Geoffrey said automatically, and Magnus said, "Battle is battle. The clash of arms and the toll of the dead is noise and destruction, whether it be thy Shire-Reeve who doth command, or the counts."

"I would rather have peace lost from armies than from bandits," Phebe declared hotly.

"I cannot like any man who fights our King and Queen," Cordelia declared, "no matter how the cause they claim doth glitter with goodness. He who fights not for Their Majesties, fights against the Law they seek to uphold." She turned to Geoffrey. "Join him? Nay, brother. If aught, thou shouldst join battle against him, and work his downfall."

Geoffrey frowned. "Dost thou truly think so?" He shrugged. "Well, then, as thou wilt. I'll not contest, when thou and Magnus do agree—the more especially when Gregory is of a mind with the two of thee."

Phebe gave a nasty laugh. "Hast thou no mind of thine own, then?"

"Only for matters that interest me. For affairs of state, I care not, so long as there be battle and glory within it. Nay, I'd as liefer fight against thy Shire-Reeve as for him."

Phebe laughed again, but in disbelief. "Nay, assuredly thou mayest do as thou wilt! Go, bear thy swords of lath against the Shire-Reeve! For what matter can mere children make, when armies clash?"

Cordelia's face darkened, and her chin came up. "Mayhap more matter than thou canst know, when those children are the High Warlock's brood."

Phebe stared. Then, slowly, she said, "Aye, they might, an they were such highborn children. Art thou truly they?"

Gregory tugged at Cordelia's skirt. "What is 'highborn'?"

"A deal of nonsense that grown folk speak," she answered impatiently.

"'Tis only the highborn who can think so." Phebe frowned, stroking the pouting fullness of her lower lip.

Abruptly, she seemed to come to a decision. Her face cleared, and she beamed down at the children. "Nay, surely, two fellows so brave as thyselves must needs strengthen any army! Wilt thou not, then, come with me to the Shire-Reeve?"

Her voice was velvet and silk; her heavily-lidded eyes seemed to glow into theirs. She stretched out a hand in welcome.

Magnus and Geoffrey stared at her, their eyes fairly bulging.

"Come, then," Phebe breathed, "for I am of his army, too."

Magnus took one wooden step toward her. So did Geoffrey.

"Nay!" Cordelia cried. "What dost thou? Canst not see the falseness in her?"

"Be still, small hussy," Phebe hissed.

But her brothers seemed not even to hear her. They moved toward Phebe—slowly, almost stumbling, but moving. She nodded in encouragement, eyes glowing.

Inside the children's heads, Fess's voice said, "Beware, Magnus, Geoffrey! The woman uses her beauty as she would use you!"

"Why, she cannot use us, if we fight willingly," Geoffrey muttered.

Gregory threw himself toward them, catching Geoffrey's hand. "What spell is this? Nay, turn! How hath she entranced thee?"

"Knowest thou not?" Phebe breathed. "Thou, too, art male, though very young. Wilt thou, too, not come to fight for the Shire-Reeve?"

"Nay, never!" Gregory stated. "What hast thou done?"

"Thou'lt learn when thou art older, I doubt not," Phebe said with scorn. "Away! Thou hast no worth yet! But thy brothers . . ." She gazed at the two elder boys, running the tip of her tongue over her lower lip. "They will come to me." She held out both hands. Gazing up at her, Magnus took one. Geoffrey took her other hand. Smiling in triumph, she turned away, strolling down the footpath with Magnus and Geoffrey to either side. She spared one quick, scornful glance back over her shoulder at Cordelia.

The forsaken sister clenched her fists. "Oh! The hussy! Quickly, Gregory! We cannot let her take our brothers!"

"But how can we stop them?" Gregory asked.

"I know not! Oh! What manner of witchcraft is this, that I have never heard of?"

"Nor never will, from the look of thee," Phebe called maliciously. But the path seemed to explode in front of her, and she pulled back with a cry of alarm.

"Puck," Magnus muttered.

Phebe cast him a quick look of horror, then stared at the elf in the pathway in front of her. "It cannot truly be!"

"Yet it is!" Puck leveled a finger at her. "And I adjure thee, witch, to break this spell! Release these boys, ere thou dost rue it!"

The threat seemed to restore Phebe a little. She straightened, looking down her nose at him. "What glamour is this! There be no elves, nor any spirits! Thou mayest cease thine enchantment, child—I'll not believe it!" And she stepped forward on the pathway.

"Hold!" Puck's voice was a whiplash. "Ere I give thy body the semblance of thy soul, and make thy face the image of thy virtue!"

The girl blanched. "Thou couldst not truly!"

"Could I not, then?" The Puck's eyes glittered. "And art thou not the harpy who doth delight in tormenting men? What semblance wilt thou have, then?"

Slowly, Phebe's eyelids drooped, and her full lips curved

into their smile. Magnus and Geoffrey stared up at her, spell-bound, but her gaze was now for Puck. "Thou art male," she purred, "and great of spirit, though small of stature. Nay, then, canst thou not imagine my delights?"

Puck snorted in derision. "Nay, nor can I think thou hast any! What! Canst thou truly think thyself the equal of a fairy lady? But look into *mine* eyes, lass, and learn what charms may be!"

And she was looking into his eyes, of course, to try to cast her spell over him—but now she found that she could not break her gaze away.

"Now, regard," Puck said softly, coming closer. His eyes glittered as he sang,

> "Golden slumbers kiss thine eyes!
> Do not wake till moon doth rise!
> Sleep, pretty wanton, do not cry,
> And I shall sing a lullaby!
> Rock her, rock her, lullaby!"

Her eyelids drooped, and kept on drooping. They closed, and she nodded, as Puck's voice went on in eldritch singing. Her head jerked up once, and she blinked, trying valiantly to stay awake—but Puck kept on singing, and her eyes closed. She sank to the ground, head pillowed on one arm, and her breast rose and fell with the slow, even rhythm of sleep.

Puck smiled down at her, gloating.

Then he turned to the two boys who stood staring dumbly down at the sleeping peasant maid, and clapped his hands in front of Magnus's face. "Waken! What! Wilt thou let a woman lead thee by the nose?"

Magnus's head snapped up as he suddenly came out of his trance.

Puck had already turned to Geoffrey. "Wake! For thou hast lost thy battle ere it began!"

Geoffrey's head whiplashed; then his eyes focused on Puck. "Battle? What fight is this?"

"Why, the struggle for thy will, my lad! What! Wilt thou let a woman lead thee into fighting for a man thou knowest to be evil?"

Geoffrey's gaze darkened. "Nay! Never would I!"

"Yet thou didst!" Cordelia came up. "Thou didst, and only Robin's rescue did save thee from it!"

Geoffrey turned to her, hot words upon his tongue; but Puck said, "Remember," and the boy froze, appalled as he suddenly remembered how he had let himself be caught.

Puck nodded, watching his face. "Aye. So easily wast thou mastered."

"It will never happen again!"

But Magnus, more carefully, said, "I pray not."

"Pray strongly, then—for any man may be caught by women's beauty, and few are the men who have not been. Yet not 'men,' neither, for that man is not a man, who may be so entranced by a woman that, at one sight of her, he doth forget all that he hath undertaken, all that he doth strive to do, all duty that remains. Nay, an he doth, then the woman hath mastered him—and how can he then be a man?"

But Cordelia had a gleam in her eye. "'Tis a power to be desired."

"Aye, for a lass—but 'tis one to be proof against, for a man. There be many good women, yet there be many also like to this Phebe, who will very willingly use their charms to govern men, an they can—so be not overly concerned with the pleasures they promise."

Cordelia frowned, looking as though she wasn't too sure she liked this line of talk. She couldn't really object to it, given the provisos Puck had stipulated; but she could set the record straight. "'Tis a foul slut, belike." She wasn't sure what a slut was, but she'd heard grown-ups use the term, and knew that it was an insult. "Yet though this Phebe hath a certain tawdry sort of prettiness, it cannot be the sole source of her power."

Puck agreed. "There's truth in that. She is a common milk-maid, look you, and, though she is attractive, I've seen far more beauteous women among the ranks of mortal females."

"Doubtless there is some element of the projective telepath in her, too," Fess said. "She is quite probably a minor witch, though she knows it not—an esper who can project her own thoughts effectively enough to hyponotize instantly. And, since she thinks her greatest strength is her physical attraction, her projective ability is naturally linked to it. Thus her effect on men is mesmerizing, both literally as well as figuratively."

"What doth he say?" Geoffrey asked.

"That she is an enchantress," Gregory summarized.

Geoffrey cast him a look of annoyance, but he couldn't argue.

"Yet surely she's enough a hazard so that the knight who rules this parish would stop her," Magnus insisted. "How cometh she to be yet free to work such havoc, Puck?"

"Why, for that she hath not begun it till two days agone," Puck sighed. "Bethink thee, lad—from what she said, this Shire-Reeve whom she doth support, did begin his work directly after thy mother and father went wandering. Ere he can stop her, the parish knight must learn how she doth turn young men away from his service—and how is he to find that out, when all she doth is chat with them?"

"But can he not see that she doth twist them to her purpose?" Cordelia protested.

"There's no law 'gainst that, and if there were, I doubt me not there'd be few weddings. Nay, lass—our goodly knight must needs decide that teasing can be treason—which thou dost know, since thou hast seen it; but grown men would have trouble crediting it."

"Aye," Cordelia said. "They are puffed up with importance. How could they deign to notice so small a thing? It would quite make them seem much smaller than they wish to be."

Puck eyed her with a new respect. "Thou wilt be most dangerous, when thou art grown. Yet thou hast the right of it—men who are surfeited with their own importance, scarce can bring themselves to acknowledge things so small as jests and rumors. That's the reason whispers are so hard to guard against, and thus can do great damage."

Geoffrey frowned. "I do begin to comprehend. Papa hath told me that rumor can bring down armies."

"This may be one reason," Puck agreed. "Another is that within the featherbed of rumor, there's ofttimes a pea of truth, and who can tell what is and is not false? What proof is there that this Shire-Reeve doth not work for Their Majesties, and for the kingdom's good? Only what we ourselves have heard from this wench."

"And how could the knight credit what she doth say?" Cordelia murmured. "She's but a milkmaid, and she speaks against the King's Reeve."

Puck nodded. "Thus, how's the knight to know the Shire-Reeve will speak him false? Or that thou wouldst speak truly?"

"Aye." Magnus's mouth tightened. "We're but children, and she and the Reeve are grown-ups."

"Yet wilt thou do better when thou art grown?" Puck asked.

"Be sure, I will!" Geoffrey stated. "Children or milkmaids, high or low, I'll hearken to them all, and give full thought to all I hear!"

Puck nodded, satisfied. "Now thou dost begin to comprehend. All folk must be allowed to speak their minds, whether thou dost think them wise or foolish—and thou must weigh what they do say, on chance that the most unlikely of them may be right. Therefore thou must needs see it enshrined in the highest Law of the Land, as thy father doth seek to do. If thou dost not, evil men may keep good folk from learning of their evil deeds."

"Why, how shall they do that?" Magnus questioned.

"By punishing all who speak against them in even the slightest way," Puck explained. "If thou dost let the law prohibit certain words, then evil men will punish folk that they dislike, by claiming they did speak the words prohibited."

"So." Magnus frowned down at Phebe. "Much though we dislike what she hath done, we must not bind her over to the knight?"

"Nay, that thou mayest do—but thou canst not forbid her to speak, even though thou dost know that she will lie, and claim she did naught of what thou sayest. Thou must needs *prove* she did as thou dost say."

"Which we cannot, of course." Magnus's mouth tightened. "Yet is there naught we can do to keep her from working her havoc, Puck?"

"Why, warn all the lads of the village about her, of course." Puck grinned. "And if they do heed thee, she'll have naught to do but rage."

"If," Cordelia said, darkly. "Can we do naught with her, then?"

Puck shrugged. "Leave her, and let her sleep. Come, children—let us seek out her commander."

"The Shire-Reeve?" Geoffrey grinned. "Nay, then! We'll have battle from him, one way or another!"

9

"Where does this Shire-Reeve quarter, then?"

Magnus asked the question clearly enough, but his eyelids were drooping.

"In Luganthorpe village," Puck said, the light of the campfire flickering on his face. "'Tis but two hours' march, in the morning."

"What else have the elves said about him?" Cordelia stroked Gregory's hair, head pillowed in her lap. His eyes were closed; he was already asleep.

"Only that he doth gather his army of plowboys, even as Phebe did say," Puck answered, "and that he hath sallied forth against a pack of bandits in the hills."

"And be there truly so many bandits as she did say?" Geoffrey asked, between yawns.

"As many, and as quickly risen."

For a moment, Geoffrey came fully alert. "Such doth not happen without planning and readying."

"Nay, it doth not." Puck's eyes glittered. "There be some that have prepared these folk for thy parents' disappearance, children."

"Then we shall fight them!"

"That thou shalt not! 'Tis the King's place, not thine." Puck smiled. "Yet I think we may be of some small service to him. . . ."

"Now—seize them!"

Rough hands grabbed the children; other hands whipped coils of rope around them, pinning their arms to their sides. An ugly man with a steel cap laughed into Cordelia's face. She recoiled at the reek of his breath.

A horse's scream, flashing hooves, and Fess was rearing, battering at the steel breastplates. The men shouted in panic and leaped back.

"Nay!" one cried. "'Tis but a horse! Have at him!"

The others turned with shouts, two jabbing at Fess with pikes. Fess slashed at one, who leaped back; then the great horse whirled toward the other, slamming down with his full weight. The man skipped back, but a hoof grazed his shoulder and sent him spinning. Another leaped in to replace him.

"Haul those brats away!" the eldest shouted, and four other men hoisted the children.

Fess wheeled from one attacker, back toward the man holding Geoffrey, then pivoted toward the one holding Cordelia. While he did, a soldier stabbed upward with a pike. The point rang against the steel under Fess's horsehair, and the black stallion turned back toward him—but his movements had slowed. The children heard his voice in their heads: *Sollldierzz . . . musst not take . . . children . . .*

Abruptly, Fess's legs went stiff, and his head dropped down, swinging loosely from the neck, nose almost grazing the ground.

He hath had a seizure! Cordelia thought.

I shall be revenged upon these scum who have hurt him! Geoffrey's thoughts were dark with anger.

The soldiers braced themselves, eyeing the stilled horse with trepidation. Then one reached out and thrust against Fess's shoulder. When the horse didn't respond, he thrust harder. Fess rocked back, but made no reaction. "Is it dead, then?" the soldier asked.

"We'll make it so." The other soldier swung his pike up to chop with the axe-blade.

"Away!" barked the oldest man. "'Tis a witch horse; leave it. Dost thou wish to have its ghost pursue thee?"

The soldier leaped back and crossed himself quickly.

The oldest man looked about the clearing to make sure everything was under control. He was a grizzled bear of a man in his fifties. "Dost thou have them, Grobin?" he called.

"Aye, Auncient! Though they have struggled some." Grobin came up, holding Geoffrey and Magnus kicking and squalling one under each arm. He chuckled. "Eh, they are mettlesome lads!"

"What shall I do with this one?" A hulking man in a steel cap and breastplate came up, tossing Gregory like a ball. The child wailed in terror.

Cordelia, Geoffrey, and Magnus's gazes snapped to the thug, and he came within a hairsbreadth of death that moment.

But he never knew it, for the grizzled bear of a man they called "Auncient" said, "Why, take him to Milord Count, even as these others. Come!"

The soldiers slung the children over their shoulders as though they were bags of potatoes. Their steel-clad joints knocked the wind out of the children, but even as Geoffrey struggled for breath, his face hardened and his eyes lost focus. Magnus's thought echoed in his mind: *Nay! They've done naught to merit death!*

Geoffrey glared at him; but he held himself back.

Wherefore hath Puck not driven away these clods? Geoffrey demanded.

He must not see need enough, Magnus answered.

'Tis true . . . We are not harmed . . . But Geoffrey's thoughts were dark.

Peace, brother, Magnus consoled him. *Thou wilt have free rein to work havoc, when we're sure these men work evil.*

The soldiers trooped through patches of moonlight into a larger clearing nearby and brought the children up to a knot of horsemen. At their head sat a man in full armor, on a huge mount. As the soldiers came up, he lifted his visor. "Well done, Auncient."

"I thank you, Milord." The auncient touched his forelock in respect. "'Twas easily done, of course."

"What was that scream, and the shouting that followed it?"

"A war-horse sprang upon us—but he froze of a sudden, as though he'd been cursed." The auncient crossed himself. "Are there sorcerers in this wood, Milord?"

"'Tis no matter, an they side with us." The nobleman was frowning down at the children. "What wast thou about, babes in the woods? How came ye here alone?"

A soldier shoved Magnus. He glared up at the nobleman. "We search for our parents."

A fist slammed into his ear, shooting pain with a loud crack. Through the ringing that followed it, he heard the auncient growl, "Speak with respect! Thou dost address the Count of Drosz!"

Magnus fought hard to control his temper and keep from hurling the knight off his horse with an unseen hand. It helped to promise himself that someday, the auncient would pay for that box on the ear—but it helped more to wonder at the nobleman's identity. "Drosz? But we are in the County of Glynn!"

"Well enough," Drosz said, with a grim smile. "He doth know his place in the countryside, if not in his rank."

"Wherefore hast thou come?" Geoffrey's gag had been removed, too.

"Why, to conquer Glynn's county." Drosz turned to Geoffrey with a contemptuous smile. "Why else would a nobleman be abroad in another's demesne?"

"But thy county is within Duke Hapsburg's lands, and we stand now within Earl Tudor's feif! Will not thy Duke bid thee hold, ere thou canst come to Glynn's castle?"

Drosz laughed. "Nay, foolish bairn! I am Hapsburg's vassal. Thus any land that I seize will enlarge his demesne!"

"Yet Tudor must needs then declare war on Duke Hapsburg," Geoffrey pointed out.

"And if he doth?" The count shrugged. "What matter?"

"Why, there will be battle!" Cordelia cried.

The count nodded. "There will."

The children stared at him, unnerved. *He cares not a whit if he doth plunge two whole provinces into civil war!* Cordelia thought.

Aye, not a whit. Magnus glowered up at the count. *Surely he doth know the death and suffering he will cause!*

That matters naught, to him, Geoffrey explained. *Naught, against the prospect of glory and power.* Aloud, he said, "Surely Glynn left a home guard. Doth none oppose thee?"

"None," the count confirmed. "'Tis as though he hath disappeared from the face of the earth, and his family with him; and his knights, not knowing what to do, have lain down their arms."

Geoffrey stared, outraged. "Assuredly he would have given commands to defend!"

"Defend what? He is gone, and his wife and bairns with him! His knights have none to turn to for direction—and they have not the rank to deny another nobleman's commands. Nay, they do not oppose me, save one or two." He dismissed them with a wave of his gauntlet—which he had probably done.

"Then thou art master of this county, also," Magnus said. "Why hast thou wasted time seizing mere children?"

"Credit me with some sense, young one." The count's smile was brittle. "There's not a nobleman in the land that doth not know the faces of the High Warlock's children."

The children were silent. The count chuckled, gloating,

looking from one little face to another.

"Then!" Magnus spoke with anger. "Then an thou dost know our rank, wherefore hast thou permitted thy minion to strike me!"

"Why, for that thou art my prisoners now, and subject to me." The count lounged back in his saddle with a toothy grin.

Magnus's eyes narrowed. He wondered if the nobleman was only stupid, or really so rude and arrogant as to treat another nobleman's children with contempt. "Well, then, we are thy prisoners." But the tone of his voice did not really acknowledge it. "What purpose can we serve in thy conquest?"

"Why, thou art hostages, ignorant child! And while I do hold thee, neither Earl Tudor, nor Duke Hapsburg, nor even King Tuan himself will dare to attack me, for fear of the powers of the High Warlock's brood!"

Magnus was silent, glaring at him. Then, just as Geoffrey started to speak, he said, "Thou mayest hold our bodies—but thou dost not command our powers."

The fist exploded against his ear again, and his head filled with the rough mocking laughter of the soldiers. Through the ringing, he heard the count gloating, "Thou wilt do as thou art bid, boy!"

Magnus just barely managed to hold onto his temper—and that, only because he could tell Geoffrey was about to erupt. *Nay!* he thought. *There are too many of them! We cannot fight a whole army alone!*

We cannot submit without fighting, either! his brother thought back in boiling rage.

Nor will we! Yet save thy power for the moment when it will suffice to topple them, the whiles they fight another army!

Geoffrey held himself in, but just barely. He glowered up at the Duke and thought, *But will there be another army? Will there truly?*

Never doubt it, Magnus assured him; and,

Puck will see to it, Gregory added.

As though he had overheard, one of the knights moved his horse up next to Count Drosz's mount and advised, "My lord, hear me, I implore thee! 'Tis known far and wide that the Wee Folk do hold these children under their especial care!"

"What! A grown man, and thou dost yet believe in the power of the Little People?" Drosz scoffed. "Assuredly, Lan-

gouste, thou must needs know that elves can be no threat to
we who are clad in Cold Iron!"

Langouste glanced over his shoulder with apprehension.
"My lord, I implore thee! Do not scoff at the power of the
Wee Folk!"

"Power?" Drosz laughed and scooped something out of his
saddlebag. He held it up for Sir Langouste to see. "Behold the
bane of the Little People, and the counter to all of their
powers—a handful of nails! Common nails! They cannot
even stand against these! See!" And he whirled, hurling the
sharp iron points into the underbrush. A scream tore from the
thicket, and another, and another, a dozen or more, all about
them. As they faded, the children saw the count was laughing.

"Nay, then," he assured his men, "'tis even as thou dost
see. These elves must quail before armed might. Any man
who wears Cold Iron need not shrink from them."

Cordelia stood trembling, wide-eyed with horror, and
Geoffrey was quaking with rage. Gregory stood like a statue,
staring at the count.

But the nobleman only smiled, and turned his horse toward
a gap in the trees, calling "Ride!" and trotted off into the
night.

His men threw the children across their horses' backs in
front of their saddles, and followed the count; but they were
pale, glancing at one another with wide, apprehensive eyes.

The horses' backs jolted into the children's stomachs, driving the wind out of them with every step; they had to gasp for
air between hoofbeats. They gritted their teeth and bore the
pain, while their thoughts flickered back and forth.

He hath injured a dozen elves at least, Cordelia thought,
outraged, *and may have slain some.*

And he doth not respect his neighbor's demesne, Geoffrey
added. *He doth respect naught but force of arms.*

There may be good within him, but we have not seen it,
Magnus replied, *and that which we have seen is vile. Canst
thou bethink thee of any cause to spare this count?*

Nay!

Nay!

Nay!

We are agreed, Magnus thought, with the weight of a
judge's sentence. *We will await opportunity.*

They jolted on down the trail, gasping for snatches of

breath between hoofbeats, but every sense was wide open now, waiting for the opportunity. Trees blurred past on both sides, dark in the moonlight. Magnus turned his head, craning his neck to peer ahead, trying to see where they were going, but it was no use; the darkness was too complete in this leafy tunnel. Only scraps and patches of moonlight glinted through.

A roar shook the wood, and something huge and massive humped up from the forest floor right in front of the count. Red eyes burned through the darkness. Horses screamed and reared, throwing their riders, trying to turn, trying to gallop away; but they slammed into each other in the confines of the trail, in panic.

The count fought his bucking, twisting horse to a standstill, crying, "Stand and fight! For whatever it is, it cannot stand against Cold Iron! Dismount and draw your swords!"

The few soldiers who hadn't been thrown leaped down; their comrades struggled to their feet, drawing their blades and staggering after the count, tripping on tree roots and stumbling in holes, but charging toward the hulking, roaring shape.

It saw them coming and bellowed, lashing out at the count with a huge dark paw; claws like scimitars slashed past him. His mount screamed and pawed the air, twisting away.

The soldiers lurched and tripped on something that heaved upward against their feet. They cried out in fear and anger, tumbling down in a crashing clatter. A host of little forms rose among the tangled mass of men and struck downward with six-inch cudgels, right at the base of the skull between helmet and collar. Soldiers yelped and stiffened, then slumped, unconscious.

The count's horse bucked and plunged, trying to turn; but the count fought it, yanking on the reins, crying "Hold, cowardly beast! I'll not flee an enemy!"

"Brave man," boomed a voice without a body. "Thy courage doth thee credit—but no advantage."

And the count rose up from his saddle—up and up, so far that his horse was able to whirl about under him and bolt away from the horrible midnight ogre. The nobleman bellowed in rage just before he slammed into a huge tree trunk and slid downward toward its base. Even as he slid, he shook his head, trying to clear it, groping for his sword; but it hissed out of its sheath by itself. He jolted to the ground and immediately lurched up, trying to stagger to his feet—and dropped back with a howl, clutching at his throat where his own sword's point had lanced him. He looked up, wide-eyed, and saw the blade floating in midair, its point circling right in front of his eyes. He shrank away and, finally, horror crept into his eyes.

The monster gave one last roar and shrank in on itself, disappearing.

For a brief moment, the trail was absolutely silent.

Then Puck's deep voice rumbled through the night. "Well done, children! Thou didst seize the moment, and gave excellent aid!"

"'Twas our pleasure." Geoffrey stood slowly, rubbing his wrists where the rope had bound them.

"Pleasure indeed." Cordelia glared at the count while an elf cut her bonds with a bronze knife. "'Tis I who wielded his sword—and almost could I have wished he'd driven himself harder against it."

"That 'almost' is not enough. Who did lift him from his saddle?"

"Geoffrey and I." Magnus flexed his fingers, trying to restore circulation. "I wish we could have thrown him harder."

"Nay! Cease!" the count roared, jerking his arms forward; but the sword feinted at his eyes, and he froze with a shuddering gasp. Behind him, a rope yanked his wrists together and knotted itself tightly, while Gregory stared at it. Elves whipped rope around his ankles, then yanked on his wrists, and he fell with a howl.

"Take away thy thing of Cold Iron," Puck said with distaste, and Cordelia sent the sword spinning off among the trees. Geoffrey watched it go with longing, but said not a word.

"He is harmless now," Puck rumbled. "Again I thank thee, children; thou hast ably done thy part. Now leave us."

"What! Leave?"

"Nay, Puck! Wherefore?"

"We have helped to fell him, and we should have some say in . . ." But Magnus's voice trailed off as he stared at Puck's face. There was a hardness to the elf that he'd never seen before, and a glint at the back of the Old Thing's eyes that made him shudder and turn away. His brothers and sister saw it, too, and went with him.

"Forget not thy father's faithful servant," Puck rumbled, "thy father's and thine. Do not leave him to rust."

"Fess! Oh, aye!" The children exchanged looks of guilt and hurried back along the trail toward the place where the count's men had ambushed them.

They came upon the great black horse in a patch of moonlight, standing with his legs out stiffly and his head between his fetlocks. Magnus floated up and reached under the front of the saddle, pushing the lump that was the reset switch. He felt it move and, slowly, the robot lifted its head, blinking and looking around at the children, dazed. "Wwwhaat? Wwwherrrre . . . ?"

"Bide thee." Cordelia laid a gentle hand on his nose. "Wait till thy mind hath cleared."

"Thou didst have a seizure," Magnus informed him. "Bide."

Fess was silent, looking from child to child as the haze cleared from his eyes. Finally he said, "Did the bandits capture you?"

"Aye, but we did escape," Gregory piped up.

"Or were rescued, more aptly," Magnus corrected.

"They were not bandits," Geoffrey added, "but soldiers of Count Drosz."

"Drosz?" Fess lifted his head. "What was his business here? This is not his demesne."

"Nay, but he did seek to seize it."

"Why did his men abduct you?"

The children glanced at one another, trying to find the right way to break the news to Fess.

"Did he seek to use you as hostages?" the robot demanded.

"He did," Magnus admitted.

"And I stood idle! May my . . ."

" 'Twas not thy fault," Magnus said quickly, staving off a flood of self-recriminations. "And there was naught to fear, truly—Puck and his elves did free us."

"Though we did aid them." Geoffrey couldn't hide his pride.

"Praise Hertz!" Fess sighed. "But where is he now?"

"The count?" Gregory asked. "Or Puck?"

"Both are farther along the trail, where the elves did seize the Count," Magnus explained. "He lies bound hand and foot —but what the Wee Folk do with him, we know not."

A single, lasting shriek tore the forest night, echoing among the trees, then ended abrubtly.

The children stared at one another, shaken. "What . . .?" gasped Magnus.

"It did have the sound of a human voice," Geoffrey said, with foreboding.

Leaves rustled beside them, and Puck moved out into the moonlight with Kelly behind him. "'Tis done, children," Puck rumbled. "None will ever fear Count Drosz's evil again."

They looked at each other wide-eyed, then back at Puck, with the question on the tips of their tongues; but the look in Puck's face held them silent.

Gregory looked down at Kelly. "What hath upset thee so?"

"Leave him," Puck said quickly, and turned to Kelly. "Thou hast done bravely this night, elf."

"It may be that I have," Kelly muttered, "but I'll never be proud of such work."

"Nay, but neither shouldst thou regret it! Bethink thee, the man had slain and pillaged as he marched into Glynn. Elves had seen him slay folk with his own hand, a dozen times at the least—and this night alone, he wounded a score of elves, some grievously; and Mayberry lies dead."

The children were silent, eyes round. They all knew that elves and fairies did not have immortal souls, as they had, and that when an elf died, his existence ceased utterly.

Kelly's face firmed with conviction, taking on the look of old flint. He nodded slowly. "'Tis even as ye do say. Nay, 'twas just . . ."

"Merciful," Puck rumbled.

"Even so. Nay, I'll not be ashamed of this deed I've done, neither."

"What deed?" Gregory asked, but Magnus said, "Hush."

"We elves have but saved Their Majesties a deal of trouble and vexation, children," Puck assured them. "Had we left it to them, the end would have been the same, but with far greater fuss and bother."

Shocked, the children stared at him.

Then Geoffrey protested, "But thou hast no authority over life and death, Puck!"

"All captains have, on the field of battle," Puck answered, "and this was battle in truth. Did Drosz not come in war?"

"Mayhap." Geoffrey frowned. "Yet 'twas 'gainst Glynn he marched, and 'twas for Glynn to . . ."

"Nay." Puck's eyes glinted. "Glynn might answer for mortals—but not for Wee Folk."

Geoffrey opened his mouth again.

"Nay, do not contend!" Puck commanded. "Be mindful, in this the authority lieth not in the person, but in Justice!"

Geoffrey slowly closed his mouth.

"Yet 'tis not thus that Justice is done," Gregory protested. "For a lord, it hath need of a court, and of other lords!"

"That is mortal justice," Puck answered, "but 'twas for crimes 'gainst Wee Folk the count did answer this night—and the Little People have had their own notion of Justice for as long as Oak, Ash, and Thorn have grown. At the least, 'twas quickly done. Nay, I've known far rougher justice from mortal men."

The children were silent in the moonlight.

Then Magnus said, "I bethink me 'tis time to go home, Puck."

10

There really was no reason not to stay and pitch camp right there, but Puck led them away into the night nonetheless—he had some sense of mortals' feelings, and thought the children would feel a bit strange sleeping nearby. So he led them away into the dark, pricked here and there by shafts of moonlight. They were very quiet behind him and, after his own black mood had lightened a little, Puck tried to cheer them by singing an elfin tune. The eeriness of its halftones fitted with the gloom about them, but after a few verses, the children began to feel a sense of calm pervading them. The huge old twisted trees looked less like menacing monsters and more like kindly grandfathers, and the bits of moonlight that lay on their leaves looked like jewels. The vines draping loops from huge branches began to seem like bunting hung for a festival, and the dry leaves underfoot a multicolored carpet. Within the hour, the children found themselves walking through a faerie forest with a silver brook cutting across their path ahead, prattling happily as it danced over rocks. A gilded little bridge arched over it and Cordelia breathed, "What enchantment is this thou hast woven with thy song, Puck?"

"Only to let thee see what is truly there," the elf answered. "There is ever magic and wonder about thee, if thou wilt but open thine eyes to it." He set foot on the bridge, and so did Gregory behind him.

"Ho! Ho!" boomed a voice like an echo in a chasm, and two huge hands with long, knobby fingers slapped onto the side of the bridge.

"'Ware!" Puck shouted, stepping backward, but keeping his face toward the bridge. Gregory bumped back into Geoffrey, who dug in his heels and braced himself as Cordelia bumped into him. Magnus managed to stop short and murmured, "Then again, in forests of fantasy, fantastical creatures abide."

"Ho! Ho!" A great ugly head popped up over the edge of the bridge, with a thatch of shaggy hair like a bunch of straw, eyes like saucers, a lump of a nose, and a wide mouth that gaped to show pointed teeth. "Ho! Ho!" it cried again, and a spindle-shanked leg swung up, slamming down a huge flat foot. But the body that leaped up onto the bridge was only four-feet high, though the chest was a barrel and the shoulders were three-feet across. Its arms reached down to its ankles, and its hands were almost as wide as its head. It clapped them with a sound like a cannon shot. "Children! Yum!"

The children crowded back against each other. "What— what is it, Puck?"

"A troll," the elf answered. "They do live beneath bridges —and are always a-hungered."

The troll grinned, nodding. "Children! Soft, tender! Yum!" And it rubbed its belly.

"So I had thought," Puck said, tight-lipped. "Step back, children! Leave the span to the creature!"

They stepped back—except for Geoffrey. The boy stood like a rock, brow clouded. "I do wish to cross, Robin. What is this thing to gainsay me?"

"One who can rend thee limb from limb with those great hands," Puck snapped. "Stay not to argue, lad."

The troll chuckled deep in its throat and swaggered forward, flexing its hands and drooling.

"Canst thou not defeat it?" Geoffrey demanded.

"Belike," Puck answered, "and belike none will be hurted. Yet 'tis not certain, and I'd liefer not chance it."

"*Thou* not chance it?" Magnus scoffed. "Speak truly, Puck —what wouldst thou do, an we were not here?"

A gleam shone in Puck's eye. "Aye, an thou wert not here, I would soon have it dancing in rage the whiles it did try to catch me, and would have its head 'twixt its legs and its arms tied in knots, like enough! Yet thou *art* with me, and I've no wish to chance it! Now, *back!*"

Reassured, the children retreated, though reluctantly.

"No, no! Not get 'way," the troll cried, and came at them with a sudden rush.

The children leaped back with a cry, and Puck howled, "'Ware!" A torch suddenly flared in his hand, thrusting up at the troll's nose. It squalled and leaped back, swatting at a burn spot on its loincloth. Puck stepped away, the torch disappearing, watching the troll warily.

It finished dousing the spark and looked back at him with huge, witless eyes, drooling and grinning as its glance flickered from child to child. It took a tentative step forward, then hesitated. "What if troll do? Children flee!" It pulled its foot back, shaking its head. "No, no! Mustn't go! Stay on bridge! Children have to cross, soon or late!" It relaxed, gazing from one child to another with a toothy grin. "Children have to cross!" Then it fell silent, totally at ease, watching, waiting.

After a little time, Cordelia asked, "Must we cross, Puck?"

"Assuredly we must!" Geoffrey answered. "And if the foul monster will not step aside for us, then we must needs remove it!" He stepped forward, hand on his dagger.

"Hold thy blade!" Puck's hand clamped on his. "I have told thee once I do not wish to fight! He who fights when he need not is either a fool or a knave!"

Geoffrey reddened, but held his place.

"Puck hath the right of it," Magnus acknowledged.

"But why dost thou speak of it?" Gregory asked, puzzled. "How can there be a question? Wherefore ought we fight for the bridge, when we need but fly over it?"

Geoffrey stared at Magnus, astonished. Magnus stared back, then grinned sheepishly. "What fools were we not to see it!"

"Aye," Cordelia agreed. "What banty roosters art thou, so intent on the challenge that thou couldst not see a foot into the air?"

"And where were thy words, whilst we did debate it?" Geoffrey demanded. "Naetheless, the laddie hath the right of it. Up, folk, and fly!"

"But what of Fess?" Magnus said.

"Don't concern yourself with me," the great beast replied. "This creature would not find me a tasty morsel."

They drifted up into the night air, wafting across the stream. The troll howled in frustration. Geoffrey laughed and swooped low, taunting. The troll leaped, snatching at the boy's ankle. Geoffrey howled with dismay as the troll yanked him down with a chuckle, straight toward its great maw. The boy yanked his dagger free and bent to stab, while his siblings cried, "Geoffrey!" "Be brave—we come!" And they all swooped back for him.

But a diminutive figure leaped up onto the troll's hand just as it was about to bite, a green-clad figure that howled, "Ye foul Sassenach! Would ye gobble up babes, then?" And it

struck with a small hammer, right on the blob of a nose. The
troll howled and clapped a huge hand over its proboscis—and
Geoffrey yanked his foot free, soaring upward, pale and trembling. Kelly hopped down off the troll's hand, a bit pale himself, and darted for the end of the bridge. The troll roared and
stamped at him, but the elf was too quick, and vanished into
the night.

"Bless thee, Kelly," Geoffrey cried.

"Aye, and bless thy stars, too," Puck snapped, right next to
him in midair. "What possessed thee to taunt him so? Foolish
boy, now get hence!"

Geoffrey's jaw tightened, but he obeyed without an argu-
ment for once, and swooped away after his brothers and sister.

Below, the troll watched him go, rubbing its nose and muttering to itself. Then a slow grin spread over its face, and it
swaggered bandy-legged toward the far side of the bridge,
chuckling deep in its throat, sniffing the night breeze and following the scent of the children.

As the trees closed behind them, Cordelia looked back.
"Puck! The troll hath come off the bridge! It doth scent the
night air . . . it doth follow our trace!"

Puck frowned, darting a quick look back. "'Tis not the
way of that kind. Then again, they're seldom so thwarted.
Summer and Fall! These are thy woods; thou dost know them
better than I. Where shall we find safe hiding?"

"Come!" Summer cried; and "Follow!" echoed Fall.

Fess, who had followed them, crossing the bridge after the
troll, blundered off in the wood with a great crash, hoping to
distract the monster.

The children for their part tried to follow Fall and Summer,
but it was slow going—the fairies failed to remember that the
children couldn't dodge through a net of brambles, or dive
through a twelve-inch hole beneath a shrub. "Hold!" Puck
cried to them. "These great folk cannot follow wheresoe'er
thou dost lead!"

"Eh! We regret!" Summer bit her lip, glancing back at the
sounds of rending and thrashing, and the booming "Ho! Ho!"
far behind. "We'll seek to lead thee through ways large
enough," Fall promised.

And they did, though they still tended to underestimate
what "large enough" meant. The children grew sore from
stooping through three-foot gaps in the underbrush and weary
from pushing aside springy branches. But they kept at it, for

the crashing and booming "Ho! Ho!" was growing louder behind them. Festoons of vines glided by them, silvered by moonlight; spider webs two-feet across netted the sides of their way, glistening with dewdrops. Cordelia looked about her, enthralled, and would have stopped to gaze, enchanted, if her brothers had not hurried her on, darting glances back over their shoulders.

"Where dost thou lead us?" Magnus panted.

"To a secret place that only fairies know of," Fall answered.

"Courage—'tis not far now," Summer urged.

It wasn't; in fact, it was only a few more steps. Gregory was following along in Cordelia's wake when suddenly he tripped and lurched against a screen of vines twined together. But the screen gave beneath his weight, and he went bumping and thumping down a hillside with a single yelp of dismay.

"Gregory!" Cordelia cried, and leaped after him.

The boy landed at the bottom with a thud and a thump, and a sister right behind him, who caught him up in a hug almost before he'd stopped sliding. "Oh, poor babe! Art thou hurted, Gregory?"

"Nay, 'Delia," Gregory answered, rubbing at a sore spot on his hip. "'Tis naught; I'm no longer a babe . . . Oh, 'Delia!"

He looked about him in rapture. She followed his gaze and stared, too, entranced.

It was a faerie grotto, only a dozen yards across, like a deep bowl in the midst of the woods, lit by a thousand fireflies and walled by flowering creepers and blossoming shrubs, roofed by blooming tree branches and floored with soft mosses. An arc of water sprang out of one wall in a burbling fountain, to fall plashing into a little pool and run tinkling and chiming across the floor of the grotto as a tiny brook.

"'Tis enchanted," Cordelia breathed.

"In truth, it is," Fall said beside her. "Long years ago, an ancient witch did fall and sprain her ankle here. The Wee Folk aided her, sin that she had always been kind to them; we bound her hurt with sweet herbs and a compress of simples, and murmured words of power o'er it, so that the grasses took the hurt from out her, and healed her. In thanks, she made this dell for us and, though she is long gone, her gift yet endures."

With a crash and a skid, her two brothers shot down the side of the grotto. Their heels hit the moss and shot out from under them, landing them hard on their bottoms. Magnus yelped, and Geoffrey snarled a word that made Cordelia clap her hands over Fall's ears.

"I thank thee, lass," the fairy said, gently prying Cordelia's fingers away, "but I misdoubt me an thy brother could know a word I've not heard. Still, 'tis most ungentlemanly of him to say it!" She stalked over to glare up at the seated boy, fists on her hips. "Hast thou no consideration for a gentle lady, thou great lob?"

Geoffrey opened his mouth for a hot answer, but Magnus caught his eye, and he swallowed whatever he'd been about to say.

"I prithee, forgive him," Big Brother said. "He is young yet, and 'tis hard for him to be mindful of manners when he is hurted." That earned him a murderous glare which he blithely ignored, and turned back to his sister. "I take it from these presents that thou art not greatly hurted, nor our brother neither."

"Thou hast it aright," she confirmed. "Yet never have I so rejoiced in a mishap. Hast thou ever seen so lovely a covert?"

Magnus looked up, saw and stared. Cordelia realized that he hadn't really noticed his surroundings, nor had Geoffrey. Even he was looking about him with awe. "'Delia! Is this some magical realm?"

"'Tis a faerie place," Summer told him, "and 'twas made for us by a good witch."

"'Tis enchanted," Fall agreed. "Hush! Canst thou not hear the chant?"

They were all quiet, and heard it softly—a murmur of musical tones, like the wind blowing through the strings of a harp, overlaid with the chiming of the fountain and its brook.

"What is it, then?" Magnus murmured.

"The wind blowing midst the vines," Fall answered.

"And what is this!" Gregory cried. He scrambled down to the center of the grotto, where light glittered from the facets of a huge crystal that sprang from an outcrop of rock.

"'Tis some great jewel, surely." Cordelia was right behind him.

"Nay." Fall smiled, stepping up next to the huge stone. "'Tis only a stone, though a pretty one. These glistening planes are but its natural form."

"Nay, I think not quite." Magnus came up behind her. "'Tis that kind of stone which Papa terms quartz, an I mistake me not."

"'Tis indeed." But Gregory's gaze was glued to the crystal.

Magnus nodded. "And I've seen quartz aforetime. Rarely doth it show surfaces so flat—and when it doth, they are scarce larger than a finger. There hath been some skilled working in this."

"Nay." Summer disagreed. "It hath been there sin that the witch did make this place."

"She made this crystal with it." Gregory's voice seemed distant somehow—diminished and drawn. "It did not merely grow; she did craft it."

Geoffrey frowned. "Why hath his voice gone so strange? . . . Gregory!"

"Hist!" Cordelia seized his hand, pulling it away from their younger brother. "He doth work magic!"

For Gregory's face had taken on a rapt expression, and his eyes had lost focus. Deep within the crystal, a light began to glow, bathing his face in its radiance.

"Surely it must hurt him!" Geoffrey protested.

"Nay." Magnus knelt on the other side of the crystal, watching his littlest brother's face intently. "It cannot; it is he who doth make use of it. Let thy mind look within his, and see."

They were silent then, each child letting his mind open to the impressions from Gregory's. They saw the crystal from his point of view, but its outlines had dimmed; only the bright spot where the moonlight cast its reflection on it was clear. As they watched through his eyes, that gleaming highlight seemed to swell, filling his vision but growing translucent, as though he were gazing into a cloud, into a field obscured by fog. Then the mist began to clear, growing thinner and thinner until, through it, they could see . . .

"'Tis Mama!" Geoffrey exclaimed, in hushed tones.

"And Papa!" Cordelia's eyes were huge, even though it was her mind that saw the vision. "Yet who are those others?"

In the vision, their mother and father sat side by side at an oaken table in a paneled corner with flagons before them, chatting with other grown-ups sitting there with them. One the children could identify—he was obviously a monk, for he wore a brown cowled robe; even the yellow screwdriver-handle that gleamed in his breast pocket was familiar. But the others . . .

"What manner of clothing is that?" Cordelia wondered.

Indeed, their clothes seemed outlandish. Two of the

grown-ups, by the delicacy of their features, were probably women, but their jerkins were almost identical to those the men wore. One of the men was lean, pale-skinned, and white-haired, his eyes a very pale blue, his face wrinkled; the other was much younger, but quite fat, though with a good-natured smile. And the third was stocky and broad, but also rather ugly. . . .

" 'Tis Yorick!" Cordelia gasped.

"He who was King Tuan's Viceroy of Beastmen, till lately?" Geoffrey stared. "I' troth, 'tis him! Yet what strange manner of garb doth he wear?"

Indeed, Yorick was dressed just like the other grown-ups, in some weird form of tight-fitting tunic that was fastened up the front without buttons.

" 'Tis he," Magnus agreed. "Yet how doth he come to be with them?"

"At the least, they have found themselves good folk to accompany them," Cordelia observed.

"Why certes, thou dolt!" Geoffrey snorted. "Would our folk e'er find aught else?"

Cordelia whirled toward him, a sharp retort on her tongue, but Magnus touched her arm. "Nay! Thou wilt disrupt the dream! Abide, sister! Be patient! Watch our parents whilst thou may!"

"Oh, aye!" Cordelia held still, concentrating on the vision. "Yet 'twas ill of them, to so leave us. Oh! How dare they go wandering without us?"

"I misdoubt me an they did it by choice," Geoffrey said, with sarcasm.

"He hath the right of it, for once," Magnus agreed. "At the least, sister, rejoice that they do live and are well!"

"Oh, aye!" Cordelia cried, instantly contrite. "How selfish of me! Praise Heaven they are not hurted!"

But even as she said it, the vision began to fade. Cordelia gave a wordless cry of longing, but the mist thickened, obscuring their parents and their friends, till cloud filled the crystal again.

"At the least, we did see them for some little while." Magnus stared at the darkening crystal with huge eyes. "Godspeed, my father and mother! And bring thee back to me quickly!"

Then the crystal was only a glittering bauble again, and Gregory's eyes closed. He swayed, kneeling, then slowly toppled.

Cordelia leaped forward and caught him, cradling his head in her arms. "Oh! Poor lad! Magnus, it hath quite exhausted him, this seeing!"

"'Tis only weariness, sister," Magnus reassured her. "He must needs rest some little while; then he will be well."

"An we have that 'while' thou speakest of." Geoffrey looked up, turning toward the entrance to the grotto with a frown.

"What dost thou hear?" Magnus was instantly alert, holding very still, straining his ears. Then he heard it, too—a crashing through the brush and a distant "Ho! Ho!" coming nearer.

"The troll!" Cordelia exclaimed. "Oh, it must not find this wondrous place!"

"I fear that it will," Geoffrey said, tight-lipped. "It doth follow our trace, and will track us here soon or late!"

"A great blundering monster such as that, entering in amidst all this dainty beauty?" Cordelia cried. "Such a creature would destroy it quite!"

"Nay, it will not." Magnus rose, hefting Gregory's unconscious body, but with great effort. "It will not come in . . . if we . . . are gone."

"Thou must not leave!" Summer insisted, hands upraised to stop him.

"Aye! 'Tis not safe," Fall agreed. "The monster will follow and catch thee!"

"Aye . . . but it will not have come in here, if . . . we have fled."

"Will it know that, though?" Cordelia demanded. "Nay! It will follow our trace in, then will follow it out again—but Heaven alone knows what havoc it will wreak while here! Nay! Set down thy brother, and aid me! That troll must not enter this grotto!"

"In that, we agree." Summer and Fall said in chorus. "Faerie magic is thine to command. How shall we stop the creature?"

A glitter caught Magnus's eye, and he turned, staring at the tracery of a dew-coated web. "With thine aid, I can at least think how to slow it when it doth seek to enter."

"Slowing the thing will not save this grotto! Oh!" Cordelia stamped her foot, glaring at Gregory's unconscious form. "Waken, lob! Canst thou not find a way to stop this monster?"

"Do not seek to rouse him." It was a deep baritone; Puck stood by her knee, frowning up at Gregory. "That seeing drew greatly on his strength; thy folk must be far indeed from us."

"Yet how shall we stay this troll, Robin?"

"An Magnus can slow it at the entrance to this grotto, I may know how to banish it—unless I mistake the creature's nature quite." Puck grinned. "At the least, we could watch from safe hiding and try. Art thou willing, children?"

"Well, if it must be safe hiding, it must," Geoffrey sighed. "What is thy plan, Puck?"

When the troll came blundering and bellowing to the grotto, they were ready for it.

It followed their trail up to the hole in the vines, went on past it, slowed, stopped, and looked around, confused. Then a grin split its face, and it turned to swagger back, sniffing as it went. As it came to the hole in the vines, its grin widened, and it shouted, "Aho!" It bent over, sniffing from side to side, then turned toward the hole with a chuckle. It stepped forward . . .

And blundered into an invisible wall.

The troll stepped back, frowning, but whatever it had come against clung to it and it swatted around trying to bat the substance away. But the effort was for naught, and it bellowed in anger, kicking and thrashing.

"It is wrapped in the spiders' webs," Geoffrey reported.

"Small wonder, when there were a thousand of them, one on top of another," Magnus answered. "Now, 'Delia, lead us. Think, brother."

Geoffrey glared at the troll, but his mind concentrated on Cordelia's thoughts.

Cordelia was thinking of birds—many birds. Sparrows, robins, bluebirds, crows—hundreds of them. Magnus picked up on the sparrows, imagining a horde of them as vividly as he could. Geoffrey took robins, lots of robins, flocking together to practice flying south for the winter.

The troll roared in full anger now, struggling with more and more strength but less and less effect. As it struggled, bits of it began to flake off against the spider webs, taking on independent life, wriggling through the holes the troll tore in its invisible cocoon, clawing loose and fluttering away into the night.

"'Tis even as Puck thought!" Geoffrey cried. "The troll is a thing made of witch-moss!" And he redoubled his efforts, glaring furiously at the monster.

The birds were fluttering out of the churning chrysalis by the dozens now—robins, sparrows, and bluebirds flying away, huge crows flapping into the night with cawing cacophony that masked the troll's shrunken, high-pitched roaring— and as they fluttered away, the thrashing shape grew smaller and smaller.

Finally, it was small enough to crawl through one of the holes it had torn—and a foot-high troll came waddling and tumbling down the side of the grotto wall with roars that sounded like a kitten's mew.

"Eh, the poor thing!" Cordelia said, and her vision of bluebirds vanished like a soap bubble. She leaped up, arms outstretched—but Puck caught at her skirt. "Nay, lass! Small it may be, yet 'tis even now a vicious, voracious monster! Hold out thy hand to it and it will take thy wrist with its teeth!"

"Think, brother!" Magnus commanded, and Geoffrey obeyed with a will. As Cordelia watched, appalled, the troll's form blurred like a wax doll too close to the fire. The colors of its face, hair, and body flowed, blending into an even pinkish mass which still wobbled toward them, pinching in the middle, dividing, splitting apart. Then each half stretched, darkening, and slabs of its substance shelved out, moving up and down, as its form coalesced and hardened—and a crow flew away into the night, cawing. A sparrow hopped after it, chirping.

Then the grotto lay empty, and silent.

Cordelia stared, eyes huge and tragic.

"Do not feel guilt, sister," Geoffrey snapped. "It would have eaten thee, an it could have."

"'Twas never a thing of its own," Puck pointed out, "for it had no mind—only an impulse, a blind, clawing need. 'Twas born of an old wife's delight in a children's tale, and had no more substance than a fevered dream."

"'Tis almost as though it had never been," Cordelia whispered.

"Never think it!" Geoffrey insisted, and Magnus nodded, his face hard. "It would have bitten thee with teeth hard and sharp, and devoured thee with an actual hunger. 'Twas real enough, sister—real enough."

11

It was still dark when Kelly shook them, one by one, calling softly, "Wake. The sun rises over the pastureland, children, even though ye see it not. We must begin the day's journey. Wake!"

The children rolled over with an assortment of groans. "But we were awake so late last night, Kelly," Gregory pleaded.

"And 'twas quite wearying," Geoffrey seconded.

"Wearying! Sure and I thought ye did love a good fight!"

"I do," the boy yawned, "yet 'tis wearying nonetheless."

"Wherefore ought we to wake, when Puck doth not?" Magnus groused.

"He rose up before ye, and went ahead to spy out the countryside. Ye'll not go unwarned into danger again, says he! So come, awake!"

"Let me sleep a bit more," Cordelia murmured, burrowing her head back into her rolled-cape pillow.

But a velvet nose nuzzled her cheek, and she looked up to see the unicorn standing over her, silver in the dark. With a glad cry, she leaped up to throw her arms about the creature's neck.

The boys rose more slowly, but with much chivying, Kelly managed to persuade the children to wash. With a splash of cold water on their faces and a double handful of wild berries in their stomachs, they felt bright enough to trudge out of the forest.

They came into pastureland, and the cool, moist air, coupled with the sight of the early sun, raised their spirits enough so that they began singing as they wended their way down a cow-track, with Fess, who had finally found them again after their adventure with the troll, trudging contentedly behind them. Geoffrey even felt lively enough to fly a few feet every other bar.

At the top of his third flight, he suddenly fell silent and

dropped back to earth hissing, "Hush! 'Tis four hulking thieves, or I mistake quite!"

Gregory bobbed up to take a look, but Magnus caught him by the ankles and hauled him back down. "Nay! If there be evil men, it most becomes children to be unseen and unheard!"

They went forward in silence, stealing into the hedgerow at the edge of the field and peeking out. They saw a dusty road. Off to their right, it met another such track to form a crossroad, marked by a huge stone cross. To their left, four beefy men came swaggering along, guffawing and bellowing.

"Eh, but didn't he run, though!"

"'Twas well for him, or we'd have left his carcass for crow-meat!"

"Nay, nay! We could ha' guv him as fancy a funeral as any village priest!"

"Surely we could have—he'd paid dearly enough for it." The biggest man chortled and held up a leather bag as big as his head.

"Aye," growled the shortest and most burly man, "yet we've not split it up into shares! And if I don't have mine soon, Borr, 'tis your corpse we'll bury, not his!"

Anger sparked in the eyes of the man called Borr, but he managed to smother it under a cardboard smile. "Eh, now! Would I cheat ye, Morlan?"

"Only an I did let ye," Morlan rumbled.

The anger glinted in Borr's eyes again, but he managed to keep the smile in place. "Why, comrade! Never would I! 'Tis only that we did need to be far enough from the ambush, lest that fat merchant might summon the Reeve!"

"So ye said," one of the other thugs growled, "but we're far enough now."

"Aye." Morlan pointed at the stone cross. "Yon's Arlesby Cross. 'Tis two miles we've come. Is that not enough?"

"Aye, 'tis indeed!" Borr agreed. "And there's the offering-stone before the rock! Others may leave food for the fairies on it—but 'tis in my mind 'twill make an excellent counting-table for us! Come, comrades!"

The four men strolled up to the cross.

They are robbers! Gregory thought.

Thieves, who've robbed a fat merchant, Geoffrey agreed.

'Tis outrage! Cordelia's thoughts were fiery. *What harm had that poor man done them?*

Ask rather, who would harm them for robbing him?
Geoffrey retorted.

Magnus set his hand on his dagger.

A small hand grasped his thumb with an iron grip. "Nay!"
Kelly hissed. "Ye cannot save the poor merchant now—his
gold's already stolen!"

"We might return it to him," Magnus pointed out.

"'Tis not worth hazarding yerselves!"

"'Tis no hazard," Geoffrey grated.

"Mayhap ye are right—yet reflect! The Puck is not by ye
now, if ye're wrong!"

Geoffrey hesitated.

The four robbers squatted down around the offering-stone,
and Borr upended the bag. Coins tumbled out, and the men
hooted delight.

"One for ye, Morlan!" Borr shoved a gold piece toward the
squat man. "And one for ye, Gran—and one for ye,
Croll . . ."

"And all for me!" rumbled a voice like the grinding of a
millwheel. Out from behind the stone cross he came—eight-
feet tall at least, and four-feet across the shoulders. His arms
were thick as tree trunks, and his legs were pillars. The cudgel
he swung in his right hand was as big as Magnus, and probably heavier. His shaggy black hair grew low on his forehead;
his eyes seemed small in his slab of a face, and his grin
showed yellowed, broken teeth. "Nay, then!" he boomed.
"Bow down, wee men! 'Tis your master Groghat who
speaks!"

The robbers stared at him for one terrified instant. Then
they leaped up and ran—except for Morlan, who swept the
coins back into the bag before he turned to flee.

Groghat caught him by the back of his collar and yanked
him off his feet. Morlan squalled in terror, and Groghat
plucked the moneybag out of his hands before he threw him
after his mates. Morlan howled as he shot through the air,
spread-eagled, and Borr yowled in pain as Morlan crashed
into him. Gran and Croll, the fourth robber, kept running, but
Groghat passed them in a few huge loping strides and slewed
to a halt, facing them with a scowl and a lifted bludgeon. "I
bade thee bow!"

Gran faced him, knees trembling and face ashen. Slowly,
he bent his back in a bow—but Croll whirled toward the trees
at the side of the road.

Groghat's club slammed into the man's belly, and the robber fell, curled around the agony in his midriff, mouth spread wide, struggling for the breath that would not come. The giant stood over him, glowering down at Morlan and Borr.

Slowly, they bowed.

"'Tis well," Groghat rumbled. "Be mindful henceforth—I am thy master. Whatsoe'er thou dost steal, thou shalt bring three parts out of four unto me."

"Nay!" Morlan bleated. "'Tis we who do steal it, we who run the risk of a hang . . ."

The huge club slammed into his ribs and something cracked. He fell, screaming.

"And do not seek to withhold aught," Groghat bellowed over the noise, "for I shall know, soon or late, who hath taken what, and shall find thee wheresoe'er thou dost roam!"

"Nay!" "Nay, Groghat, we never would!" "Three parts out of four to thee, Groghat, ever, henceforth!"

The giant glared down at them, nodding slowly. "See thou dost not forget." He nudged Morlan with his foot. "Take thy fools, and be gone."

"Aye, Groghat! Even as thou sayest!" Gran knelt to pull Morlan's arm over his shoulders. Morlan screamed in pain.

Borr stood looking up at the giant. He was trembling, but he plucked up his courage to ask, "Art not afeard of Count Glynn? Assuredly, thou art mighty—but how wilt thou fare an he doth come against thee with an hundred men, armored?"

Groghat laughed, a sound like marbles rolling down a sheet of iron, and pulled something out of the wallet that hung from his belt. "Look and see!" he bellowed.

Borr took a hesitant step, eyeing Groghat warily.

"Nay, be not afeard!" the giant rumbled. "I'll not smite thee now. Come and see!"

He doth wish them to look, Geoffrey thought. *He doth wish to boast.*

Borr looked down into the giant's cupped palm and his breath rasped in, harsh with dismay. "'Tis Count Glynn's signet ring!"

"The same," Groghat laughed, "and I assure thee, I did not find it by the side of the road!"

Borr lifted his gaze to the huge face, trembling. "Hast thou then slain him?"

"What! Throw aside a counter for bargaining? Nay!"

Groghat laughed with contempt. "What would I do then, if the Duke and his horse and foot came against me, eh? What would I do *now?* Nay, ask!"

"What wouldst thou do now, if the Duke came against thee with all his horse and all his men?" Borr asked, quavering.

"Why, bid him, 'Hold, or I will slay them! Slay Count Glynn, and his wife and babes!'" Groghat cried. "Would he charge me then? Nay!"

He holds them imprisoned! Cordelia thought, appalled.

We must rescue! Geoffrey clenched the nearest branch so hard his knuckles whitened.

"Hold fast," Kelly hissed, laying a hand on his shoulder. "He will not kill them, as thou hast now heard. No further harm will come to them—yet it might, to *thee.*"

"Aye, quake!" Groghat laughed, "Tremble, and rightly! For 'tis I who rule this county now, and all must pay me tribute!"

"Aye, Groghat!" Borr was nodding so quickly it seemed his head might fall off. "All shall be as thou dost say, Groghat!"

"Be sure that it will," the giant rumbled. "Will you or nill you! Nay, be assured—I will not take all thou dost steal. Wherefore ought I? For then thou wouldst steal no longer, and I wish thee to—to keep garnering gold for me. Yet thou wilt give to me three gold pieces of each thou dost steal, and three of each four silver and copper, also!"

"Aye, Groghat!" "Even as thou dost say, Groghat!"

"Be sure of it!" The huge club hissed through the air and slammed into Borr, sending him flying with a yelp. Groghat laughed as he tied the moneybag to his belt. "That will ensure thy memory! Forget me not! Now up, and away—the whole day lies before thee, and thou hast much stealing to do for me!" And he turned away, guffawing and beating the money-bag in time to his footsteps as he strode away down the road.

Borr and Croll hauled themselves to their feet, groaning.

"Here, then! Aid me with him!" Gran cried.

Borr turned, frowning at Morlan, then nodded. "Aye. He did, at the least, fight the ogre." He reached down.

"Not the arm—he hath broken ribs on that side," Gran cautioned. Together, they helped the moaning man to his feet.

"'Twill heal, Morlan, 'twill heal," Gran soothed.

"Yet will we?" Borr muttered as they turned away. "We must now rob whether we wish to or not!"

"Oh, be still! Thou knowest thou didst wish to," Morlan groaned.

"Aye," Borr admitted, "yet to keep only one coin out of four!"

"'Tis one more than thou wouldst have otherwise," Morlan growled. "But help me to a bandage and a bed! Then give me two days, and I'll aid thee in robbing again!"

And they went off down the road, grumbling and moaning.

"Nay, 'tis scandalous!" Geoffrey hissed, as soon as they were out of hearing. "Will the roads not be safe for any man now?"

"At the least, we know now why Count Glynn did not summon his knights to battle Count Drosz," Gregory pointed out.

"Even so," Magnus said with a scowl. "There will be no government henceforth—he who hath seized rule, will do naught but take money!"

"'Tis outrage!" Geoffrey exclaimed. "The Count can no longer protect his people—and this giant will encourage bandits, not stop them!"

"No woman or child will be safe now," Cordelia whispered.

"Out upon him!" Geoffrey cried. "Let us slay this vile giant!"

"Nay, children, stay!" Kelly warned. "'Tis not a common man ye would fight now, but a monster!"

"And was that dragon a garden lizard?" Geoffrey countered.

"'Gainst that dragon, thou hadst the power of the unicorn to aid thee—but what aid will she be 'gainst a fell man of that size? Nay, Groghat might catch and hurt her!"

"Oh, nay!" Cordelia cried, flinging her arms about the unicorn's neck.

Kelly pressed his advantage. "And thou didst have the Puck's magic to strengthen thine. Wilt thou not wait till he doth rejoin thee?"

"But this monster must not be left an hour, nay, a minute, to strike terror into our neighbors!"

"And who will take up the reins of governance when he hath dropped them?" Kelly demanded. "Nay, ye must free the count and his wife and children ere thou dost seek to battle the giant!"

"Why, then, lead us to them!" Geoffrey said.

"Thou carest not which battle thou hast, so long as thou hast battle," Cordelia scoffed.

"Thou dost me injustice!" Geoffrey turned on Cordelia, clenching his fists.

"'Tis true." Magnus slid artfully between them. "Thou must needs own, sister, that thy brother doth contain his hunger for fighting 'till he doth find a brawl that will aid other folk!"

"Aye, 'tis true," Cordelia sighed, "and here's a brawl that will aid them surely."

"Then let us to it!" With the children safely sidetracked, Kelly could let his own anger boil up. "The gall of him, to strike at a woman and babes! Onward, children! For we'll find and free that count, and he'll call up his knights! Then may ye aid him in making that giant into a doormat for the town gates!"

"Aye!" the children shouted, and followed the leprecohen.

The boys decided flying was faster, but Cordelia wouldn't leave her unicorn, so they flew down the road to either side of her, with Gregory perched astride the unicorn's neck just in front of Cordelia with an ear-to-ear grin, thumping the poor beast's withers and howling, "Giddyap! Giddyap!"

"Wherefore hath the beast come to tolerate him, yet not us?" Geoffrey called to Magnus.

His big brother caught the blackness of his mood and shouted back, "Mayhap because Gregory is so tiny. Contain thyself, brother!"

Geoffrey lapsed into a simmering glower.

Fess brought up the rear with Kelly dodging between his hooves and howling, "Ye great beast! Tread more softly!"

As they rode, clouds drifted across the sky, and the day turned gray. Kelly lifted his head and sniffed the air. "Sure and it's rain I'm smelling!"

"An analysis of local meteorological conditions indicates a high probability of precipitation," Fess agreed.

Thunder rumbled, not terribly far away.

"Ought we not seek shelter?" Cordelia asked.

"'Twould be wise," Kelly agreed, and swerved off the road into the trees. "Turn, Iron Horse! At the least, the rain will reach us less beneath leaves."

Thunder rumbled again, and the first raindrops sprinkled the road as the children turned to follow Kelly. They thrashed their way through the underbrush at the side of the road. After fifty feet or so, the forest floor became relatively clear, as the deep shade of the towering trees cut off sunlight from the small growth. There were still roots and saplings, so the unicorn and the robot-horse couldn't really run. They hurried as quickly as they could, though, trotting. Kelly led the way, dodging saplings and vaulting tree roots.

"'Tis a hut!" Geoffrey cried, pointing.

The children looked up, then swerved off after him with glad cries. The unicorn followed, responding to Cordelia's nudge.

"Nay, children!" Kelly cried. "Will ye not heed? There's something about that hut I like not!"

But the children ran blithely on.

He frowned up at Fess. "Hast thou naught to say? Do ye not also mislike it?"

The great black horse nodded.

Kelly ducked into a hollow at the base of a tree and dropped down, cross-legged, folding his arms. "I'll not move from here! Do as I do, ye great beast—will ye not? Let's bide here without, and watch and wait, so we can spring to their aid if they need us."

Fess nodded again, and crowded up against the tree, to block the rain from Kelly's doorway.

The two older boys shot through the window. The unicorn pulled up short at the doorway. Cordelia sprang down, and hammered on the panel. It swung open, and Geoffrey stood there. "Who would it be, calling at this time of the day? Eh! We have no need of your ware!"

"Oh, be not so silly!" Cordelia ducked in through the doorway, hauling Gregory with her. She stopped and looked around in surprise. "Doth none live here then?"

"If one doth, he is not at home." Geoffrey looked around at the empty interior. Gregory scuttled past his hip.

Cordelia turned to look up at the unicorn. "Will you not come in, then?"

The unicorn tossed her head and turned away, trotting back toward the wood.

"Come back!" Cordelia cried.

The silver beast turned and looked back, tossing her head and pawing the turf. Then she whirled away, trotting off among the trees.

"Hath she left again, then?" Geoffrey said hopefully.

"Oh, be still!" Cordelia turned back, tilting her nose up. "She doth but seek her own form of shelter. I misdoubt me an she doth not trust housen."

"Nor do I." Magnus was looking around the hut with a frown. "How can this chamber be so much larger than it seemed from the outside?"

Cordelia shrugged and went to sit on a three-legged stool by the fireplace. "All houses do seem smaller from without."

"Yet 'twas not a house—'twas but a hut of sticks! And here within, 'tis a solid house of timbers, with walls of wattle and daub!" Magnus went over to the table set against one wall and frowned up at the shelves above it. "What manner of things are these?" He pointed from one bottle to another. "Eye of newt . . . fur of bat . . . venom of viper . . ."

"They are the things of magic," Gregory said, round-eyed.

Magnus nodded somberly. "I think that thou hast the right of it. And they are not the cleanly things, such as old Agatha doth use when she doth brew potions, but foul and noisome." He turned back to his brothers and sister. "This is a witch's house, and worse—'tis a sorcerer's!"

The door slammed open, and a tall old man hunched in, face and form shrouded by a hooded robe. A yellowed beard jutted out of its shadow, wiggling as he swore to himself, "What ill chance, that such foul weather should spring up! What noisome hag hath enchanted the clouds this day?" He dropped a leather pouch on the table in the center of the room. "At the least, ere dawn, I gained the graveyard earth I sought —so the trek served its purpose." He yanked off his robe, muttering to himself, went to hang it by the fire—and stopped, staring down at Cordelia.

She shrank back into the inglenook, trying hard to make herself invisible.

The old man was tattered and grubby, wearing a soiled tunic and cross-gartered hose. His face was gaunt, with a hooked blade of a nose and yellowed, bloodshot eyes beneath stringy hair that straggled down from a balding pate—hair that might have been white, if he had washed it more often. Slowly, he grinned, showing a few yellow teeth—most of them were missing. Then he chuckled and stepped toward Cordelia, reaching out a hand blotched with liver-spots.

"Stand away from my sister!" Geoffrey cried, leaping between them.

The sorcerer straightened, eyebrows shooting up in surprise. "Eh! There's another of them!" He turned, saw Gregory and, behind him, Magnus, hunched forward, hands on their daggers—but he saw also the fear in the backs of their eyes. He laughed, a high, shrill cackle, as he whirled to slam the door shut and drop a heavy oaken bar across it. "I have them!" he crowed, "I have them! Nay, just the things, the very things that I'll need!"

"Need?" Dread hollowed Magnus's voice. "What dost thou speak of?"

"What dost thou think I speak of?" the sorcerer spat, whirling toward him. He stumped forward with a malevolent glint in his eye. "What manner of house dost thou think thou hast come to, child?"

Magnus swallowed heavily and said, "A sorcerer's."

"Eh-h-h-h." The sorcerer nodded slowly, a gleam in his eye. "Thou hast sense, at the least. And what doth a sorcerer *do*, lad?"

"He doth . . . doth brew . . . magics."

"Well! So thou knowest that little, at least! Yet the better sorcerers do seek to discover new magics—as I do. For I am Lontar, a sorcerer famed throughout the countryside for weird spells and fell!"

The children stiffened, recognizing the name of the man who had cursed old Phagia.

Again, the gap-toothed grin. "And I've found one that will give me power over every soul in this parish! Nay, further— in the county, mayhap the whole kingdom!"

Gregory stared up at the old man's eyes and thought, *He is mad.*

"Hush!" Magnus hissed, clapping a hand onto his shoulder, for Gregory had not cast his thoughts in their family's private way. But Lontar's grin widened. "Patience—he is young. He knoweth not yet that all witch-folk can hear one another's thoughts. But I . . ." he tapped his chest. "I am more. I can make others hear *my* thoughts—aye, even common folk, lowly peasant folk, with not one grain of witch-power in their brains!"

The children were silent, staring at him.

The sorcerer cackled, enjoying their fright. "Yet 'tis not thoughts alone I can send, nay! For years I have studied, trying and trying, again and again, whetting my powers with one weird brew after another—yet I have learned the craft of it,

aye, learned it until I can work this spell without drinking
even a drop of the potion, nor a whiff of its fumes! First with
mere earthworms, then with the robins who came for them,
then with field mice, rabbits, wolves, bears—all, all now
cower before me! All shrink and howl, turn and flee, when I
do cast this into their brains!"

"Cast what?" Even Geoffrey could not quite disguise the
dread in his voice.

"Why . . . pain!" The sorcerer cackled with high glee. " 'Tis
pain, pure! Pain, searing pain, as though thy head did burn,
and thy whole body did scream with the stings of a thousand
bees! 'Tis pain, pain, the root of all power—for pain doth
cause fear, and fear doth make all to obey! Yet!" He speared a
long, bony forefinger straight up. "My work is not done! I
cannot yet go forth, to take rule of the county! For I've not
done with the last task!"

"And what task is that?" Magnus's voice trembled in spite
of all his efforts; he could feel the feared answer coming.

"Why, people! Casting the pain into the minds of real people! With bears I have done it, with wolves, but never with
people!" The sorcerer's eyes glittered. "To make human brains
flame, to make mortal folk scream at my mere thought! And
why have I not? Why, 'tis that I've never found folk with
whom I could attempt it! Long have I sought some, to use for
my learning—yet never did they come, strangers and alone,
into my wood. Ever, ever did they come accompanied, three
or four grown ones together—or they had folk who would
seek them, an they did not return!"

"So have we!" Geoffrey said stoutly. "We too have folk
who will scour this forest, an we come not home!"

"Thou dost lie." The sorcerer leveled a forefinger at him.
"Never have I set eyes upon thee before; thou art not of this
parish; thou art come from afar. And thou hast come without
parents! None do so—save orphans! Or ones who do flee!"
He cackled with glee at his own cleverness. "Nay, none will
come seeking thee—and if they did, who would know where
thou hast gone?"

"But the count!" Magnus cried, grasping at straws. "The
count would call his men out against thee!"

"The count!" Lontar crowed. "Nay, there is no count! Dost
thou not know? A giant did seize him! A giant did break down
the door of the count's castle in the darkest hour of night, did
thrust the count and his family into a bag, and commanded all

the knights and men-at-arms to put down their swords on pain of their lord's death! Then he clapped all those proud warriors in the deepest, dark dungeons, and hauled the count and his family away into his own hidden prison. The count? Ah, the count shall do naught! Nor can he, when I've learned to use my torture spell to its fullest! He, even he, shall not resist me—nor shall Groghat the giant! Even him shall I humble, even him shall I bring to his knees, screaming with the pain that sears through his brain! None will resist me; all will bow down!"

Suddenly, Gregory stilled, staring at him, unblinking.

"And I'll begin it with *thee!*" The old sorcerer spun, leveling a forefinger at Cordelia.

"Nay, thou shalt not!" Rage flared in Magnus in a moment of pure hate, every gram of emotion directed at the old sorcerer. Geoffrey's wrath joined his, and Cordelia's terrified anger.

Gregory cried, "I have it!" and instantly his brothers and sister found in their minds the old sorcerer's method for concentrating thought and projecting pain. With it came memories of the pain and terror of little animals, spurring the children to greater anger, and greater, as their fear and wrath focused into the old sorcerer while Cordelia screamed and screamed, the force of her horror tearing through the old man's brain with her brothers' hatred and rage behind it, stabbing through from temple to temple, searing his mind with his own techniques until his howl turned into a raw, hoarse scream. His body stiffened, hands curling into claws; he stood, back arched, for one frozen instant, then collapsed in a heap on the floor, totally silent.

The children stared, appalled, anger evaporating in an instant. Finally, Cordelia spoke. "Is . . . is he . . ."

Gregory was staring intently at the old body. "His heart hath stopped."

"We have slain him!" Cordelia cried, in dismay.

"More to the better!" Geoffrey snapped.

But Magnus said, "Nay! We must not have blood on our hands, an we can prevent it! What would Mama and Papa say?"

"That he is a vile, evil man," Geoffrey answered.

"But they would say also that we must spare his life, an we can." Cordelia knelt down by the body, gazing intently at Lontar's face. "What we have done thus far they would approve, for we have done it only in defense of ourselves—and I thank you, my brothers!" She gave each of them a warm look of gratitude that made even Geoffrey forget his anger for a moment; then she turned back to the sorcerer. "Now, though, 'tis another matter. Now we can spare his life—and we will, an we can start his heart to beating once again!"

"How canst thou do that?" Geoffrey questioned; but Magnus joined Gregory and Cordelia beside the waxen body, staring down.

"Be guided by me," Cordelia breathed, "for this is women's work, in this land. Squeeze the left of the heart, when I bid thee—now!"

With telekinesis, they massaged the heart. All three of them thought a squeeze on the left-hand side of the heart, then let go immediately.

"Now, the right side," Cordelia instructed, and they all squeezed together. "Now the left again . . . now right . . . left-right . . . left-right . . . left-right . . ."

They kept at it for several minutes while Geoffrey stood back glowering, his arms folded.

"It doth beat of its own," Gregory reported.

"Aye," Cordelia agreed, "but faintly. Keep pressing, brothers, but softly now."

Gradually, bit by bit, they lightened the pressure till, finally, the old man's heart was beating regularly again. Cordelia breathed a long, shaky sigh and sat back on her heels. "'Tis done!"

"Mama would be proud of thee," Gregory said, beaming.

"And of thee." Cordelia managed a tremulous smile before she sighed again. "Eh, brothers! I hope that never again shall I come so close to causing another's death!"

"If thou dost," Geoffrey growled, "I trust he will deserve it as deeply as this one did."

Cordelia frowned down at the old sorcerer. "He hath caused great suffering, 'tis true."

Gregory frowned, too. "Mama and Papa hath said that when a person's heart is stopped too long, the brain can suffer hurt."

"Aye, and full damage." Magnus scowled, concentrating. The room was silent a moment while his brothers and sister watched him; then he nodded. "All is as it should be. From what I can tell, there is no damage done."

"There should have been," Geoffrey hissed.

Magnus glanced up at him, irritated, but said nothing—he couldn't really disagree.

"Yet I think he will not be so quick to offer injury again," Cordelia said thoughtfully.

"Aye . . . yet let us be certain." Magnus glared down at Lontar's unconscious face. The old man twitched in his sleep, and Magnus said, "Lay words, Gregory."

The little boy's face screwed up for a moment, then relaxed.

So did Magnus. He wiped his brow with a shaky smile. "An aught will restrain him, that will."

His brother and sister nodded. They had heard the thought Magnus and Gregory had implanted in the old man's mind. "From this time forth," Cordelia said, "if he doth so much as think of causing pain to another creature . . ."

"Every time," Gregory agreed, "each and every."

And they turned and went out the door, closing it behind them, leaving the unconscious sorcerer to waken in his own good time—with an association arc buried in his mind. If ever again he thought, even thought, of causing pain to somebody else, he would feel a twinge of the agony the children had given him stabbing through his own brain, and a small child's voice echoing in his ears:

"Thou must not be so nasty!"

12

They came out of the hut to find rain still falling lightly about them.

"I will gladly choose a wetting, over housen with that monster!" Geoffrey declared.

Cordelia shivered and hugged herself, but said bravely, "I, too."

"Kelly knew it from the first." Magnus looked glum. "We should have hearkened to him; he would not come near."

"Nor would my unicorn," Cordelia said softly. "Alas, poor beauty! Doth she suffer from this wetting?"

"She doth know the ways of the wood." Magnus looked about him, frowning. "Kelly! Wherefore art thou? Hast thou abandoned us quite?"

"Nay, he hath not," said a deep voice by his knee, "nor have I."

"Robin!" Cordelia exclaimed, overjoyed, and Geoffrey said, "I thought thou hadst gone to spy out dangers ahead of us."

"Aye, but I did not know thou wouldst turn from the homeward path. Yet thou hadst need to; I will own, thou hast done well."

"Well! We were near to being slain in agony!" Cordelia cried.

"Thou wouldst not have been," Puck said, with full certainty, and Kelly stepped up beside him, nodding. "If there had been any true danger, children, yer great black horse would have stove in that sorcerer's door, and elf-shot would have struck him senseless."

"I think he was so already," Geoffrey growled.

"Mayhap," Puck agreed, "yet he did not have so much power as the four of thee."

But Magnus was frowning at Kelly. "How didst thou know what did hap within?"

"Through a brownie, who hid by the hearth. Long have the Wee Folk forsaken that place; yet when they saw thee go in, one crept through a mousehole to watch."

"Fie upon it!" Geoffrey plopped down cross-legged, arms folded tight, head hunkered down. "Will we never truly win a fight by ourselves?"

"Why, so thou didst," Puck answered. " 'Twas thou four who didst best that sorcerer, children."

"As thou didst know we would," Magnus accused.

Puck shook his head. "If thou hadst not been able to join all thy four powers together, then might he have hurted thee."

"Then," Geoffrey retorted, "elves would have saved us."

"That they would have," Puck agreed. "I have sworn to thy parents that I would protect thee. Never wilt thou lack for elfin guards. Yet they did naught, in this instance—the victory was thine, and thine alone."

"The day shall come," Geoffrey vowed, "when I shall win broils without even thy warding, Puck."

"So it shall, when thou art grown," the elf allowed. "Yet for now . . ." He looked from one little face to another. "We must join forces. What thou didst, thou didst well. Now let us return to thy chosen goal."

Geoffrey looked up, frowning. "To free the count?"

Puck nodded. "Yet I bethink me, we must have greater force than a band of elves and four small children, even ones so powerful as thyselves. Kelly!"

"What would ye?" the elf muttered.

"Hie thee to King Tuan, and ask of him some few knights and a hundred foot. 'Tis a castle we must breach, not some mere peasant's hut."

Kelly nodded. "A catapult with it?"

"Aye! See to it thou art there and back within the half of an hour!"

"Were the cause not so vital," the leprecohen growled, "I would never heed so much as one of yer commands!"

"Thou wouldst, or thou wouldst truly hop to it!"

"Yet the cause *is* vital," Kelly said hastily, "and I am gone." And he was, with the sound of arrow feathers whipping past an archer's ear.

"Come, children!" Puck turned away toward the roadway. "To Castle Glynn!"

· · ·

"The half-hour is up," Gregory reported.

Puck spared him a glance of annoyance. "Must all thy folk carry clocks in their heads?"

"Only Gregory." Magnus gave his little brother's shoulder an affectionate squeeze. "Yet where is Kelly, Puck?"

"Here."

The unicorn and robot-horse stopped; Magnus and Gregory dropped down to the road. The leprecohen stepped out of the brush, slapping dust out of his breeches. "Sure and it's a hornet's nest ye did send me into!"

"Nest of hornets?" Puck frowned, arms akimbo. "Explain thyself, elf!"

"There's little enough to explain. The king can spare us no knights, nor no footmen neither."

"What!"

"Surely he would not deny us!"

"How could the King forget his High Warlock's children?"

Kelly shrugged. "What grown folk will credit the words of children, when great affairs of state do loom?"

"Yet how is't this king would not hearken to the Puck?" the bigger elf demanded. "Say, Kelly!"

"Oh, he's hearkening to ye, well enough—or to Brom O'Berin, his Privy Councillor, which comes to the same thing, when Brom's doin' yer askin' for ye. But he's facin' the same task a hundredfold, in the South—and the East and the West too, for that matter. And the North, now that I mention it."

Puck scowled. "Thou dost speak in riddles. Explain."

"Why, 'tis no more nor less than this—that every petty lord has of a sudden risen 'gainst his neighbor. Their dukes do naught to prevent them, for they're far too occupied with fighting one another, themselves."

The children stared, horrified. "And the King must beat them back into their castles, one by one?" Geoffrey whispered.

Kelly nodded. "Do ye wonder he can spare ye no horse nor foot?"

"Nay, not a bit."

"But how comes this?" Magnus asked. "I can comprehend how any one count might rise in war 'gainst his neighbor—but that all might do so, together...!"

"'Tis conspiracy," Geoffrey stated.

They were all quiet, turning to him. Then Magnus nodded.

"Aye. 'Twas planned, was it not?" He turned back to Puck. "Where *did* Mama and Papa go?"

"Thou must needs now know," the elf said sheepishly. "We did follow their tracks to a pretty pond in the woodland. There we found marks of a scuffle, and their tracks did cease."

"Even as they did when we were stolen away to Tir Chlis," Magnus whispered.

Gregory looked up, interested.

"Even so," Puck agreed.

"'Twas no mere mishap, nor the work of a moment's passion." Geoffrey spoke angrily, to hide the creeping fear in his belly.

"Nay." Cordelia shivered, and the fear was plainly written on her face. "It must have been well plotted. Yet how could they know where Mama and Papa would go?"

"They must needs have lured them in some fashion," Geoffrey returned, "and set up their engines of enchantment along the path to that pond."

"Set them up days in advance, and waited and waited," Gregory agreed. "Such weighty spells do require much apparatus that I wot not of."

The children were quiet. It wasn't all that rarely that Gregory admitted that he didn't know how something worked—but it was unusual for him not to know.

"And," Geoffrey summarized, "whosoe'er did plot to kidnap Mama and Papa, did plot also to have all the barons rise up at one time."

"Yet how could they do so?" Cordelia asked, puzzled.

Geoffrey shrugged impatiently. "There are a hundred ways, some of which I know."

"This set of events falls into a pattern characteristic of SPITE, your father's anarchistic enemies," Fess interjected.

"Groghat must be hand in glove with them," Geoffrey cried. Then, suddenly, he looked thoughtful. "Aye, there is truth in that, is there not?"

"Sure and there is," Kelly agreed. "From what we saw of him, I'd be well surprised, if he had wit enough to plan such as this."

"More a dupe than a partner." Puck nodded.

"Yet what of their enemies?" Magnus asked, frowning. "Papa hath said SPITE is opposed by VETO, which is composed of those who seek to rule all, with an iron fist."

"Yes—the totalitarians," Fess agreed.

They were all quiet, thinking. Then Gregory said, "Mayhap the Shire-Reeve?"

Geoffrey's head snapped up. "Aye, thou hast the right of it!"

"And thou children art like to be caught in the warring," Puck said. "I like it not."

"Yet we are like to be caught in such warring in any case." Cordelia spread her hands. "Would not we be marked, Puck?"

The elf was silent for a moment. Then, slowly, he nodded. "I had not thought to set spies to watch thy house."

"Thought!" Kelly scoffed. "Wherefore would ye need to think? If there be great lumbering fools sitting out in the forest watching the High Warlock's house, how could elves fail to notice them?"

"There's truth in that," Puck agreed, and turned to the children. "Yet these enemies of thy father's have spells we wot not of, with which they can watch."

The children were quiet. Then Cordelia said, in a very small voice, "Dost thou say we ought not to go home?"

"I misdoubt me of it," Puck said grimly, "yet I'll set elves to watching for watchers."

"Then where can we hide?" Gregory asked.

"In any place," Puck answered, "yet never for more than one night."

"Then Count Glynn's castle is as good as any other," Geoffrey insisted. "We have but to defeat one giant, to hide there."

"How shalt thou?" a huge voice roared, and a net of thick ropes dropped down over them.

Kelly howled, darted through the mesh, and ran. Puck disappeared. The unicorn tossed her head, knocking the net aside, and bolted, with Gregory and Cordelia on her back—but Groghat swung his stick like a baseball bat, knocking the two children off. They slammed to the ground. Pain stabbed through their sides, from head to hip, and the world seemed to swim about them. They heard Groghat's hoarse bellow and Fess's screaming whinny of rage, abruptly cut off with a huge crash.

"Thou hast hurted him!" Geoffrey cried, thrashing against the mesh. "Fiend! Thou hast broke our father's horse!"

"I'll break more, ere I'm done," Groghat bellowed. He scooped up Cordelia and Gregory with one huge hand, tossed them into the net with their brothers, and yanked on a draw string. The whole net shut up like a bag. Groghat threw it over his shoulder with a roar of laughter and strode off over the fields, chanting a victory song.

Jumbled in together, jouncing with every step, the children held a conference that the giant couldn't hear.

He is large, Geoffrey admitted, *yet there is but the one of him.*

And he hath but four limbs, Magnus agreed.

And but one brain, Gregory pointed out. *Gently, 'Delia!*

Big Sister had him bundled against her tummy for cushioning, to protect him from the jouncing. *As gently as I can, babe. Hold tightly to me.*

Nay, siblings, Magnus thought. *We have slain a vile sorcerer, and restored him to life again . . .*

More's the pity, Geoffrey added.

And from him, Gregory continued, *we have learned a spell for causing great pain.*

Never shall we use it! Magnus thought instantly. Then he reconsidered. *Mayhap—for Groghat . . .*

He is ours, not we his, Geoffrey said, with finality. He looked around, frowning through the mesh. *Puck did but now say we would not lack for guards—yet I see him not, nor Kelly neither.*

Thou wouldst not, Magnus reasoned, *yet be certain—an we cannot finish what we begin, they will.*

Cordelia's thoughts were tinged with blood. *An he hath broke our Fess . . .*

I misdoubt me of that, Magnus thought back at her. *Fess hath been in many battles, and hath scarcely lost horsehair. Yet he will need one to turn him on again.*

Aye. Geoffrey glowered. *Naetheless, I am not therefore minded to spare this foul giant. What say you, brothers and sister? Shall we slay him now, or later?*

They were quiet for a moment.

Nay! Geoffrey protested. *Surely thou dost not truly think to let him live!*

For a while, at least, Cordelia thought.

Aye, Magnus agreed. *We did wish to go to Castle Glynn, did we not? Wherefore ought we not let him take us there?*

Then, too, Gregory added, *I have never seen a real giant before.*

• • •

Yet it was not Castle Glynn that Groghat brought them to, but
a craggy old ruin deep in the forest.

He stamped into the great hall, halted before a fireplace
where a huge fire roared, loosed the drawstring, and upended
the bag. The children squawked as they hit the floor, and
Groghat crowed, "Now, then! I've new toys to play with!"

The children picked themselves up, and there was murder
in Geoffrey's eye. Magnus laid a restraining hand on his arm
and said, "Hast thou never had playmates, then?"

For a moment, there was a lost, frozen look in Groghat's
eyes. Then it thawed into a grin, and Magnus noticed that the
giant's eyeteeth were longer than any of his other teeth. "Thou
art the toys, not the players," Groghat growled.

"Indeed." Geoffrey cocked his head to the side with the
dangerous glint still in his eye. "What game wilt thou play?
Ninepins?"

"Jackstraws, more likely," Groghat grunted. "What, child!
Dost not realize thou art in danger of thy life?"

Geoffrey simply stared at him.

Magnus said quickly, "There are many things we do not
realize. We are, after all, but innocents in a rough world. Wilt
thou not explain to us?"

For a moment, Groghat seemed baffled. Then he looked
suspicious. "What manner of things?"

"Why, many things." Magnus was all innocence.

Groghat sat on a bench slowly, leaning back on a table with
one elbow, eyeing them warily.

"Poor giant." Cordelia fairly oozed sympathy. "Thou hast
had little of gaming in thy life, hast thou not?"

"What need have I of games?" Groghat rumbled.

"But who hath not?" Magnus spread his hands. "I'll wager
thou hast never even played at riddles!"

"Riddles?" Groghat frowned. "What game is this?"

"Why, 'tis simply done." Cordelia beamed. "One of us will
tell a riddle, and if thou canst not puzzle it out, thou must
needs answer any question we ask."

"Thus will we gain knowledge," Magnus said brightly,
"and thou wilt gain amusement."

Groghat sat there gazing at them for a long moment, and
Magnus began to think they might have stretched their luck
too far. Then the giant rumbled, "It may prove amusing, in
truth. Well, then, as thou wilt. What is thy riddle?"

They all heaved a sigh of relief. Then Magnus recited,

> *"Arthur O'Bower has broken his band;*
> *He comes roaring up the land.*
> *The King of Scots, with all his power,*
> *Cannot turn Arthur O'Bower."*

"Aye!" Cordelia cried, glints dancing in her eyes. "Say to us, then—what is this Arthur O'Bower?"

Groghat's brow knotted in consternation, and the children waited in suspenseful silence while the giant gazed into the fire. Finally he turned to Magnus with a look of impatience. "'Tis nonsense! No one man could stand against all the might of a King, especially an he hath broken with his band of men!"

"Nay, certes 'tis nonsense," Magnus agreed. "'Tis all for fun."

"Aye, it is that," Groghat agreed reluctantly. "Tell me, then—what is Arthur O'Bower?"

"Why, the wind!"

"Wind . . ." Groghat stared at them for a moment.

Then he threw back his head, roaring a laugh. "Nay, of course! Now I see, now I know how this game is played! Nay, then, let *me* ask *thee* one!"

"Nay!" Magnus held up a palm. "First, our question! One question that thou wilt answer, ere we ask another riddle!"

"Dost thou not remember?" Cordelia urged.

Groghat scowled at them for a moment; then he almost smiled. "Well enough, then, claim thy forfeit. What is thy question?"

"Wast thou born a giant?" Cordelia asked. "Or didst thou but grow larger?"

Groghat scowled, but answered, "I cannot say surely, for I do not remember—yet the ill folk who reared me did tell me I was a wee, puny thing when the stranger brought me to their cottage."

All four children looked up, suddenly bursting with curiosity.

"Now, my riddle." Groghat leaned forward. "Tell me what is silver above and pale below."

"Why, 'tis . . . WHUF!" Geoffrey broke off with Magnus's elbow in his ribs.

"Silver above . . . pale below?" Magnus frowned. "Let me see, could it be . . . Nay, a lizard's green above . . . Nay, it's . . . Why, I have it! 'Tis a rock!"

"Nay, thou'rt wrong!" Groghat crowed. "Where hast thou ever seen a silver rock?"

"High in the Crag Mountains," Cordelia answered, "but Papa told us 'twas 'fool's gold.' What is the answer?"

"A fish, children! Hast never seen a fish?"

"Only when it's cooked and on my plate," Magnus fibbed. "What is thy question for us?"

"Question? Why . . ." Groghat thought a minute. "Let me see . . . question . . . Um."

The children waited.

Finally, Groghat said, "What manner of horse was that I overthrew? Never before have I heard a horse crash!"

Anger kindled in Geoffrey's eyes, but Magnus said, "An enchanted horse. I know not the crafting of the enchantment; 'tis Papa's horse."

"Enchanted?" Groghat looked up. "Is thy father a wizard, then?"

"Ah-ah! No question without a riddle!" Cordelia held up a palm. "And 'tis our turn.

> *"A little wee man in a red, red coat,*
> *A staff in his hand, and a stone in his throat.*
> *If you'll tell me this riddle, I'll give thee a*
> *groat!"*

Groghat's brow knitted again. "What is a 'groat'?"

"Papa said 'twas a very small coin. What is the little wee man?"

"Little wee man . . . Let me see . . ." Groghat gazed off into space. "It could not be an elf, no, for I've never seen one with a stone in his throat. I have never seen one at all, come to that. Are they real, I wonder?"

"They are."

"Magnus!" Cordelia chided him. "He must tell his riddle ere thou dost answer!"

"Oh! Aye, I erred!"

But Groghat grinned. "I care not. But I cannot tell what thy wee, wee man is."

"'Tis a cherry!" Cordelia cried. "The staff in his hand is the stem, and the stone in his throat is the pit. Now tell me—if thou wast so small a babe, how didst thou come to be so great?"

Groghat smiled, and Cordelia was glad she'd chosen the

more complimentary adjective. "The stranger who brought me to the old couple, brought them also a potion to put in my stew at every meal." He frowned. "He brought, too, a gold coin; therefore did they care for me. Yet they cared for the gold more."

And he doth revenge himself upon them, by being mean to all folk he doth meet, Gregory thought.

Thou hast the right of it, Magnus agreed, *but what was in the potion?* Aloud, he said, " 'Tis thy riddle now."

Groghat stared off into space, thinking.

Papa hath told us of a lump of flesh, in the base of the skull, that doth direct how much we grow, Gregory answered. *Whate'er the potion was, it must have acted upon that bit of flesh.*

Magnus nodded. *Yet who was the stranger?*

Papa's enemy, Geoffrey thought instantly. *It matters not from which side.*

"What is it," Groghat asked, "that is brown in the spring, green in the summer, and scarlet in the autumn?"

Gregory started to answer, but Cordelia clapped a hand over his mouth. "Let me think . . . green . . . scarlet . . ." She sighed and shook her head. "I cannot say."

"Nay, thou canst not!" Groghat guffawed, slapping the tabletop. " 'Tis a tree, foolish child!"

'Why, so 'tis," she cried, fairly beaming. "What is thy question?"

Groghat remembered. "Is thy father a wizard?"

"Nay, he's a warlock. And my riddle is: How can there be a chicken that hath no bone?"

"A chicken that hath no bone!" Groghat stared. "Nay, tell me—for I'd be greatly pleased to dine on fowl that did not crunch!"

"Then thou hast but to fry an egg!" Cordelia said triumphantly.

Groghat stared. Then he threw back his head and roared with laughter, slapping his leg.

Doth he eat chickens whole? Geoffrey wondered.

Aye, and without plucking the feathers, I doubt not, Magnus answered.

"Now let me see . . ." Cordelia pressed a finger against pursed lips. "What question shall I ask?"

Wherefore doth he roam the countryside? Magnus prompted.

"Wherefore dost thou roam the countryside?" Cordelia repeated. "Thou hast a pleasant enough lair here, if thou didst put it in repair."

"Why, for that I hate all craven knaves who take orders!" Groghat exploded. "Ever did the old man who reared me give orders: 'Do this! Fetch that!' And I grew wearied, and did resolve that, when I grew large, never more would I do another's bidding! Therefore do I spit on all craven knaves who obey, and make it *my* commands they answer to!" He leaned back against the table, gazing at the children and brooding. "Thee, now—thou showest no sign of fear, nor of doing another's bidding . . ."

Could he begin to like us?

Would we want him to?

Papa's enemies do use this poor puppet to help to bring chaos to the land, Geoffrey thought, *and he knoweth it not— he, who is so proud of not doing another's bidding!*

'Tis true, Magnus agreed, *and I doubt me not 'twas Papa's enemies in SPITE, who do hate all government, that did bring him to the old couple and paid them. Yet wherefore do not Papa's other enemies in VETO, who wish to rule all Gramarye with an iron glove, not attempt to stop him?*

Why, for that it will be all the easier for them to step in and conquer all when there's no government left, and no large army with it, but only small armed bands of bandits, Geoffrey answered.

I mislike the way he doth look at us. Cordelia's thoughts were tinged with apprehension.

"'Tis time to discover whether thou wilt obey me or no," Groghat rumbled.

Quickly, Gregory thought, *I have been tracking the paths his thoughts flow through when they tell his arms or legs to more, or his muscles to tighten or loosen to hold his balance. They all do meet at the top of his belly in one great knot.*

'Twould hurt him greatly, an thou didst twist it with thy thoughts. Cordelia shied from the idea.

Greatly daring, Magnus demanded, "'Tis mayhap more to the point, to know whether or not another doth command *thee*."

Anger flared in Groghat's eyes. He surged to his feet, bellowing, "Dost thou slander me, bug? Who could command such as I?"

"The man who did bring the potion that fed thee," Magnus answered, with a stroke of insight. "Thou dost have pain if thou dost not drink it, dost thou not?"

For a long moment, Groghat just stared at him, his eyes burning.

Suddenly, his head snapped up, looking toward the window. His lips curved into a wicked grin, and he chuckled. "What is this I hear?"

The children strained their ears, but heard nothing. "I cannot guess," Magnus admitted. "What is it?"

"A maiden," Groghat said, with a throaty laugh, "and naught else—a lone maiden, wandering in the woodland. Nay, she must not go without escort!" He whirled away to the door.

As he opened it, he whirled back, stabbing a huge finger at them. "Do not think to wander—for this door shall be barred and, if thou dost seek to climb from the window, thou'lt fall to they death!" Then he was gone, and the door boomed behind him.

The children stared at each other in the sudden silence.

"Thou'lt not heed him, I trust," came a voice from the hearth.

The children spun about, startled. "Puck!" Cordelia squealed in delight.

"Wherefore art thou amazed? Did I not assure thee thou wouldst be guarded?"

"Truly," Magnus admitted. "Canst thou find a broom for Cordelia, Puck? Then we can fly out the window."

"'Tis in the corner, yon. Thou hast but to clean ten years' worth of cobwebs from it."

"Ugh!" Cordelia flinched at the sight.

"Art thou so squeamish, then?" Magnus sighed. He went over to pick up the broom and clean it.

"Puck," Geoffrey asked, "what will the giant do with the maiden, when he doth catch her?"

"Eat her, belike," Cordelia said wisely.

"Mayhap summat of the sort," Puck said nervously. "Come, children! We must rescue!"

"Why, certes, we will," Geoffrey said, surprised, "but wherefore dost *thou* say we must, Robin?"

"For that this maiden ever did cry, ''Ware, Wee Folk!' ere she did pour out filthy wash-water, and did ever leave a bowl of milk by her hearth for the brownies. Shall the Wee Folk desert her now, in her hour of need? Nay!" He raised his voice.

> *"Ye elves of hills, brooks, standing lakes, and*
> *groves,*
> *And ye that on the sands with printless foot*
> *Do chase the ebbing Neptune, and do fly him*
> *When he comes back; you demi-puppets that*
> *By moonshine do the green sour ringlets make,*
> *Whereof the ewe not bites; and you whose pas-*
> *time*
> *Is to make midnight mushrooms, that rejoice*
> *To hear the solemn curfew! Thine aid she doth*
> *require,*
> *Who hath ever paid the tributes which thou dost*
> *desire!"*

He was silent a moment, his head cocked to one side; then he gave a satisfied nod. " 'Tis well. Come, children."

He started toward the window. Puzzled, they followed him, Cordelia dragging the broom.

Howling exploded outside.

The children stared at one another. "What noise is *that?*" Magnus cried.

Geoffrey grinned.

"Come see," Puck invited as he hopped up to the window-sill.

The boys levitated, drifting up behind him. Cordelia followed on her broom. They flew out the window, drifting over the woodland to a meadow, bisected by a cow path. A young girl was fleeing away from them, running flat out for all she was worth.

"The Wee Folk did afright her with the semblance of a bear," Puck explained.

"It truly doth sound like one." Geoffrey peered down, then slowly grinned. "Whatever thy folk have done, Puck, they have done well!"

Below them, Groghat was stamping and howling as though he were demented.

"What have they done?" Cordelia gasped.

"Only cozened a hiveful of bees into thinking the giant's a

field of sweet flowers," Puck said innocently.

"'Tis strong magic indeed." Gregory remembered Groghat's odor.

"Aye, but if they stop, he'll pursue her—or go home to find thou art gone, and run amok through the woods seeking his captives. And there are still the count and his family in the dungeons, on whom he might wreak his vengeance."

"Then we must put him to sleep," Magnus said firmly. "Come, Gregory. Where is this thought-path thou hast found?"

Gregory visualized Groghat's nervous system for them, and they all struck together, a massive stimulation of the solar plexus. Groghat folded as though the wind had been knocked out of him—which it had.

"He sleeps," Gregory reported.

"Recall thy bees, Puck," Magnus requested.

Puck was silent a moment, then smiled as a buzzing cloud lifted from Groghat and headed back into the woods.

Magnus sat back with a sigh of relief. "'Tis done."

"Aye." Geoffrey gazed down at the giant. "Good folk may travel the High Way again."

"Not yet," Cordelia corrected. "Those loutish robbers do still hide in the forest."

Geoffrey lifted his head, a slow grin stretching his lips. "Why, then, we'll hale them out!" And he turned away, reaching for his dagger.

"Thou shalt not!" Puck's hand closed around his wrist. "When thou art grown, thou mayest do as thou dost please, and hazard thyself as thou wilt—yet for now, thou wilt leave such measures to those grown-ups whose office it is!"

Geoffrey turned back, frowning. "But he lies imprisoned!"

"Then let us free him!" Cordelia clapped her hands. "Oh, please, Puck!"

"Certes," the elf agreed. "There should be no danger in that. Yet wilt thou leave thy father's horse for the crows?"

"Fess!" Cordelia pressed a hand to her lips. "I had forgot!"

"The bird that could harm Fess must needs be an iron crow," Magnus assured her, grinning. "Naetheless, we assuredly must not leave our stalwart companion. Come, let us seek him."

He banked away toward the forest, and the others sailed after him.

• • • •

The great black horse lay on its side, eyes clouded.

Cordelia knelt by him. "Pray Heaven he's not truly hurted!"

"I doubt it quite." Magnus dropped down beside the robot and felt under the saddlehorn for the enlarged vertebra that was the hidden circuit-breaker. "Papa hath told me that Fess's 'brain' is enclosed in padding that can withstand shocks fifty times greater than the pull of the earth . . . There!"

The amber eyes cleared. Slowly, the great head lifted. "Whaaat . . . wherrrre . . ."

"Self-diagnostic," Gregory said quickly.

The robot held still.

"What hast thou said, sprat?" Geoffrey frowned, worried.

"I know not—only that 'tis something Papa doth say, when he's afeard Fess may be hurted. What is its meaning, Magnus?"

"Iddt cuezzz uh brrrogram that eggzamines mmy circuits forr dam-mage," the great black horse put in, "then mmy phyzzical strugdyure. In this instanzze, mmy circuitry is unnn-damaged, and therre izz only a slllight weakening inn mmy left hind leg."

"Oh!" Cordelia's eyes widened. "How may we mend it?"

"It is unnn-nezessary ad this timme. Stannd aside, dzhildren."

They leaped up and stepped back as Fess lurched, scrambling to his feet. "Yet will not the weakening prove harmful, an thou art embattled?" Geoffrey protested.

"The probability of such stress-failure is .97," Fess acknowledged. "When we return home, I shall see to its replacement. Yet for now, I am safe enough." He lifted his head suddenly, looking off toward the north. "Your friend has returned, Cordelia."

They all turned, to see the unicorn step out of the wood. Cordelia ran to embrace her with a glad cry. The unicorn nuzzled the girl's face, then cocked her head in question. "Gladly!" Cordelia cried, and leaped up sidesaddle. The unicorn trotted toward the boys, but halted ten yards away.

Puck smiled, pleased. "Now, children—shall we fetch that count thou dost seek?"

"And his children," Cordelia added.

The count was in his dungeon, eating bread and water. His wife was in the cell next door, encouraging her children in

their efforts to dig their way out with a spoon. She knew they
didn't have a chance, but it kept them busy. Needless to say,
she was overjoyed when the young Gallowglasses let her out.
So was the count.

"I shall call up my men!" he cried.

"First thou must needs go back to thine own castle,"
Magnus reminded him. "Be wary and go by the northern
path."

"Wherefore?"

"For that we left the giant sleeping by the southern pasture,
and he may be wakening now."

"And we have met a poor old witch in the south who was
accursed by a foul sorcerer; we left them sleeping, too," Gregory added.

"And there is a peasant wench who doth work her wiles to
persuade all the young men to join with the Shire-Reeve,"
Cordelia put in.

"All this, in a few days' time!" The count shook his head.
His lady tactfully didn't mention that she had told him he
should pay a little more attention to the monsters in the underbrush.

"All lie to the south," Magnus explained. "Sin that thou art
afoot, we do think thou wouldst be wisest to go toward the
north."

The count didn't argue. He and his family faded into the
forest, moving fast.

Magnus turned to confer with his brothers, sister, and
elves. "The count and his family are freed, and the giant is
vanquished; I doubt me not he will prove small trouble, an we
can muzzle his master."

Puck frowned. "Thou speakest of true danger now. These
Cold-Iron warlocks have thy father's manner of magic; I ken
not how to counter it."

"Ye couldn't counter a dance step," Kelly scoffed. "Ye
don't seek to undo these Cold-Iron spells—ye bedevil the
sorcerers!"

Puck gave him an irked glance. "I've some small experi-
ence in that, too. I'd have no fear for my own sake—but 'tis
too great a risk for the children."

Geoffrey lifted his head, incensed, but Gregory said,
"They may hold our Mama and Papa."

The children stared at one another, then at Puck. "'Tis
true," Magnus said slowly. "Where else would Papa's enemies

hold those they've captured, but in their own castle?"

"They do not use castles," Puck reminded. "They may issue their orders from a manor house, or a church—or even a peasant hut, for all that."

"For all that, and all that," Kelly grumbled.

Puck frowned at him. "Of what nation didst thou say thou wert?"

"Any but yers," Kelly retorted.

"I prithee, hold," Magnus cried. "If Mama and Papa are prisoners within the keep of these star-warlocks, we must hale them out."

The room was quiet for a moment; Puck and Kelly exchanged looks of misgiving.

"We will help thee to find them," Puck said at last, "if thou wilt promise me solemnly to stay in the forest nearby, and never go into the fighting."

The children exchanged glowers, and Geoffrey looked fit to burst. Finally, though, Magnus said reluctantly, "We do promise, Puck."

"Most solemnly?"

"Oh, aye, most solemnly," Geoffrey said in disgust.

"Well enough, then." Puck nodded, satisfied, and turned away to the dungeon stair. The children followed.

"Though how," wondered Magnus, "could any prison hold our mother and father?"

"In drugged slumber," Geoffrey answered. "Come, brother—let us search!"

13

"Yet wherefore have we gone south again?" Cordelia spoke to Puck, but her eyes were on the brace of partridge that Magnus turned slowly on the spit over the campfire.

"Aye," Gregory said, and swallowed before he went on. "We have journeyed northward thus far, Puck. Dost thou mean to take us home now?"

The elf shook his head. "I have an itch in my bones that tells me thou art right to seek thy parents. Whether thou wilt find them or no, thou art right to seek them."

"Yet rebellions commonly start far from Runnymede," Magnus pointed out as he turned the spit. "Wherefore do we turn our steps once again to the Capitol?"

"'Tis not a rebellion we face," Puck answered. "'Tis a host of rebellions, and their leaders do wish to topple the throne at first chance. They must, therefore, stay near the Royal Mere."

Geoffrey nodded. "'Tis sound."

"I rejoice that I meet thine approval," Puck said, with withering sarcasm. Geoffrey watched the partridge turn, blithely unwithered. He swallowed, though.

"Yet surely we're amiss to go farther into the forest," Magnus said, frowning. "Will they not hold their center in the Capitol itself?"

"Nay," Geoffrey answered, "for no other reason than that we'd seek them there. Puck hath the right of it; they'll as likely be in the forest near Runnymede, as any place else."

"With modern communications, the 'center' can be any-place—or many places," Fess explained. "Still, if there is a spies' nest, it would most logically be near Runnymede, as Puck has suggested."

"Fess agrees with thee," Gregory informed the elf.

"I have heard," Puck grunted. "'Tis not witch-folk alone who hear thoughts."

"Art thou not pleased?"

"I cry his mercy," the elf said dryly.

"Have you any method in mind for locating this hypothetical headquarters?" Fess asked.

"Set a spy to catch a spy," Puck retorted, "and I've more of them than any mortal band."

Leaves rustled, and two fairies flitted up, close enough to be seen in the firelight.

"Summer and Fall!" Cordelia cried in delight.

The two fairies dropped dainty curtsies. "We have come to repay thy good aid."

"Who did summon thee?" Kelly snorted.

"Why, the Puck," Summer answered. "'Tis our wood, do ye not see; we know who moves in it better than any."

"What *doth* move?" Puck asked softly.

Fall turned to him. "'Tis warlocks thou dost seek, is it not?"

"Warlocks, aye—or sorcerers, more likely."

"We know of them," said Summer. "They have a great house quite deep in the forest, at the foot of the mountains."

Puck looked up at Geoffrey. "'Tis but three hours' ride from Runnymede."

"And I doubt me they would ride," the boy returned.

"'Tis two days' walk, though, for a mortal," Fall cautioned. "Thou art witch-bairns; can ye travel no faster?"

Magnus started to answer, then glanced up at Fess.

"Do not delay for my sake," the robot assured them. "I shall follow your thoughts, and will arrive not long after yourselves. The unicorn, I doubt not, will find Cordelia no matter where she goes. I ask only that you not risk any great hazards till I am with you."

"We will fly with winged heels," Magnus assured the fairies.

"Or broomsticks," Summer said, with a smirk.

It was a big half-timbered house with white stucco that had mellowed to ivory with age—or what looked like age; for "Who would ha' builded a house so deep in the woods?" Magnus asked.

A hut would have been understandable, maybe even a cottage—but this was a two-story Tudor house with wings enclosing a courtyard.

"Nay, none would have built here," Geoffrey whispered, with full certainty. "'Tis Papa's enemies have made this place, and that not much longer ago than Magnus was born."

"If 'tis so big, it must be ripe for haunting," Cordelia whispered.

Her brothers looked at her in surprise. Then they began to grin.

The guard's eyes flicked from screen to screen, from one infrared panorama of the clearing outside the headquarters house to another, over to a graph-screen that showed objects as dots of light on crossed lines, then to a screen that showed sounds as waveforms, then back to the picture screens again. He was bored, but knew the routine was necessary—HQ was safe only because it was guarded.

A long, quavering sound began, so low that the guard doubted he'd heard it at first, rising gradually in pitch and loudness to a bass, moaning vibration that shook the whole building. The guard darted a look about him, then whirled to the score of screens that showed views of the inside of the house. Finally, he stabbed at a button and called, "Captain! I'm hearing something!"

"So am I," a voice answered out of thin air. A moment later, the captain came running up, shouting to make himself heard over the noise. "What is it?"

But as soon as he started talking, the sound stopped.

The two men looked about them, waiting. Finally, the captain said, "What in hell was that?"

"Right," the guard answered. Then he saw the captain's face and said, "Sorry. Just trying to lighten the mood."

"I don't need light moods, I need answers! What did your screens show?"

"Nothing," the guard said with finality. "Absolutely nothing."

The captain scowled at the screens. "How about the oscilloscope?"

"Nothing there either."

The captian whirled back to him. "But there had to be! That was a noise—it had to show as a waveform!"

The guard shook his head. "Sorry, Captain. Just the usual night-noise traces."

"Not the outdoor scope, you idiot! The indoor one!"

"Nothing there, either." The guard glared at him. "And if we could both hear it, *one* of the mikes should have picked it up."

They were both silent for a moment, the guard watching the captain, the captain gazing about him, frowning. "What," he said, "makes a noise that people can hear, but microphones can't?"

"They are worried," Gregory reported, "and afeard, though they hide it."

"No mortal can fail to fear the unknown," Puck said, grinning. "'Tis bred into thee from thine earliest ancestors, who did first light campfires 'gainst the night."

They crouched in a dry stream-bed near the house; the stream had been diverted indoors to fill out the water supply. Bracken had grown up in it, enough to cushion the children as they lay against the side on their stomachs.

"Is that why we waited for night?" Geoffrey asked.

"It is," Puck answered. "Thy kind fears the dark, though some of ye hide it well."

"What shall we give them next?" Cordelia asked.

Puck turned to her with a smirk. "What wouldst *thou* fear?"

The captain sat in the watch officer's office, gazing out the window. What could that noise have been? Of course, old houses are always settling—but this house wasn't really old, it just looked that way!

Well, on the other hand, new houses settle, too—he knew what kind of shoddy workmanship they tried to pass off these days. But settling wouldn't make a noise that lasted so *long!*

Outside, something flitted by; he barely saw it out of the corner of his eye. He frowned, peering more closely. There it was again, just a flicker—but enough to need checking! He pivoted in his chair and pressed a touchpoint on his desk. "Check the visual scan, northeast quadrant, quickly!"

"Checking," the guard's voice responded.

The captain waited, glaring out the window. There it was once more—still a flicker, but lasting a little longer this time. He could almost make out a form . . .

"Nothing," the guard stated.

The captain cursed and whirled back to the window.

The shape danced between two tree trunks a hundred-feet

from the house, at the edge of the security perimeter. It was pale, glowing, and vaguely human in form. In spite of himself the captain felt the hairs trying to stand up on the back of his neck. He was a materialist—he knew nothing could exist if it couldn't be weighed or measured. If he saw it but the cameras didn't, it couldn't really be there; it had to be an hallucination. And that meant . . .

Unless somebody else could see it, too. He stabbed at another touchpoint and barked, "Sergeant! Come in here!"

Two minutes later, a third man stumbled in through a side door, hair tousled, blinking sleep out of his eyes. "What . . . what's moving, Captain?"

"Ghosts," the captain gritted. He pointed out the window. "Tell me what you see."

The sergeant stepped over to the pane, puzzled. Then he stared. "They're not real!"

"Well!" the captain heaved a sigh. "At least you see them, too!"

"What?" the sergeant turned to him. "Did you think you were dreaming, sir?"

"No, just hallucinating. Now, you've seen them—go look on the monitors, will you?"

Frowning, the sergeant turned and went out into the hall. A few minutes later, his voice sounded right next to the captain's ear. "Right you are, sir. There's nothing on the monitors."

"That's what I thought." The captain stared out at the darkness, numb. There were three of them now, flitting from one tree trunk to another. Or else it was just one, moving very quickly. . . . "Check all the sensors."

A few minutes later the sergeant reported, "Nothing on infrared, sir," and the guard's voice said, "No radiation . . . no new concentrations of mass . . . no RF reflection . . ."

"They're not real." The captain glared out at the glowing, dancing forms in indignation—but under that emotion was a growing dread. The things were there, no doubt about it—it wasn't only him; the sergeant had seen them, too. But how could they be there and not leave any trace on the sensors?

Gregory looked up at Magnus and Geoffrey. "Canst thou sustain this illusion, brothers?"

The two bigger boys knelt side by side, sweat starting on their foreheads, deep in concentration. "Long enough," Magnus answered.

" 'Tis hard, casting this picture into their minds," Geoffrey muttered. "The groaning was easier."

"Then make them hear it again," Magnus grunted. He waited a moment, then asked, "How doth it work on them?"

"They do begin to fear," Gregory reported. " 'Tis not great, and buried deeply—but it hath begun."

"So much the worse for them," Cordelia declared. She turned to Fall. "Hast thou the spiders?"

"Aye, a thousand for each door. They have begun spinning a giant web before each portal."

" 'Tis well." Cordelia turned back to Magnus. "Are the elves in place?"

Her brother looked the question at Kelly. "Aye," the leprecohen grinned, "and greatly delighted they are."

"Then let them laugh," Cordelia declared.

A hideous cackling rang through the house from every nook and cranny.

"Trace!" the guard shouted. "*That* sound shows a waveform, Captain!"

"At last! Something real!" The captain hit a touchpoint on the wall beside the desk and a siren whooped throughout the house. Agents tumbled from their cots, bleary-eyed and fuzzy-brained, hearing the captain's voice booming near their ears, "Search every place large enough to hold a loudspeaker!"

They searched. Behind the terminals, behind the stacks of boxes of organic powder, throughout the storerooms they searched—but they found nothing more than spiderwebs, curiously without spiders. As the siren faded, they heard what they were looking for—or its evidence; shrill, manic laughter, at exactly the right pitch to set their teeth on edge and make chills crawl up their backbones. Inside the closets they searched, around the hearth and inside the chimney—but they didn't peer into the crannies between the stones. Down in the time-lab, up on the landing pad, under each cot they searched —but they didn't pull out the wainscoting. Inside every desk drawer, behind every toiletry, inside the cabinets they searched—but they didn't look inside the pipes, or behind the mirrors in the bathroom.

It was just as well they didn't. They wouldn't have believed what they found, anyway. Even if they had, it wouldn't have made them feel any better.

In every nook more than two inches wide with a foot of space behind it, an elf crouched. Inside the walls, in back of the baseboards, and behind the food synthesizer hid pixies, shooing away mice—and from every minute crack and each open grille echoed their laughter, growing more and more hilarious with every passing moment.

"It's mass hallucination!" the captain bellowed. "It couldn't be anything else!"

"How about sabotage?" called a civilian official.

"From where?"

"Bid them coax the mice to where they can see these fellows," Magnus instructed Kelly.

The elf protested. "Why not the Wee Folk?"

"We dare not let the Big People find them! 'Tis too dangerous," Cordelia explained.

Geoffrey nodded. "And, too, if they did find something that could explain the noises, they might become able to bear their fear."

"Assuredly, we do not wish that," Kelly grinned, and he turned to instruct an elfin courier.

Inside the house, elves coaxed mice into mouseholes that the men didn't know existed. Quivering, the mice stared out at the huge beings who were hurrying from place to place, peering and seeking, growing more and more frantic with each passing minute.

Cordelia closed her eyes, opening her mind to the kitchen mouse. "Aye, I can see them. That cup, there . . ."

The cup shot off the counter and flew through the air, narrowly missing a plainclothes agent. The agent's head snapped around watching it; he winced as it smashed itself to smithereens against the wall. He looked about with a sudden stab of foreboding . . .

. . . and saw the saucer spinning right toward his nose.

In the watch office, the captain heard a crash. He spun about to find the terminal cover in a dozen pieces and molecular-circuit gems strewn about in a circle.

At the guard station, the terminal beeped. The guard turned toward it, wide-eyed, and saw a mass of print scrolling frantically upward on its screen.

The print stopped abruptly.

Slowly, the guard stepped toward it, scanning the letters. "Regulations concerning surprise inspections..." He darted frantic glances at the screens, but they were all blissfully peaceful. He stabbed at a touchpoint and called, "Captain... I think somebody's trying to tell us something..."

But a civilian agent down the hall suddenly ducked as a vision pickup wrenched itself out of the ceiling and went whistling past his ear to smash itself to bits on the wall. The agent screamed, "Poltergeist!"

With sweat dripping off his brow, Magnus asked, "Have the gnomes tunneled under the foundations?"

"Aye," Kelly reported. "A score stand under each corner —and the Puck is with them."

Magnus nodded. "Tell them the contest hath begun."

"It's enemy action!" the captain said to an agent, white-faced and trembling. "That High Warlock has to have figured out where we are, and he's sending an army of espers against us!"

"The High Warlock is missing," the agent snapped. "Remember?"

The whole room shivered.

The agent looked up, white around his eyes. "What the hell was *that?*"

At the guard station, the desk suddenly heaved upward as the floor bucked beneath. The guard toppled over, howling, "Earthquake!"

"If it's an enemy action," the agent said to the captain, "it's a damn good one!"

The floor again heaved upward a foot, then dropped back down. The agent and captain tumbled shouting to the floor.

Out in the hallway, a civilian agent grabbed at a door frame for support, but the jamb jumped under his hand.

"Enemy action, supernatural, or just unexplained phenomena—it's lethal!" The agent jumped to his feet and stabbed a touchpoint on the desk. "Everybody evacuate!"

"They might come out at any number of places," Geoffrey said angrily.

Gregory shook his head. "They wished the house to be proof against burglars— so they filled the windows with slabs of glass so thick they cannot be broken, and cannot be opened."

"Then there are but the two doors," Magnus said, grinning.

"They come!" Cordelia cried.

The door slammed open and the men came running out at full speed—and slammed into a huge net that had been spun by a thousand spiders. It stretched, but it held. The men flailed about, howling, but the web closed behind them, netting a bagful of a dozen agents at each doorway.

Then up to the front doorway strode the High Warlock.

Higher than usual—he was nine feet tall if he was an inch, crowned with flames where he should have had hair, and his eyes were glowing coals.

The chief agent stared up at him in horror. "But you were kidnapped!"

"Didst thou truly think any trap could hold me?" the High Warlock boomed.

The agent plucked up his nerve. "One of *our* traps might have—but what can you expect of an anarchist? Of course their trap didn't hold!"

In the gully, Cordelia read the man's mind, and whispered to Magnus, "He doth speak truth—he knoweth not how Mama and Papa were captured."

The High Warlock boomed, "Yet thou didst collaborate with them! Even now, thine agent doth seek to seize power!"

"None of our men are trying a damn thing," the captain yelled, and the agent said, "Go talk to SPITE about it."

"They lie," Cordelia said. "Their thoughts leapt to the Shire-Reeve; he hath been their man for many years, and they have told him exactly what they wished him to do when the chance came."

"As it hath." Geoffrey frowned. "But that chance was not of their making?"

"Nay," Cordelia answered.

Magnus was silent, face screwed up in concentration, staring over the rim of the gully at the house and the nearest bagful of agents, into whose minds he was casting the simulacrum of his father.

"Who doth support thy Shire-Reeve in the other counties?" the High Warlock boomed.

"How the hell did you know about . . ." the captain burst

out; but the agent silenced him with a gesture. "We aren't supporting any locals."

"Yet a dozen came to his mind," Cordelia reported, "faces, and some names, one for each dukedom and earldom. And the Shire-Reeve is above all of them."

"Thou dost lie poorly," the High Warlock sneered, "yet thou wilt be in no further danger this night. Farewell." He turned, and stalked away into the darkness.

The VETO agents watched him go, stupefied.

After awhile, the captain looked up at the house. "Everything seems quiet."

The agent shook his head. "That doesn't matter. The High Warlock knows about this HQ. We'll have to abandon it and build another one."

"Sir!" the sergeant hollered. "The net's loose!"

"Loose?" "Let me see!" "Let me out!"

"Rank!" the agent bawled. "Squirm aside! Out in order of seniority."

He scrambled out of the bag with the captain right behind him. The agent stood, dusting himself off, but the captain looked up at the house, frowning.

"Don't get ideas," the agent growled. "We can't stay here."

"Y'know," the captain said, "that guy was awfully big, even for the High Warlock."

"What are you saying?" the agent asked.

"And his voice was kind of low-pitched for a human being, you know?"

"Yes, sir, now that you mention it." The sergeant stood up beside him.

"And come to think of it," said one of the junior agents, "the High Warlock speaks modern English, not Elizabethan."

A mile away, the children sat down with Puck, Kelly, and Fess to try to make sense out of the new information.

"'Tis not our VETO enemies who did kidnap them," Magnus stated.

Cordelia nodded. "That much is clear. Therefore we must seek elsewhere for them."

"But what will happen an we do not find them before Groghat and the barons have brought down Their Majesties?" Geoffrey asked, frowning. "Or the Shire-Reeve hath taken the throne?"

The children were silent for a moment.

Then Gregory said, "We must prevent that."

"Nay!" Puck cried. "There be some matters that be too dangerous even for witch-children!"

"But we cannot let them ruin our land, Puck," Cordelia pleaded.

"You cannot stop them, either," Fess murmured. "Puck is right in this, children. You can be of great assistance to adults —but you cannot fight such powerful, grown enemies by yourselves. They will defeat you, and you may be slain."

"Heed him," Kelly advised.

They were silent for a moment. Cordelia rose and went to her unicorn, hugging it for comfort.

Then Geoffrey rose too, dusting off his hands. "Well, then! If we cannot find them of ourselves, we must find Mama and Papa, that they may do it!"

"Aye," Magnus looked up, his eyes kindling. "And we may begin by seeking out Papa's enemies from SPITE."

"There is none," said Summer, "not in all this forest, nay, nor any of the farmlands about."

"Truly," Fall agreed, "not in all this earldom of Tudor— neither a great house, nor a warren of caves."

"Sure, and 'tis as they say," Kelly agreed. "In all the King's lands, 'tis the same—in all of Runnymede, no sign of any sort of a 'headquarters,' as ye call it. I've sent for word from the fairies there, and I know."

"Nor is there one in any county in Gramarye," Puck added. "I, too, have called for word from all fairies, aye, and elves, too, and nixies, and pixies, and pookas and sprites; from bu- chawns and kobolds, from gnomes and from goblins . . ."

"We do believe thee," Magnus said hastily, to cut off Puck's listing of spirits. "Yet surely these 'anarchists' do coor- dinate actions. Must they, therefore, not have a center?"

"A geographical center is not necessary," Fess reminded them, "any more than it is for the witches and warlocks. Just as any of you can communicate with a leader, no matter where he is, so can the anarchists, with their transceivers and view- screens."

"Yet the folk of VETO could have done so, too!"

"True," Fess admitted, "but a central administrative base is more in keeping with their pattern of thought. SPITE's anar- chists have the goal of destroying central coordination, so they are much more likely to manage without its physical symbol."

"Yet they must have a leader," Geoffrey insisted, "a commander! No action can be taken in concert without one!"

"It is theoretically possible," Fess demurred, "though it has never occurred."

"What manner of men are these," Cordelia said in disgust, "who embrace the very thing they abhor, in order to destroy it?"

Fess tactfully forebore to mention that she was not the first to have had that particular insight.

"An they have a commander," Geoffrey said stoutly, "we have someone to question. How can we find him, Fess?"

"That will be extremely difficult," Fess admitted. "In fact, if they adhere to their usual pattern, they will have several commanders, each of whom has all the data that the others have, and any one of whom is capable of coordinating the entire operation."

"They are nonetheless commanders," Geoffrey said staunchly.

"'Tis their pattern in all things," Fall said. "Fairies from other counties have told us of plowboys and shepherds who go to join the forces of bandits; and of giants and ogres, who have begun to wreak terror, but do not leash outlaws; of sorcerers who do seek to seize power, and counts who do battle one another, but never the bandits. Each county seems to have one of each of these, and a monster, too. If 'tis not a dragon, then 'tis a manticore or a cockatrice."

Geoffrey reddened with anger. "Commander or not, they have been well enough guided to unleash this chaos on our land in a day!"

"'Tis horrible," Cordelia stated, pale and trembling. "Oh! The poor peasant folk, who must suffer the woes these evil ones do inflict!"

Gregory clung to her waist, round-eyed with horror.

"And we can do nothing," Magnus breathed, "for this is beyond what four small children can do."

"Aye," Puck agreed. "That is work for thy mother and father, when they do return."

"But will they return?" Cordelia said in a very small voice.

"Oh, they shall!" Gregory looked up at her with total certainty. "They shall find their way home again. None can keep them from us."

Somehow, no one even thought of doubting him.

Then Magnus's face hardened, and he turned to his brothers and sister. "Yet in our own country, we need not allow so much misery! In Runnymede and in this southern tip of Tudor, we can hold sway! Not of our own doing, 'tis true —but by bringing the Wee Folk, and the other goodly creatures . . ." he nodded toward Cordelia's unicorn ". . . to act against these . . . these . . ."

"Nasty men!" Gregory cried, his little face screwed up in indignation.

Magnus froze, trying to look severe. Then Cordelia giggled, and Magnus grinned. "Aye, lad, these nasties! Yet we *have* brought Puck and Kelly and their folk to league 'gainst these 'nasties,' and we can do it again and again, till they are all rendered harmless! Runnymede at least can be kept safe, and the King shall have a sanctuary of peace into which to retire!"

"Aye!" Gregory shouted. "We shall seek out the nasties, and lock them in gaols!"

"And while we are about it," Geoffrey said grimly, "we can ask certain questions of them."

"Out upon them!" Cordelia cried. "With which shall we begin?"

They all fell silent, staring at each other in consternation.

"Who," Gregory asked, "is the greatest of nasties?"

14

"'Tis well asked," Magnus admitted. "Who can be chief among them? Who can be leader of they who seek to eschew leadership?"

They were walking down a forest path in the general direction of the main road, trying to puzzle it out.

"They do not truly lack a leader," Geoffrey asserted, "though they claim to. I heard Papa speak of this, of a time; there's one whose word they heed."

Magnus frowned at him. "I have not heard of this. What name had he?"

"I do not know," Geoffrey confessed, "nor did Papa. Yet he seemed certain that there was such an one."

"Mayhap thou hast heard of this, Robin?" Cordelia asked.

"As much as Geoffrey hath," Puck said, "yet no more. Thy father seeks some philosopher, some writer of ill-formed ideas, whose thoughts these foes of governance do adhere to. He doth give no orders, seest thou, but doth suggest some actions."

"Yet Papa doth not *know?*" Gregory inferred. "He doth but guess?"

"Nay; 'tis something more than that," Puck said. "He's certain that this philosopher exists, but only doth *think* the others follow his words."

Geoffrey shook his head, frowning. "I misdoubt me of it. No band of men can take any action an they have no commander. Their deeds would lack coherence; each would do what the others have done. There would be only repetition of the same work, in many places."

Magnus nodded slowly. "Now that I bethink me of it, their actions may bespeak just that."

"Hold!" Puck stiffened. "Here comes one hot-foot!"

Summer and Fall popped up, wide-eyed. "An elf hath told us, and we have gone to see! His words are true!"

"What words are those?" Cordelia asked.

"'Tis a band of peasants," Fall explained. "They do march along the King's High Way, bearing scythes and brandishing sickles—and a boy doth march before them!"

Cordelia was puzzled. "Before them? Doth not his mother keep him close?"

"Nay, nay!" Summer protested. "The lad doth lead!"

The children stared.

Then Geoffrey scowled. "Can this be true? That a whole band of grown folk would allow a mere boy to lead them?"

"Quite true," Fall assured him, "for the lad who leads them claims to be thyself."

The children stared, thunderstruck.

Then Magnus found his voice. "How can this be? Could a peasant lad have such audacity?"

"Nay!" Geoffrey cried, "for who would credit him? What proof could he offer?"

"The best, for one whose claim is false," Summer answered. "He is the spit and image of thyself."

Geoffrey stood rigid, the color draining from his face. Cordelia saw, and took a step backward before she realized what she was doing.

Then the boy erupted. "The louse and recreant! The vile bit of vermin! How durst he? How could this overweening rogue have the gall and bile to present himself as *me*? Nay, take me to him straightaway, that I may carve his gizzard for his tombstone!"

But the two fairies stepped backward, appalled by his wrath.

"Wilt thou not, then?" Geoffrey shouted. "Nay, I must . . ."

"Throttle thy wrath!" Magnus snapped, and Geoffrey whirled to face him, crouching for a leap; but his brother said, more calmly, "What warrior will confront another in hot blood?" and Geoffrey froze. He stared at Magnus for a moment, then answered, quite reasonably, "Why, he who shall lose."

Magnus nodded. "'Tis even as our father hath said, and we've seen the truth of it in himself. Nay, then, brother, be mindful—a rogue who would claim to be *thee* must needs be competent at battle. Thou must needs have thy wits about thee when thou dost face him."

"Even so," Gregory breathed.

Geoffrey stood, gazing at him for a minute; then he nodded, and slowly straightened up, relaxing—but every muscle held a tension that still bespoke firmly-bridled anger. "I thank thee brother. I am myself again." He turned to Summer and Fall. "My apologies, sweet sprites, for such unseemly wrath."

"'Tis warranted." But Fall still stared at him, her eyes huge.

"Wilt thou take me to him now?" Geoffrey asked.

The fairies nodded, and turned away wordlessly, running lightly down the path.

Geoffrey's mouth tightened in chagrin, and he launched himself into the air to follow them.

His brothers wafted after him. Cordelia's unicorn kept pace.

"I have ne'er seen him so angered," Cordelia murmured to Magnus.

"I do not wonder at it," he answered. "But we must watch him closely, sister, or he'll rend that whole peasant band apart."

Magnus halted them with a raised hand. "'Ware, my sibs! I mislike this!"

Beside him, Geoffrey nodded. "'Tis not natural."

A hundred yards away, the village stood, a handful of houses circling a common—but with not one single person in sight.

"Where have the goodfolk gone?" Cordelia wondered.

"To follow my fetch," Geoffrey grated, "or to attend him."

"'Tis the latter." Magnus pointed. "Seest thou not the flash of color, here and there, between the cottages?"

His brothers and sister peered at the village.

"I do," Fess said, "and I have magnified the image. There are people there, many of them—but their backs are toward us, and only one voice speaks."

"Cordelia," Magnus said, with total certainty, "bid thy unicorn bide in the forest till we come. And thou, Fess, must also wait in hiding."

Cordelia's face clouded up, but Fess spoke first. "I am loathe to leave you, as you know, Magnus. Why do you wish me to wait?"

"For that the safest way to come upon them is to slip into the crowd, and worm our ways to the fore. Thus may we discover whether this double of Geoffrey's is any true threat or not, and if he is, may we thus take him unawares. Therefore I pray thee, hide and wait."

"Well enough, then, I shall," Fess said slowly. "But I will hide nearby, and listen at maximum amplification. If you have need of me, you have but to call."

"Be assured that we shall," Geoffrey said, his face taut.

Cordelia slipped off the unicorn's back and turned to stroke the velvet nose. "I must bid thee await me, beauteous one." Tears glistened in her eyes. "Oh, but thou wilt not flee from me, wilt thou? Thou wilt attend?"

The unicorn nodded; Magnus could have sworn the beast had understood his sister's words. He knew better, of course —Cordelia was a projective telepath, as they all were; it was her thoughts the unicorn understood, though the sounds may have helped. She tossed her head and turned away, trotting off toward the shelter of the trees.

"Come, then," Magnus said. "Cordelia, take thou the eastern point with Gregory. Geoffrey will take the center, and I the western edge. We shall meet in the front and center."

The others nodded, tight-lipped, and they spread out as they approached the village. Fess accompanied them, but stopped behind one of the cottages, waiting, head high, ears pricked, as the children silently infiltrated the crowd.

The "crowd" consisted of perhaps a hundred people, only a few dozen of whom, to judge by their carrying scythes and pitchforks, had come in off the road with the juvenile rabble-rouser. But he was doing his level best to convert the other threescore to his cause; as the children stepped in between grown-ups at the back of the mob, they heard him telling atrocity stories.

"Thus they have done to a village not ten miles hence!" the boy cried. "Wilt thou suffer them to so serve *thy* wives and bairns?"

The crowd in front of him rumbled angrily. Scythes and pitchforks waved.

"Nay, thou wilt not!" The boy stood on a wagon, where they could all see him—but he failed to notice the four children who slipped in from the space between two cottages. "Thou wilt not suffer bandits to rend thy village—nor wilt thou suffer the lords to amuse themselves by warring in thy fields, and trampling thine hard-grown corn!"

The mob rumbled uncertainly; apparently they hadn't heard this line before. Bandits were one thing, but lords were entirely another.

"Thou wilt?" the boy cried, surprised. "Then I mistook

thee quite! I had thought thou wert men!"

An ugly mutter answered him, and one man at the front cried. "'Tis well enough for thee to say it, lad—thou hast not seen the lordlings fight! Thou hast not seen how their armor doth turn our pike blades, nor how their swords reap peasant soldiers!"

"I have not," the lad answered, "but the Shire-Reeve hath!"

The crowd fell silent, astonished.

It was quiet enough for Geoffrey to hear the words Magnus whispered in his ear: "We know now whence he cometh!"

Geoffrey nodded, and his eyes glittered.

"The Shire-Reeve hath fought in lordlings' armies!" the false Geoffrey cried. "When young, he fought for the Queen against the rebels! Again he fought, chasing out the Beastmen from our isle! And anon he fought, when Tudor called, against the depredating bands of other nobles—and he hath grown sick at heart, from seeing all their wanton waste!"

"Yet how can he, a man of common birth, stand against a belted knight?" a man in the crowd called.

"Because his rank is royal!" the boy called back. "He is the King's reeve, for all the shire! And if he doth now bid the nobles cease their brawling, can any say him nay?"

The rumble agreed, gaining heart.

"Come follow me, and I shall lead thee to him!" cried the lad. "Come join the Shire-Reeve, and fight 'gainst those who do oppress thee!"

"This swells too greatly," muttered a baritone by Magnus's knee. "We must spoke his wheels." A second later, a voice from the middle of the mob called, "How dost thou know where thou mayest find him?" The men in that location looked around, startled, but the boy answered,

"We know that he doth quarter in the town of Belmead. We've but to go, and attend his pleasure!"

"And will he welcome us?" called a voice from another part of the crowd, "or will he think we come against him?"

Again, men turned to look, but the imitation Geoffrey answered, "How could he think thus? Assuredly he'll welcome thee!"

"How couldst thou know?" cried another disembodied voice from a third quarter. "What lad art thou, to speak thus?"

The boy reddened. "I am the High Warlock's son, as I have told thee! Dost thou doubt my word?" And he turned to call out over the crowd, "Can any call me false?"

"Aye!" Geoffrey cried. "*I* call thee false!" And he sprang into the air, arrowing straight toward the wagon, landing straight and tall, turning to look out over the crowd proudly, then turning further, to glare at the imposter.

The boy stared, thunderstruck. So did the crowd, confronted by two Geoffreys—and indeed, the imposter was Geoffrey's exact double, matching him inch for inch and feature for feature. A frightened murmur began.

"How sayest thou now, O false one?" Geoffrey demanded. "Tell us thy *true* name!"

The boy's chin lifted. "I am Geoffrey Gallowglass, the High Warlock's son! And who art *thou*, who doth dare to walk in my semblance?"

"Thou liest, rogue!" Geoffrey shouted. "How durst thou claim my place?"

"Thy charges shall avail thee naught," the double answered, "for 'tis plain to any *I* am the true Gallowglass!"

A shriek of rage pierced the air, and Cordelia shot over the heads of the crowd on her broomstick, leaping down to the wagon and crying, "Thou liest, rogue! This is my brother, Geoffrey Gallowglass! And I am his sister, the High Warlock's daughter Cordelia!"

A double explosion cracked, and Magnus stood behind her with Gregory at his hip. "She speaks good sooth! And I am Magnus, the High Warlock's eldest!"

"And I his youngest!" Gregory piped. "We all now tell thee, goodfolk, that thou hast been deceived!"

"Even so!" Magnus shouted to the crowd, and clapped the real Geoffrey on the shoulder. "*This* is my brother, the true Geoffrey Gallowglass! He whom thou hast followed is a false and lying knave!"

Geoffrey cast them all a brief, warm look of gratitude, while the imposter stared, appalled. But he recovered quickly and cried aloud, "They all conspire against me! Why, these four are no more brothers and sister than I am a cockerel! Their claim is false, for *I* am the true Warlock's child!"

A fearful mutter swept through the crowd, as Cordelia howled in anger and leaped at the boy. Her brothers caught her and held her back, though, and Magnus said evenly, "Nay," then cried aloud for the crowd, "Nay, thou hast no need to claw him with thy nails! Thou art a witch; thou hast but to think him ill!"

Cordelia's eyes glittered, and the boy said quickly, "Oh,

aye, belike thou art truly witch-brats! Indeed, I saw thee fly —but that's no proof that thou art the High Warlock's brood!"

"What proof hast *thou?*" Geoffrey retorted.

"Why, this!" and the boy rose five feet into the air, smoothly and easily. A rumble of awe and fear rose from the crowd.

"What proof is that?" Geoffrey sneered, rising up to match him, but Gregory murmured to Magnus, "Ah, then! He is, at the least, truly a warlock!"

"'Tis the only aspect of him that is true," Magnus growled back.

"Show other proof," Geoffrey taunted, "that I may match and best thee!"

The boy reddened, and disappeared with a bang. Its echo sounded from across the common, and everyone whirled, to see him standing on the roof of a cottage. "Match this an thou canst!" he cried.

"What warlock cannot?" Geoffrey retorted. Air boomed in to fill the space where he'd been, then blasted atop the cottage next to the one on which the young warlock stood, as Geoffrey appeared next to its chimney.

"They look alike, and both work magic!" someone in the crowd cried. "How can we tell which one is true?"

"Why," Cordelia answered proudly, "by their moving lifeless objects! For the High Warlock's lads, alone of all the warlocks in Gramarye, can move things other than themselves!"

The fake paled, but he bounced back instantly, sneering at Geoffrey, "Dost need a lass to speak for thee?"

"Why," Geoffrey retorted, "art thou envious because thou hast no sister?"

"Thou liest, rogue!" the imposter shouted. "My sister bides at home!"

"For such a fib, thou shouldst be caned," Geoffrey snapped, and a quarterstaff wrenched itself out of the hands of a peasant who shrank back with an oath. The stick shot spinning straight toward the false Geoffrey. The boy saw it coming and leaped into the air; the stick passed under him, and he turned to Geoffrey with a taunting laugh.

"Wherefore didst thou move thyself, rather than the staff?" Geoffrey demanded.

The boy frowned. "It did not please me to do so!"

"Then thy pleasures must change," Geoffrey said, with a sour smile. "'Ware, from thy back!"

The imposter spun about, just in time to see the whirling staff make a great half circle and come spinning back at him. He howled, throwing himself flat on the rooftop, and the staff passed over him. As he scrambled to his hands and knees, it paused and lashed one quick spank across his bottom. He went sprawling with a cry of rage, but Geoffrey's yell of accusation was louder. *"Now* wherefore didst thou not seize the stick with thy mind?"

The imposter stood up slowly, glaring in fury, but made no answer.

"Thou didst not because thou *canst* not!" Geoffrey cried. *"I* am the true Geoffrey Gallowglass!"

"Thou art the true liar!" the boy shouted back. "Thou didst move that staff no more than I did! 'Twas thy tame witch who did move it for thee!"

Cordelia howled in indignation, but Gregory said reasonably, "Whether my brother be the true Geoffrey or not, *thou* must needs be false—for all Gramarye doth know that the High Warlock's sons can move things with their minds. And thou canst not!"

The crowd rumbled in excitement, but the boy shouted, "'Tis a lie! *No* warlock can move things by thought! If thou sayest the High Warlock's sons can, then do it thyself!"

"Why, that I shall," the six-year-old lisped, and Cordelia floated gently up into the air. She squawked in fury and whirled, trying to reach her little brother, but Magnus cried, "Aye! All know a witch cannot make herself fly! 'Tis why she doth sit on a broomstick and make it to move! *Now* wilt thou say my sister doth this trick for her brother?"

The imposter's face darkened in fury. "Even as thou dost say—'tis a girl's trick! What lad would practice it, save he who is womanish at heart?"

"Thou insolent rogue!" Geoffrey shouted in fury. "Match *this* 'girl's game,' an thou canst!"

An unseen hand seemed to snatch up the imposter and send him tumbling through the air toward Cordelia. He howled in anger and terror, but Cordelia cried, "I wish him not! Have thy rogue back!" And the spinning imposter suddenly reversed, flying back toward Geoffrey.

"Nay, keep him!" he retorted, and the boy-ball halted a

foot from Geoffrey's head, then shot back toward Cordelia. The imposter wailed and, at the top of his arc, disappeared with a bang.

"Out upon him!" Magnus called, but Geoffrey disappeared with a gunshot-crack before he finished the phrase.

The crowd burst into a fury of excited, fearful noise.

Gregory's eyes lost focus. "He hath found the imposter!"

"How could he fail to?" Cordelia said, with an impish smile. "Is't for naught thou hast spent so many hours at play with flit-tag?"

"They will cry to burn witches next, an we do not appease them," Magnus said in an undertone.

Cordelia nodded. "Do so, and quickly!"·

Magnus stared. "*I?* How shall *I* quiet this mob?"

Cordelia shrugged. "Thou art the eldest."

Magnus favored her with a murderous glare, then looked about in a frantic search for aid.

Aid was sitting in the corner of the wagon, leg propped over folded knee. "Speak to them," he advised, "and tell them the true end of the Shire-Reeve's actions. They will credit thee, for thou art the High Warlock's son."

Magnus stared at the elf, and swallowed. "Yet what shall I say to them?"

"It shall come to thee," Puck assured him, "and should it not, I shall give thee words."

Magnus gave him a long, steady look, then nodded. "I thank thee, Robin." He took a deep breath, squared his shoulders, and turned to the crowd, holding his hands up and crying, "Goodfolk, hearken! I beg thee, attend me! Give me a hearing, I pray!"

Here and there, a villager noticed and pointed, telling his neighbor, who turned, then elbowed the one next to him. One by one they quieted, until finally Magnus could make himself heard.

"'Twas an evil young warlock who did lead thee," Magnus cried, "and the mark of his evilness was this: that he called for combat! It may seem he did not—but be not deceived! If the Shire-Reeve fights the lords, 'twill be not one battle, but many! 'Twill be war—and the end of it will be, that the Shire-Reeve will battle the King!"

The crowd erupted into a fury of incredulous noise again, each man demanding of his neighbor if the charge could be true. This time Magnus just waited it out, fists on his hips, knowing they were thinking about the rightness of the Shire-Reeve now, not of the witch-folk.

Gregory tugged at Magnus's tunic. "Is't true, Magnus? Doth the Shire-Reeve truly mean to attack King Tuan?"

"I know not," Magnus confessed, "yet it doth seem likely, doth it not?"

Gregory nodded. "I see no other end to it. But doth the Shire-Reeve?"

That was enough for Magnus. If his baby brother said it was bound to happen, it was inevitable. He held up his hands, signaling for quiet again. When the crowd's babble had begun to slacken, he called out, "Good people, hear me!" and they quieted.

"He who we called brother," Magnus called out, "was the real Geoffrey Gallowglass, the true High Warlock's son! We are his brothers and sister; we are the High Warlock's brood! I tell thee, our mother and father would never approve of this Shire-Reeve's doings! Yet there is much unrest in this Isle of Gramarye at this time, and they cannot be everywhere at once to quiet it!" A neat turn around the facts, there. "Thus are we come to bear word to thee! Wait and watch, and guard thine own villages! Endure in patience and in loyalty to the King and Queen! Join not in the unrest, lest thou dost make it more furious still!"

He began to catch uneasy glances and, at the fringes of the crowd, people began to edge away.

It was the right idea, but he had to make sure he didn't make it sound like blame. "If thou art one of those who hast been cozened away from thine own village, I beg thee: Hasten! None can tell what mischief may be wreaked on thine house or crops whilst thou dost tarry. Go back, and swiftly! Guard thine own!"

Now even people in the center of the crowd began to glance around them, and the ones at the edges turned about and strode away, not caring who saw them. After all, the High Warlock's eldest had just told them they should do it, hadn't he?

Cordelia breathed a sigh of relief. "Well done, brother! Only now do I bethink me there could have been evil here!"

"Let it depart, also," Magnus said, frowning as he watched the crowd break up. "Gregory, seek! How fares our brother?"

Thunder split the peaceful air of the forest clearing, and Geoffrey looked about him, noting in an instant the debris of burned-out campfires, bones, rags, and vegetable garbage, registering the conclusion that he was in the peasant band's last campsite. It made sense—it was the nearest isolated location the imposter would have remembered, and been able to visualize well enough to teleport to.

Because he was there, of course, in the center of the clearing, with his back to Geoffrey. He whirled about, startled by the thunder-crack, and stared, appalled, at his double. "How didst thou know where to seek me!"

"Why," Geoffrey gloated, "what warlock of any real power would not?"

The boy went dead-white—but he was the kind who attacked when he was terrified. He caught up the nearest dead branch and leaped at Geoffrey.

Geoffrey sidestepped with a mocking laugh, jumped away, and caught up a tree branch of his own. The boy was on him in a second, but Geoffrey met his blow with a block and a counter. The imposter just barely caught it with the tip of his staff and swung a murderous double-handed blow at Geoffrey.

It was a mistake, for it left his whole side unguarded. Geoffrey simply leaped back, let the stick whip past him, then leaped in again, snapping his staff out in a quick, hard blow.

It caught the imposter on the side of the head, sending him spinning and down. Geoffrey stood, waiting for him to get up again, but he didn't.

Foreboding struck the young warrior. For all his belligerence, he himself had never killed, and had only once knocked someone out. Warily, he stepped around and knelt by his opponent's head, reaching down to touch the throat, alert for the boy to jump up and attack—but the imposter stayed still, eyes closed. Geoffrey felt the strong, steady beat of the boy's pulse through the artery, and sat back with a sigh of relief, which turned into a frown. *Now* what was he supposed to do?

"He hath fought the imposter, and knocked him senseless," Gregory reported. "He asks our aid."

"And certes, he shall have it," Magnus answered, "Sister, do thou, an it please thee, fly aloft o'er the forest, and spy out his place." He closed his eyes, concentrating on Geoffrey's thoughts.

"I have it." Cordelia had been mind-listening, too. "'Tis a half-day's walk to the north, not far from the High Way. I shall see thee there anon." And with no more ado, she hopped on her broomstick and swooped up into the sky.

"I thank thee," Magnus called after her, then paused to frown a moment in concentration. *Fess! There is a clearing toward the north, where these peasants did pass the night! Wilt thou find it, an thou canst, and meet with us therein?*

I shall, Magnus, the horse's thoughts answered. *I have no doubt I will find it.*

Magnus relaxed a little. The imposter might present him with a difficult decision, and he had a notion he was going to need all the advice he could get. He turned to Gregory. "Now, lad! Let the semblance of this clearing fill thy mind."

They both closed their eyes, letting themselves see through Geoffrey's eyes. A second later, thunder cracked around them; the clearing solidified, and was real.

"We are come," Magnus informed Geoffrey.

"And well come indeed," Geoffrey said heartily. *"Now* what shall we do with him?"

"Why, let Gregory lull him to deeper sleep, of course." Magnus knelt down by the unconscious imposter. Gregory followed suit, dropping into tailor's seat and closing his eyes. Magnus stared at the face, so completely like his brother's, and felt with his mind as the imposter's breathing deepened and slowed.

"He sleeps most soundly," Gregory said softly. "He will believe whatsoever thou sayest now, and answer whatsoever thou dost ask."

Magnus started to speak, but caught himself and looked up at a hissing of air, as Cordelia brought her broomstick in for a landing near them. "Well met, sister," he said softly. "Here's one for thy questioning."

Cordelia dropped down to kneel by the imposter, muttering, "Thou mightest do this thyself."

"Aye," Magnus admitted, "yet not so well as thee." It was only partly flattery.

Not that Cordelia was really about to object. Her face settled as she stared at the sleeping boy, her mind probing, asking, following question after question, drawing out seven years of information in a few minutes, at the speed of thought. Her brothers frowned down at the imposter, too, eavesdropping on his thoughts through Cordelia's mind.

They were so intent on the account of the boy's life that they did not see the huge black horse step quietly into the clearing, and move up behind them.

Finally, Cordelia sat back with a sigh. "Thou hast heard. 'Tis indeed a woeful tale."

"Aye." Gregory's eyes were wide and tragic. "Poor lad, to have never known mother or father!"

"Slain by beastmen." Geoffrey regarded his rival with sympathy. "And himself only living by chance, hidden under the fold of a blanket."

Magnus shook his head, scowling. "How cold were they who raised him! How unfeeling!"

"Aye," Cordelia said softly, "yet he loved them, for they cared for his needs."

"Therefore he sought ever to please them," Gregory finished, "and still doth."

Geoffrey shook his head with finality. "There will be no shaking his loyalty to them. He will ever cleave to these enemies of our father's."

"Yet how horrible, to set surgeons to changing his face!" Cordelia protested. "And not once, but thrice!"

"Until he became the image of myself," Geoffrey said grimly, "and his own countenance was clean forgot."

"They have taken away his face," Magnus said softly, "and taken away his sense of self with it. Yet they cannot take his soul."

"I doubt not they would, an they could," Geoffrey said darkly.

"They have allowed him a name, at least," Gregory sighed.

"Bren." Geoffrey said the name slowly, feeling its texture on his tongue. "Odd, to know another name with my face."

Suddenly, Gregory leaned forward with tears in his eyes. "Let us wake him, and tell him how vile are they who reared him! Oh! Let us bid him come home to our mother and father, and grow up with ones who care for him!"

But Magnus stayed him with a hand on his chest, shaking his head with a very dark frown. "'Tis even as we've said—'twould avail us naught. He will never believe evil of his masters; he is loyal."

"Yet what should we do with him?" Geoffrey said softly.

They were all silent, none of them wishing to say it.

"Thou shouldst slay him." Puck was there suddenly, gazing somberly about at each one of them.

They stared at him in horror.

"It would be prudent," Fess admitted. "This child has been bred to mimic Geoffrey, and to oppose him. Further, he has been indoctrinated with beliefs which are the antithesis of your own. If he lives, he will one day be your enemy—and when he has grown, he may have acquired the skills and strategy to defeat you."

"'Tis even as he saith," Puck agreed. "'Twould be best war-lore to now slay him."

The children looked at one another in guilty foreboding. Even Geoffrey's face was haunted.

"Yet thou wilt not, and therefore I rejoice," the elf went on. "To slay a sleeping child would twist thy souls to a course that could only end in devotion to evil. Nay, thou wilt let him live, and I'm glad of it."

Fess nodded in approval. "I must agree. To slay him is the course of prudence—but to spare him is the course of wisdom."

"Yet what shall we do with him, then?" Cordelia whispered.

"Why, walk away, and leave him," the elf answered. "What else?"

They were all silent.

Then Magnus stood, slowly, and turned away.

After a minute, Gregory too stood up, murmuring, "Wake when thou canst no longer hear our footsteps," and turned to follow Magnus.

A moment later, Cordelia followed him.

Finally, Geoffrey rose, face thunderous, and went after them.

Puck heaved a sigh of relief and disappeared into the brush.

As they went out of the clearing, Geoffrey said darkly, "This is unwise, brother. An we let him live, we allow a viper to flourish."

"Yet he himself hath done no evil," Cordelia pleaded. "At the least, brother, let him grow up!"

"Aye," Magnus agreed. "That much is the right of every child."

"Well, I will be ruled by thee in this," Geoffrey grumbled. "Yet I prophesy, brother, that he will bring disaster upon our heads when we're grown!"

Magnus walked on for a few paces, not answering. Then he said, "What sayest thou to that, Gregory?"

"Geoffrey is right in this matter," Gregory answered. "We must begin to prepare ourselves for that battle."

15

The children made their way through the forest, unnaturally quiet, the thought of the false Geoffrey weighing on all their minds.

Suddenly, Fall popped up next to Cordelia's knee. "There's one who doth ask for thee."

They all stared at her.

Then Cordelia found her voice. "For me?"

"For all of thee. He is of a size with thee, little lady, and hath wandered into the wood unaccompanied."

"A boy?" Magnus and Geoffrey exchanged puzzled glances. "Who could be seeking us?"

"What name hath he?" Cordelia asked.

"His name is Alain, and he doth say he is a prince."

"Alain!" Cordelia clapped her hands, and the boys grinned. "Oh, bring him! Bring him!"

Fall smiled, relaxing. "Well, if thou dost know him. Elves unseen hath led him toward thee for a day now—he did first seek thee some leagues away, near Runnymede."

The children looked at one another, wide-eyed. "Why, that cannot be far from the Royal Palace!"

"'Tis even so," Fall agreed. "He did sit 'neath a pine, calling, 'Wee folk, come and aid!' And they saw 'twas but a child, so they came near, yet not too near, and showed themselves, asking, 'What aid dost thou seek?' And he bade the elves take him to thee. Yet they would not, without thy consent; for aught we knew, he might have been thine enemy."

"Nay, he is our friend! Or as close to one as we have." Witch-children didn't find many playmates. "Wilt thou bring him to us?"

"Assuredly, an thou dost ask it." Fall ducked away, and Summer followed her.

"'Tis most dangerous for a prince to be abroad alone," Magnus said, frowning. "Doth he not know his father's ene-

160

mies could seize him and hold him hostage, to threaten the King?"

"Alain doth not think of such things," Geoffrey said, with some assurance; he'd spent enough time scrapping with the prince to know him pretty well.

"Yet assuredly, his bodyguards do! How have they permitted him to wander by himself?"

Geoffrey grinned. "I misdoubt me an they *permitted* him."

None of the children wondered why Alain was looking for them. After all, who else did he have to play with? His own brother was smaller than Gregory.

The boy came around a huge oak tree, following the two fairies who skipped before him. He wore a flat, round cap, leather breeches tucked into his boots, and a surcoat of stout green broadcloth; but the waistcoat beneath it was of gold brocade, and his shirt was of silk.

"Alain!" Cordelia squealed.

The prince looked up, saw her, and his face burst into a grin of delight. He ran toward them. The fairies dodged out of his way. He threw his arms around Cordelia, crying, "'Tis so good to see thee!" Then he whirled away to pump Magnus's hand. Geoffrey stepped up to throw him a companionable punch in the arm. Alain spun with a left hook that sent Geoffrey sprawling. He leaped up and waded in, fists clenched and grinning, but Magnus stepped between them. "Nay!"

"'Tis but in good friendship," Geoffrey protested.

"Aye," Alain agreed. "How else do two warriors greet one another?"

"With raised visors and courtly bows! Blows arouse tempers, and spoil friendships!"

Geoffrey made a rude noise. Magnus glared at him.

Gregory tugged at Alain's arm. "Where is Diarmid?"

"At home, with our mother," Alain explained. "Father bade me also to bide with her, but I could not stand it."

"Even so," Geoffrey sympathized. "'Tis hard, when battles are brewing."

"Oh, aye, but an 'twere naught but that, I'd never have disobeyed him."

"He is, after all, thy liege as well as thy father," Magnus agreed. "What matter's of great enough moment to bring thee out 'gainst his command?"

"And why dost thou seek us?" Geoffrey crowded in. "'Tis not as though 'twere playtime."

"'Tis not, in truth," Alain agreed, "but I know not to whom else I may turn. I am greatly afeard for my father." Suddenly, he looked very serious, even somber. Nothing had changed in the way he stood, but the children were somehow reminded that he was a prince.

"We can do but little," Magnus hedged. "We are not, after all, our parents."

"Yet what power we do own, is thine!" Geoffrey avowed. "What moves, Highness? Wherefore is thy sire in such straits?"

Alain looked from one to the other of them, and his eyes glowed with gratitude; but he said only, "The barons have risen in chaos, brawling and warring against one another like drunken serfs on a feast-day. Father hath marched out to pack them singly home."

Geoffrey scowled, and Magnus asked, "Do their dukes naught to bring them to heel?"

Alain shook his head. "And 'tis in my mind that they do let their vassals test the King for them, ere they do commit their own armies."

"And their sons," Geoffrey reminded. "Thy father doth still hold the heirs of the twelve great lords as hostages, doth he not?"

Alain wrinkled his nose. "Aye, and a noisome lot they are, forever swilling up ale and pestering the serving-wenches— and brawling amongst themselves."

The children nodded, without saying anything; they had understood for some time that Alain's friendly feelings toward them had a lot to do with the quality of the only alternatives available. "The dukes act prudently, then," Geoffrey said, "yet mayhap not wisely."

"Aye," Alain agreed. "This is their chance to gain Father's trust again, they who rebelled against him so long ago . . ."

(It was thirteen years.)

". . . yet they will not. Nay, he'll never trust them more, when he hath won through." The prince's face darkened, and the children knew what he was thinking without reading his mind—*if* his father won.

"But there's no question that thy father will win!" Geoffrey cried. "They are only counts. A King with a royal army should have little trouble with them!"

"Aye," Alain agreed, "yet there's this upstart of a Shire-Reeve."

The children stared.

Then Magnus frowned. "Surely a Shire-Reeve cannot be greater trouble than a count!"

"This one may be," Alain said. "He hath gathered an army in but a few days' space."

Geoffrey glanced at Magnus. "This must have begun ere our parents were taken."

Alain stared. "I had heard thy parents were stolen, and it did grievously trouble Their Majesties—but how is't thou hadst already heard of the Shire-Reeve?"

"We did meet with a peasant wench who did taunt a plow-boy 'til he did march off to join the Shire-Reeve," Magnus explained.

"She did nearly bewitch Magnus and Geoffrey into a-joining with him, too," Gregory piped up.

Geoffrey flushed and turned to swat his little brat, but Cordelia blocked his swing. "Aye, they would most gleefully have marched away with her!"

"Praise Heaven they did not!" Alain went pale at the mere thought of the Shire-Reeve with the powers of Magnus and Geoffrey behind him.

"Nay, praise Puck—for he did break her spell," Cordelia informed him. "Be sure, she was a witch of a sort." She turned to her brothers. "Do not regard me so darkly—there's no shame in being enchanted!"

But Magnus said only, "There is," and turned back to Geoffrey. "I should not think a mob of plowboys would trouble thy father—they are raw, untrained in battle."

"They have already fought with three counts, and have won," Alain said grimly, "and many soldiers from those defeated bands were eager to join with the Shire-Reeve. Nay, he hath an army as large as Father's now, though not so well-trained or experienced."

"And certes not so well led!" Geoffrey affirmed. It wasn't flattery—King Tuan was an excellent general.

"My thanks," Alain said with a bow, "and I own, I would not be concerned were it but a matter of the Shire-Reeve—but five counts have marched up behind Father's army."

Geoffrey stared; then he frowned. "'Tis odd that five should act together, when they have but lately been battling one another."

"It is, in truth," Alain concurred. "Yet I have heard Father say that many of the noblemen have taken seneschals, whom he did not like, and I think they may have counseled their counts."

The Gallowglass children exchanged glances. *'Tis those minions of SPITE that Father hath told us of*, Magnus thought.

Aye, yet he did not know that they had come as seneschals, Geoffrey answered.

Mayhap he did, but did not tell us, Gregory added.

They shared a moment of indignation at the thought that their father might not keep them up-to-date on matters of state.

Then Geoffrey turned to Alain. "Still, though, these counts are little threat, unless by hap they all attack together, and that when thy father's engaged in battle with this Shire-Reeve."

"Even so," Alain said, "yet that is just what I fear."

Gregory nodded. "The King is, after all, the greatest stumbling-block in each one's path. An he were defeated, each could seek to enlarge his own demesne without let or hindrance."

"Save for their dukes," Alain said darkly, "and if Father were..." he swallowed. "...if Father were gone, the great lords most probably would whip their vassals right smartly into their places."

"Aye, then march 'gainst each other," Magnus said, frowning, "and make one great turmoil out of our fair land."

"And whiles they were battling one another, the Shire-Reeve would no doubt serve them as he would have served the King," Geoffrey added "battling one, while another doth attack from the rear—and, by the time the dukes did band against him, his army would have grown too great to defeat."

"The fools!" Magnus cried. "Do they not see that, if they aid him now, this Reeve will presently reave them, one by one?"

Alain stared. "Dost thou think he doth seek the throne?"

"I am certain of it."

"Yet how can he?" Alain protested. "He is of common birth, scarcely a gentleman!"

"He doth see no bar in that," Magnus said. "Nay, for such an one, that is all the more reason to seek to rule!"

Alain's eyes narrowed; his face darkened. "'Tis a vile churl, then, and doth deserve to be drawn and quartered!"

Magnus nodded. "Such an one could rend this land asunder—for even an he did win to the throne, ever would barons rise up against him; they could never respect his right, sin that he hath not royal blood!"

"Nor would any man honor him," said Cordelia, "for each commoner would think, 'He is lowborn, and hath won to the throne; wherefore should not I?' And one after another would rise up to challenge him."

"The country would ever be rent in warfare," Alain groaned. "Never would there be peace!"

"Yet that is just as this Shire-Reeve's masters do wish," little Gregory said.

Alain stared. "What! How is this? Doth this miscreant have a master?"

The Gallowglasses exchanged glances. "We cannot know that . . ." Magnus hedged.

"Yet thou dost suspect it! Nay, tell me! To withhold thy good conjecture would be treason!"

"Only an we guessed truly," Magnus sighed. "Yet we have cause to think this Shire-Reeve was set up by enemies of Papa, who do seek to plunge this whole land of Gramarye into chaos."

Alain frowned. "Father hath never spoken of such."

"Papa may not have spoken to him of it," Cordelia explained. "He is loath to speak until he is certain."

I would not quite say that is accurate, Fess's voice said in the Gallowglasses' minds.

But Alain couldn't hear him, of course. He shook his head. "He should never withhold such suspicion—yet I can comprehend it; Father would tell Mother, and she is forever fretting about troubles that may come, but do not."

"Yet the trouble hath come indeed," Geoffrey said, "and we do know of our own that Papa hath enemies of another sort—ones who do wish to steal thy parents' thrones, and rule Gramarye more harshly than ever they have."

Alain stared. "Assuredly thy father must have spoken to Their Majesties of this—he must needs be certain of it!"

"Mayhap he hath," Magnus said quickly, "but thy father hath not yet seen fit to tell thee. We all are yet young."

"Mayhap," Alain agreed; but he glowered at the thought.

"Yet here's a quandary," Cordelia interjected. "Did we not, t'other night, hear one of those men say that the Shire-Reeve was one of *their* vassals?"

The children stared at one another.

Then Gregory nodded. "Aye, they did say so."

"In point of fact," Fess reminded them, "they did not *say* it; Cordelia read it in their leader's mind. Her exact words were, I believe, 'Their thoughts leapt to the Shire-Reeve; he hath been their man for many years, and they have told him exactly what they wished him to do when the chance came.'"

The children didn't quibble; they knew Fess always remembered everything exactly as it happened—Papa had used him to give evidence in family quarrels often enough.

Alain frowned. "Yet how can that be? Didst thou not but now tell me the Shire-Reeve did have support from men who wished no rule at all?"

"We did," Magnus verified, "and so we did believe. How now, my sibs? How can the man fight for both sides?"

"Why, by fighting for neither!" Geoffrey cried in excitement. "He lets each believe he's their man—but in truth, he fights only for himself!"

"Aye!" Alain caught his enthusiasm. "He doth play a double game, doth play them off 'gainst one another!"

Geoffrey nodded, eyes glowing. "They believe they use him—but he truly seeks to use *them*, taking support from each, yet plotting in private to cut out both, root and branch, as soon as he doth have power!"

"The very thing!" Cordelia concurred. "He could quite easily deceive those who seek chaos, for he doth seem to be only one more ambitious fool, seeking to gain land by battle—and his ambitions are so great that he could equally deceive those who seek to rule all the land, and with an iron fist!"

"Yet in truth," Magnus agreed, "he doth seek to gain the throne, not mere rule, and to beget kings—and this by deceit and craft, as much as by force of arms."

Alain was trembling. "Of such stuff are kings made, I fear—though very evil kings."

"This one shall not be a king," Geoffrey avowed. "Not of any sort."

Gregory chirped, "Have we found our Great Nasty?"

16

"We should take the left fork."

Magnus halted, and Cordelia's unicorn who had appeared just as Cordelia needed her, stopped, unwilling to come too close to one of the boys. Fess stepped up behind Magnus, who frowned down at the younger boy. "Wherefore, Alain?"

Alain scowled up at him, then shrugged. "It matters not. I am a prince, and I say it; therefore we should take the left."

"Yet it may not be the wisest thing," Gregory demurred.

"Hush, nutkin!" Alain said impatiently. "If a prince saith it, 'tis wise."

"Mayhap we should discover where each goes," Cordelia suggested.

"What need? I am a prince!"

Geoffrey had had enough. "Directly and to make no ado, your Highness—thou dost not yet command, nor need we yet obey."

Alain rounded on him, furious. "Thou wilt heed the Blood Royal!"

"Heed it, aye. Obey it, nay."

Alain drew back a fist, but Magnus caught it. "Be still, the pair of ye! Alain, when thou art grown, I will take thy commands, and gladly—but for now, I am eldest, and age is of greater import than rank."

"But I am a *prince!*"

"And I am the Puck!" boomed the resident elf. "The High Warlock and his wife have set me to govern their bairns in their absence, and I will—so an thou dost wish to accompany us, thou art welcome; but thou must needs mind thine elders!"

Alain scuffed at the ground with a toe.

"Even Robin will not bid us choose, when he knows not what lies at the end of each road," Cordelia said gently.

Alain looked up at her with gratitude, and for a moment, his face softened, almost to the point of idiocy.

Geoffrey saw, and smiled a cynical smile. "What! Wouldst thou heed a woman?"

Alain turned on him, fists clenching and face thunderous.

"So long as thou dost not heed my brother," Magnus murmured.

Alain looked up at him, startled, then smiled, his eyes glowing. "Thou hast ever the truth of the matter, Magnus!"

Geoffrey glared, but just then Summer and Fall popped up from the left-hand fork, shaking their heads. "There's naught down that road save a woodcutter's cot."

Puck queried. "How far didst thou pursue it?"

"To its end—mayhap a league."

Puck shrugged. "Let us hope Kelly hath found summat."

Leaves rustled, and a green top hat popped up with Kelly under it.

"Well come!" Puck cried. "What moves?"

"Naught but an army or three," Kelly said with nonchalance.

"At last!" Magnus sighed, but Puck demanded, "Whose?"

"The Shire-Reeve's." Kelly grinned. "At the least, I *think* it be he, for his arms have no crest, and his soldiers, no livery. Nay, it must needs be he, for his horses are great, rangy beasts, straight from the plow, not fit for a knight."

"What other armies are there?" Geoffrey asked.

"The King's, but 'tis on the far side of the hill, and between them lies a field of wheat."

"'Tis destined to become a field of battle," Geoffrey muttered.

"And at his back lies a river—yet there are two fords for the crossing of it, and five counts' armies beyond. None have more than a half-dozen knights and a few hundred men-at-arms—yet together, they're a force to be reckoned with."

"An they can fight in unity," Geoffrey added.

"'Tis even so." Puck turned to Alain. "Well enough—we have found the enemy. From this time forth, matters may become exceedingly dangerous—and we cannot risk the heir apparent. Thou wilt go home!" He transferred his glare to Kelly. "And thou shalt accompany the Prince, to ward him!"

"Nay!" cried Alain, and, "Niver, ye scoundrel! What! Would ye make a nanny of me?" howled Kelly.

"I am not a baby," Alain said, glowering.

"Nay, thou art nine now, and fully come into childhood. Yet thou art the heir!"

"Yet I've a smaller brother at home!"

" 'Tis for thy father to place thee at risk, not for me!"

"But he'll never do so!"

"Nay, he will—when he doth believe thou art a strong enough fighter. Yet that waits till thou art sixteen, lad, or older."

"That is seven years!" Alain wailed.

"Enjoy them whilst thou may," Puck advised him, "and I shall see thou art alive to do so. Now go to safety!"

"Wherefore do *they* stay?" Alain pointed at the Gallowglasses.

"For that they are in my care, and must stay where I do— and for that they've no parents to be sent home to. Fear not—I'll keep them as safe as thou wilt be."

"Oh, nay!" Geoffrey protested, but Alain bawled, " 'Tis not fair!"

"Nay, but 'tis merciful. Go now to thy mother!"

"I'll not take him!" Kelly declared. "My place is here, with the witch-children!"

"Thy place is wheresoe'er the Hobgoblin doth send thee. What, elf! Wilt thou question the King of Elves?"

"He is not here," Kelly snapped.

"Nay, but he hath given this brood into my care—and wilt command as I do: that the Heir have guard to his parent!"

" 'Tis thou dost say it, not he," Kelly grumbled; but he seemed wary now.

"Shall I ask it of him, then? Nay, thou canst reach to him as quickly as I! Shall we go? 'Tis but a matter of minutes, for elves."

Kelly glowered at him, but didn't speak.

Puck held his gaze level, fists on hips, waiting.

Finally, Kelly snapped, "Well enough, then! It shall be as thou dost say!"

Puck smiled. "Brave elf!" He turned back to Alain. "And wilt thou, too, be as worthy?"

"Where is the worth in retreat?" Alain burst out. "Wouldst thou have me flee from danger?"

"Aye, till thou art grown. What! Must I summon His Elfin Majesty to command thee, too?"

"He may not! I am Prince of Gramarye!"

"And he is a king, who may by right command a prince— yet his power's within himself, not his army, and can be wielded on the moment. Wilt thou go to thy home for safety, or wilt thou be kept on a lily pad?"

"Thou canst not afright me thus!" Alain declared, but he looked less certain than he sounded. "Attempt it, then—and answer to my father for what thou hast done to the Royal Heir!"

Puck reddened, and his voice fell to a deadly quiet. "Wilt thou go, or must I send word to the Queen?"

"Mummy is fifty miles distant!" Alain wailed.

"Aye, yet thy father's but half a league onward—and so is his belt."

Alain glared at Puck for a moment longer, but finally could not hold it. He collapsed with a sigh. "Even so, then. I shall go."

Puck nodded, but showed no sign of victory. He turned to Kelly and said, "Guide him, elf. And see thou he doth come to his parent ere morn!"

When darkness enveloped the forest glade, Puck moved silently among the sleeping children, shaking them and murmuring, "Wake. The moon is up, as thou must be, also."

One by one, they sat up, stretching and yawning.

"I could sleep the night through," Geoffrey sighed.

"Do so, then!" said Magnus. "Puck and I will suffice to tend to this Shire-Reeve."

"Nay," Geoffrey said quickly. "I am fully awakened."

Cordelia lay nestled against the unicorn, who lay on her side, tummy against the girl's back. Now she sat up, blinking, cuddling Gregory against her. That meant the little boy had to sit up, too, but as soon as he did, his eyes sagged shut again.

"Do thy best to waken him," Puck advised. "Thou two must be most alert, when we do return."

Cordelia kissed Gregory on the forehead and gave him a little shake, murmuring, "Waken thou, mannikin." Little Brother lifted his head, blinking; then his eyelids closed, and so did hers. Cordelia shook her head and turned to Puck. "He shall be wakeful, when thou dost return."

Puck nodded and said, "Keep safe, then. Fairies do watch thee." He turned to Magnus and Geoffrey. "Let us go. I have been to the Shire-Reeve's tent already, and long did I wait till he ceased his work with parchments, and lay down to sleep; yet now he doth slumber, and I've deepened his sleep with a spell."

Magnus nodded. "Aye, let us away."

Puck caught their hands and nodded. All three disappeared.
With a boom, air rushed in to fill the space where they'd been.

Two young men stood guard at the door to the Shire-Reeve's
tent. One had been a member of the Reeve's trained band of
armed men for several years; the other was a raw recruit, a
shepherd boy, who kept watching his veteran partner closely,
trying to imitate him, holding his pitchfork the same way the
constable held his pike.

Something exploded inside the tent. The two men whirled
about, staring. They heard the Shire-Reeve cry out, then heard
the explosion again. The two men stared at each other in
alarm, then crashed together as they both tried to jam through
the tent flap at the same time.

They tumbled in, weapons at the ready, staring about them
wildly.

"Hold up the tent flap," the veteran barked.

The shepherd turned and yanked the flap high. Moonlight
streamed in, enough to show them the Shire-Reeve's cot,
empty.

In the forest glade, the two boys appeared with a thunder-
crack, a full-grown man held horizontally between them. His
feet dropped to the ground, and he thrashed his way upright,
shaking off the boys' hands. "Witchcraft! Vile dwarves,
who . . ."

He broke off, staring at the small figure confronting him,
only as high as his knee, but with a very stony look on his
face. "Thou, who dost nail up Cold Iron over every door, and
dost never leave milk for the brownies," Puck grated, "wilt
now face the Puck!"

While the Shire-Reeve stood silent for just that one moment, Cordelia, in the shadows, stared at the quarterstaff that
lay hidden in the grass. It leaped up and cracked into the
Shire-Reeve's head. He fell like a pole-axed steer.

The Shire-Reeve awoke, frowning against a splitting head-
ache. He tried to sit up, but couldn't lift his arms to support
himself. In sudden panic, he thrashed about, trying to move
his hands and legs, but found they were lashed securely together, with the arms bound tightly to his sides. He looked
about him, panting, wild-eyed, and saw four children of vary-
ing sizes, gazing down at him. A shadow moved behind them;

he recognized it for a huge black warhorse with glowing eyes, and a chill ran down his back. Then something stepped up beside the horse into a patch of moonlight, and he saw a silver head with a long, straight horn spearing out from the forehead —and centering on him. The chill spread into his belly, and turned into dread.

"Look down," suggested a deep voice.

The Shire-Reeve did, and turned completely cold. There, in front of the children, stood a foot-and-a-half-high elf with blood in his eye.

"Be honored," the mannikin grated. "Few mortals ever do see the Puck."

The Shire-Reeve lay stiffly, panting, wide-eyed. Frantically, he strove to compose himself, to collect his thoughts.

"I know thee," Puck said. "Thou art Reginald, son of Turco, who was squire to Sir Bartolem—and thou dost call thyself 'squire' too, though thou hast no right to it, sin that thou hast never borne a knight's armor, nor cared for his horse."

The middle-sized boy started at that, then glared down at the man.

The Shire-Reeve nodded, trying to slow his breathing. He swallowed and said, "Aye." He swallowed again and said, "Then the Wee Folk are real."

As real as thou, but with a deal more sense," Puck said with sarcasm. "*We* do not make spectacles of ourselves, flaunting our power for all men to admire—or women, in thy case."

Reginald's face darkened. He was glad of the anger he felt; it helped restore him to himself.

Puck nodded toward the children behind him and said, "I can see in thine eyes that thou dost dismiss these children as being of no consequence. Thou art a fool; they are the High Warlock's brood."

Reginald stiffened, staring from one little face to another.

Puck nodded. "Aye, thou hast cause to fear them. They will have little mercy for the man who did kidnap their parents."

"I did not!" Reginald cried. "Who saith this of me? 'Tis a false lie!" And it was, in a way—he had only spoken with those odd scrawny men with the gaunt faces and the wild looks in their eyes, telling them that the King was a tyrant, and so was Earl Tudor and even Count Glynn. He had claimed to believe all the noblemen were, and had sworn he wished to destroy them all, letting the people live freely on their own, with none to oppress them. And the odd men had smiled, eyes glittering, and promised to aid him in any way they could—they were wizards, after all, and owned a kind of magic that few witches knew of.

So he had asked them to kidnap the High Warlock and his wife.

All of that passed through his mind as he stared at the elf with the High Warlock's children behind him, their faces growing darker and darker with anger. He hadn't asked enough of the weird men; he should have asked them to take the children, too. . . .

He let none of that show in his face. He only said stoutly, "I did not abduct the High Warlock!"

But the children didn't believe him, he could see it in their faces. With a sinking heart, he remembered that they were warlocks and a witch, and that they could hear thoughts. "'Tis not true!" he burst out; but the elf only said, "We had guessed already what thou hast thought. Yet who put this notion of conquest into thy mind? Was it the other wizards, they who go about dressed as peasants and speak to the common folk of their miseries? Or didst thou come to think of it by thine own self?"

"Nay, 'tis all false!" Reginald insisted. "I did but seek to keep the peace in mine own shire! And when I saw there were bandits throughout all of Tudor, I marched out against them!" He tried desperately not to think of those scabrous, tattered men coming to him when he was, very truthfully, only seeking to keep the peace, which did not take much doing—only the occasional poacher, and the peasant who drank too much on a feast day; but it was enough to earn the King's silver, and keep him in his grand, stone house. But those false peasants with the burning eyes had convinced him he could have more, so much more—the whole Earldom, perhaps even the whole kingdom! And they were right, it was possible—for he had an army now, and those magical weapons the wizards had given him! He would defeat the King, with the aid of those foolish counts. Or, rather, with the help of the other wizards, the ones who said they were spiteful, and who swore they could persuade a few of the counts to attack the King from the rear. For a moment, the fear clamored up in him—what if they did not? What if he attacked the King's army, and found himself fighting alone?

Then he thrust the fear down. It was needless; the wizards had sworn he would win, both the peasant ones and the spiteful ones.

"The King hath the aid of the Wee Folk," Puck grated, "and the magic of all the royal witches and warlocks—and even these half-fledged ones are mighty. Be sure, an thou dost fight His Majesty, thou shalt lose."

For a moment, panic seized Reginald. Could the elf speak truly? But he forced the fear down; the goblin was only trying to frighten him, to defeat him by destroying his confidence! Yet Reginald would confound him; Reginald would face the King and beat him. But he would not go on to take the title of "dictator," as the peasantish wizards wished him to, nor would he set up their odd system of officials to control every aspect of the people's lives. Neither would he continue to battle the noblemen and kill them all off, letting the serfs and peasants run riot, as the spiteful wizards wanted him to. Nay, he would seize the crown!

"Thou dost seek to establish thine own dynasty." Puck glared into Reginald's eyes, and the Shire-Reeve felt as though they pierced him to his very soul. "Thou dost seek to beget sons, who will take the title of King from thee when thou dost die."

"Nay!" Reginald said. "'Tis not one word of truth in it!" But there was, of course—and not just one word, but every word.

Puck looked up at the children. "Thou hast heard his thoughts—he doth seek to rule. Yet he hath neither the wit nor the strength for it." He turned back to the Shire-Reeve. "Thou wilt finish by serving the ends of the spiteful wizards —for of such ambitions as yours, is anarchy bred."

The Shire-Reeve stared into Puck's eyes, and realized that the elf and the children had heard even the thoughts he'd sought to suppress. With a sinking heart, he read his doom in their faces.

"What shall we do with him?" Magnus whispered.

A brawny forearm slammed into his face, and a knife-point poised in front of his eye. "Hold!" snarled a voice like a broken garlic bottle. "Witch's brat!"

On the other side of the knife, Magnus saw another soldier

with a sword pricking his sister's stomach and, beside her, Gregory at arm's length over a third soldier's head, squalling with terror, about to be thrown. Terror for his younger brother galvanized Magnus. Without even thinking, he aimed the emotion with the old sorcerer's torture-spell, and the third soldier screamed in agony, clutching his head as burning pain stabbed through it, dropping Gregory. The little boy drifted downward and landed as lightly as a feather.

Geoffrey was struggling and kicking in a fourth soldier's arms. A rock shot up off the forest floor and crashed into the second soldier's head. He gave a hoarse shout, then folded, sword dropping harmless to the ground. Cordelia stared at it, and it swooped up toward the soldier holding Magnus.

"Hold!" the man shouted. "An it comes nearer, thou'lt have a blind brother!"

The children froze.

Soldiers stared at them, warily. Then a sergeant barked, and farm boys leaped in to point pitchforks at the children.

The Shire-Reeve grinned. "Well done, Bardolf! Now, Harold—cut my bonds!"

A man-at-arms hurried over to cut through the ropes that held his master. The Shire-Reeve sat up, rubbing his wrists, then caught Harold's arm for support as he climbed to his feet.

How did they find us? Geoffrey thought.

A slender man in herald's livery stepped forth from the group of soldiers with a contemptuous smile.

He is a warlock! Cordelia thought.

The slender man gave her a mock bow. *Dorlf Carter at thy service, lady.*

I wonder that he gives us his name, Geoffrey thought darkly. *Come what may, we'll know who to hang.*

Dorlf glared at him with narrowed eyes. Then he turned to the Shire-Reeve. "Thou shouldst slay that one with no more ado, Squire."

Cordelia's gaze leaped up to him, startled. Then she glared at the pitchfork that was pointed at her tummy.

Magnus followed suit, staring cross-eyed at the dagger in front of his eyes.

The nearest soldier swung his pike up, and would have died in agony at that moment, if the Shire-Reeve had not held up a hand. "Nay, hold! These children are of too great value to be slain out of hand! King Tuan will never dare fight us, so long as we hold these!"

His face hard as flint, Geoffrey gave the telepath a stare like a poniard, and Dorlf shrieked, clapping his hands to his temples, back arched in agony.

"Stop him!" the Shire-Reeve shouted, and soldiers leaped to Dorlf's aid. "Not him, you fools—the child!"

A tendril of smoke spun up from the hand of the soldier guarding Cordelia, and he howled with pain, dropping his sword.

The knife in front of Magnus's eyes glowed cherry-red, and the soldier dropped it with a bellowed oath. Both blades landed in dried leaves; flames bloomed and soldiers shouted in panic, stamping at the blaze.

Dorlf dropped to the ground, unconscious or worse.

"Kill them!" the Shire-Reeve shouted, his face dark with anger.

The soldiers turned on the children, chopping with swords and pikes—but their weapons jerked in their hands and slammed back against their chests, knocking them into the peasant recruits trying to come up from behind.

Gregory clung to Cordelia's skirts and stared at the soldiers behind his big sister and brothers—and pebbles and sticks shot up at them from the forest floor. The farm boys stumbled backward, swearing; then their faces hardened, and they stepped forward again, arms up to guard their faces. But Gregory had found the larger rocks now, which cracked into the soldiers' heads. They bellowed in pain and retreated. One dropped his sword, and it leaped up, whirling in midair like a windmill in a gale, turning from side to side as though it were looking for someone to slice. The peasant soldiers stepped back farther, poised to dart in at the sign of an opening—but there wasn't one.

Fess's hooves and teeth seemed to be everywhere, and the unicorn's horn darted about, bright with blood—but there were a hundred soldiers, and more.

Geoffrey stepped forward, pale with rage. The soldiers in front of him knocked backward, sprawling against the ones behind them to either side as though a snowplow had hit them. The invisible plow moved onward, shooting off bow-waves of soldiers.

No, Geoffrey! Magnus thought; but his younger brother didn't even seem to hear him. He stepped forward, a foot at a time, as though he were wading through molasses. One thought, and one thought only, rang through his mind, again and again, like the tolling of a funeral bell: *The Shire-Reeve! Though I die, I will slay the Shire-Reeve!*

Magnus leaped in behind, adding his power to Geoffrey's, slamming soldiers back against one another. He didn't want to see murder—but if someone had to die, it was going to be the Shire-Reeve, not his brother.

"Slay them!" the Shire-Reeve shouted, pale with fright, and the soldiers leaped in. There were fifty of them, all grown men, and only two young boys. A wave of peasants slammed into the backs of the front rank, and the front rank pitched forward, crashing down on top of the boys. Cordelia screamed in rage, and rocks struck the soldiers nearest the pile—but they fell forward, on top of the stack. Underneath, Geoffrey squirmed, pinned to the ground, fighting for breath he couldn't get; then more soldiers slammed down on top, more and more, pinning him down, and the fear of death seeped through his every fiber. He fought back hysterically, and his brother did, too, repelling the crushing pile above them with every ounce of adrenaline shooting through them. The pile lurched, heaved—and steadied. More soldiers leaped on, and more, collapsing the bubble of telekinetic force that protected the young warlocks, jamming the huge pile of flesh down on top of them, crushing, flattening . . .

A hoarse shout rang through the forest: "For the Queen and for Gramarye!" And, suddenly, soldiers in the royal colors were leaping out of the trees around the clearing, faces shadowed under brimmed metal helmets, the blazon of the King's elite Flying Legion on their surcoats, charging in at the Shire-Reeve's ragtag peasant boys, chopping down at them with pikes, stabbing with long spears. The Shire-Reeve's men turned, with howls of terror and rage, fighting back. Pikes flashed; men dropped with blood pumping from their chests, gushing out of slashed necks. A head went flying; a headless corpse fell to the forest floor.

With a tearing scream, the huge black horse reared, steel hooves lashing out, the unicorn beside it, goring men with its silver horn. The Shire-Reeve's men howled in superstitious fear and crowded back against their own companions in a huge knot, surrounded by King's men.

Through it all raged a great chestnut warhorse with a golden knight on its back, shouting, "Onward, brave fellows!

Onward! For glory and freedom! Hurl the soldiers aside! Hack through to the core! Seize the vile recreant who seeks to slay children!"

"King Tuan!" Cordelia cried, eyes streaming.

The King it was, laying about him, hacking and hewing his way to the pile of men on top of the boys.

That pile exploded with sudden, shattering force, a dozen men flying outward, striking their fellows and knocking them down. An eighteen-inch elf stood where they'd been, face pale with fury, as the two boys scrambled to their feet, gasping for breath.

"Ga-a-a-llowgla-a-ss!" a great voice bellowed, and a small dark body shot from the King's horse like a cannonball, landing beside the two boys, laying about him, two feet high, huge-headed and black-bearded—Brom O'Berin, the King's Privy Councillor, come to defend the children who were his favorites in all the land. He leaped, kicking and slamming punches. Armed soldiers fell back from his blows. Foot by foot, he cleared the path between the boys and Cordelia, and she caught up Gregory and ran to her brothers with a glad cry.

The Shire-Reeve's men turned to face the new enemy—but they were all about, ringing in the whole clearing, crowding in by the hundred, against fifty. The Shire-Reeve's guards fought with the desperation of men who know they cannot retreat; but one young soldier cried, "Mercy! I yield me! Have mercy!" and dropped his pike, throwing his arms up, palms open. A King's soldier yanked him by the collar, hurling him behind and out of the fight, where more soldiers, coming out of the trees, stood ready to catch him and tie him up.

Seeing him still alive, other soldiers began to cry, "I yield me!" "I yield me!" The King's men caught them and pulled them out of danger.

"He is a traitor who yields him!" the Shire-Reeve shouted. "A traitor and a fool! Fight! 'Tis thine only hope—for the King shall hang thee if thou dost surrender!"

"A pardon to any man who yields him!" King Tuan bellowed. "Full pardon and mercy! I shall hang no man who was constrained to fight! Surrender and live!"

"He lies!" The Shire-Reeve screamed; but the King knocked the last bodyguard aside, and his horse leaped up to the Reeve.

The Shire-Reeve howled like a berserker in fury and stabbed at the King, sword-point probing for the eye-slits in the helmet; but Tuan's sword leaped to parry, whirled about in riposte, and stabbed down as the King lunged, full extension. The Shire-Reeve gave a last curdling scream, and his eyes glazed even as the sword transfixed him, piercing his heart. Then he fell, and Tuan yanked the sword free. "Thy master is dead!" he roared. "Yield! What cause hast thou for fighting now? Yield thee, and live!"

The Shire-Reeve's soldiers hesitated, for but a second— but that was enough for Tuan's finest. In that moment, they struck the weapons from their enemies' hands and set the points of their pikes to the throats of the Reeve's men. The enemy shouted, "I yield me! I yield me!" holding up their empty hands, and King Tuan wiped his blade and cried, "Let them live!"

When the soldiers had shackled the Shire-Reeve's officers and led them away, Tuan nodded to his own men. "Let them flee."

Glowering, the legionnaires stood aside, and the Shire-Reeve's peasants blinked up at them, trying to believe they were really free, but afraid they were not.

"I did declare I would not harm any man who hath been constrained to fight for the Shire-Reeve," Tuan said. "Now go, and tell thy fellows what hath happed here."

With a glad cry, the peasant boys turned and bolted.

As they disappeared among the trees, Brom O'Berin rumbled, "Was that wise, Majesty?"

"It was," Tuan said, with full certainty. "They will bear word to the Shire-Reeve's army, and the army will disband, each man going to his home, as most of them wish to do. The remainder will know their cause is lost with the Shire-Reeve's death." Then he turned to the children.

Four chastened and humbled Gallowglasses looked up at him with foreboding—and an apprehensive Puck eyed Brom O'Berin warily.

"We thank thee, Majesty, that thou hast saved us in our hour of desperation," Magnus managed.

"I rejoice that I came in time," Tuan returned. "Yet I trust thou hast learned not to meddle with armies again, till thou art grown!"

"Oh, aye!"

"'Twas dangerous folly, we now know!"

"We will never dare such hazard again!"

Tuan reserved his own opinion about that—and he noticed

that Geoffrey hadn't said anything. Still, he counted his winnings and decided to stand pat.

Cordelia said, greatly daring, "Yet how didst thou know we stood in such great need of rescue?"

Tuan smiled. "For that, thou hast another to thank." He turned to the trees and called, "Come forth, Highness!"

There was a moment's silence; then Alain stepped out from between the trees with Kelly beside him.

The silence stretched; then Puck muttered, "I commanded thee to take him home!"

"Aye, ye did." Kelly's beard jutted up defiantly. "Yet if I had, what would have become of the other children?"

"Would thou hadst ta'en such great caution with all those entrusted to thy care." Brom O'Berin glared at Puck.

Puck looked away. "Who could ha' known the Shire-Reeve had his own tame warlock?"

"Who should ha' known better than the Puck?" Brom retorted.

Puck bit his lip. "I cry thy worship's pardon; I mistook."

"Gentlefolk," Tuan murmured. Dwarf and elf alike fell silent, and the King bowed gravely to his son. "I thank thee for thy timely news."

Equally formally, the Crown Prince returned the bow. "I rejoice that I have been of service." He cast a glance at the Gallowglasses. "Mother was so far away—and 'twas even as Puck said: Father was scarce two miles off!"

"Let him not deceive thee," Tuan said kindly. "He was concerned for thy safety."

"As well he should have been," Brom muttered.

"And I must thank *thee,*" Tuan said to the Gallowglasses, "for thy loyalty. An all my subjects were so true and courageous, I would have little to concern me."

They stood, staring; then Cordelia, blushing, dropped a curtsy, and the boys, suddenly remembering their manners, bowed. "We are only glad that we could aid," Cordelia said.

"'Tis well for me that thou didst. Thanks to thee, this greatest threat to Queen Catharine and myself—and thy friends the princes—is removed; for, due to thine action, I took this Shire-Reeve unawares, yet with honor."

The blush spread to the boys.

Tuan turned to Alain. "Thou hast served me well this day, my son."

Alain fairly beamed.

"Yet I cannot help but wonder," Brom O'Berin rumbled, "how much of what they did was out of fear for Their Majesties, and how much was adventure." He glowered at Kelly. "Thou, I'll wager, couldst not abide the thought of being far from battle."

The elf hunched in on himself, but Puck spoke up. "The fault, my lord, was mine. 'Twas I who led them out against enemies."

"Aye, but the enemy was not the Shire-Reeve," Magnus said quickly. "'Twas a fell giant, who gave us little trouble."

Brom's head snapped up; he stared, appalled.

"Coming to fight the Shire-Reeve was *our* choice," Geoffrey seconded.

"Yet not thine idea." King Tuan bent a stern eye on his son, who seemed to shrink. "I mind me an I bade a certain person to bide at home, for the protection of his mother."

"I could not see thee go against such odds," Alain wailed.

"Bless thee for thy caring, son," Tuan said, thawing a little, "yet I've faced such odds before, and won."

With Papa's aid, Magnus thought; but he didn't say it aloud.

"Yet I cannot pretend I am not happy at the outcome of thy disobedience," Tuan admitted. "Indeed, thine aid was most fortunate."

"Fortunate indeed," Brom rumbled. "In truth, 'twas but good fortune that none of thee were slain, or maimed."

The children shrank in on themselves again.

"He doth but speak the truth," Tuan said, some sternness returning.

"We know," Magnus said, his voice low. "Had it not been for thy timely rescue, we'd ha' been crow's meat this eventide."

"Indeed thou wouldst have," Brom O'Berin agreed. "Therefore, hearken! I now command thee to get to thine home! And sweep, adorn, and wash it, that thy parents may have pleasant housen when that they return!"

"Dost thou think they will?" Magnus's eyes lit.

Brom shrugged impatiently. "A universe could not keep them from thee. 'Tis but a matter of time. Therefore, go!" He glared at Puck. "Directly, to their home! Conduct them, Robin—and let them not linger by the wayside!"

"I go, I go!" Puck cried. "See how I go!"

"Be sure, I will," Brom said.

"Thou also." Tuan fixed his son with a stern gaze. "Thou must not risk thyself further."

"Must I go home then after all?" Alain protested.

The wood was quiet while Tuan gazed at his son thoughtfully. At last he said, "Nay, I think not."

Alain grinned, delighted.

"A prince must learn the ways of battle," Tuan explained, "and this will be a proper chance for learning, now that the Shire-Reeve is felled and there's little danger. These petty barons are not like to combine against me—and, one by one, I may swat them like flies. Yet an thou art with me, my concern for thy safety will hamper me; I will not strike as swiftly and fully as I ought. Therefore must thou promise most devoutly to stay within my tent, whiles I do battle."

Some of the glow left the prince. He lowered his eyes and glowered at the ground, shuffling a toe.

"What!" Tuan cried. "Is a father's commandment not enough?"

"Nay," Alain said reluctantly. "I will obey."

"Yet I bethink me thou wilt forget, and seek to creep out to watch the battle," Tuan said, frowning.

Alain was silent.

"Therefore, I command thee—as thy liege!" Tuan said sternly. "Son or not, thou art my subject—and my vassal!"

Alain drew himself up smartly. "I am, Majesty!"

"Then thou wilt hearken to me, by thy vows as my vassal! Thou wilt stay in thy tent when battle rages! 'Tis thy duty to thy sovereign!"

Alain stared at him. Then he said, "An thy Majesty doth command it, I shall," and his face was full of devotion.

Tuan broke into a smile. "Stout lad! Come, then—for thou and I must hasten back to our army."

"Aye, my liege!" Alain came running, and jumped. Tuan caught his outstretched arm and swung him up behind, on his horse's rump. Alain threw an arm around his father's waist, and turned back to wave to the Gallowglasses.

"Again, I thank thee!" Tuan called back over his shoulder. "Now get thee home, young witchfolk!"

They rode off into the forest, and disappeared among the trees with Brom and the soldiers thronged around them.

Cordelia watched them go with a gleam in her eye.

"And what dost *thou* think, watching that handsome lad so shrewdly?" Magnus teased. "Bethink thee, thou'rt five months older—he's too young for thee."

"Yet he'll not always be so," Cordelia pointed out. "And thou, great lummox of a brother, mayest mind thine own affairs!"

"Of which thou art one," Magnus said, grinning. "Come, sister—gather up thy babe of a brother, and follow our elf."

Cordelia smiled and caught Gregory by the hand. They all turned toward the southern trail, following a chastised, but very relieved, Puck.

17

They meant to go straight home. They tried to go straight home. This time, they did everything they could to go straight home.

Could they help it if they were ambushed?

One minute they were walking down the path; the next, something huge and dark dropped over them with a roar.

"Geoffrey, defend!" Magnus cried, striking—out but the thing just flapped where he hit it.

"Have at thee, villain!" His brother threshed about, but the darkness tangled itself about him. Cordelia screamed, and Gregory bawled—and all of them fought to lift whatever the foul-smelling thing was, with their thoughts.

But nothing happened.

Outside, Fess's battle cry tore the air, underscored by the sound of meaty impacts. Something bellowed, and someone shrieked, then something big struck the ground with a metallic crash. Then the bellow sounded in full rage, and hoofbeats galloped away with a defiant, fading, whinnying scream.

"Praise Heaven!" Cordelia said. "My unicorn, at least, hath saved herself from whatever foul monsters have set upon us!"

"But Fess!" Gregory bleated. "What of gallant Fess?"

For a moment, they all listened frantically, searching for Fess's presence with their minds.

"He is disabled," Magnus said, and all of them felt terror seize them. What could be so mighty as to put the robot out of action so quickly?

There was one being who had done it before . . .

The huge voice roared with victory now, and something squeezed all around them, jamming the four of them up against each other. Then the dark foul-smelling thing yanked their feet out from under them and swung them high in the air, jumbling and knocking against one another, feet up, heads down. They couldn't see a thing, and they all screamed and yelled.

The roar turned into words. "We have them! And their guardian beast lies slain! We have them!"

"So I see," wheezed a crackling old voice, and the sound of it chilled the children. "Hold that sack tightly closed, Groghat! Let them not escape!"

"Nay, Lontar! Fear not—I'll not chance it!"

"But thou didst enchant him!" Cordelia cried to Magnus. "He cannot so much as *think* of injuring us, or any folk, without pain!"

Lontar's voice gave a high, shrill laugh. "But *I* do not hurt thee, foolish child! 'Tis Groghat who doth so!"

"And do gladly, for children who cozened me and gave me pain," the giant grumbled. "Do *thou* prevent them from disappearing, Lontar!"

"Oh, the lass cannot disappear, at the least," a feminine voice said impatiently. "That power's proper only to warlocks."

"Indeed," Lontar's voice wheezed. "And hast thou not noticed, Phebe, that these lads can move objects by thinking at them?"

"Nay, I had not," Phebe answered, her tone surly. "Hold them fast, Lontar!"

"Oh, be easy in thine heart." Lontar cackled. "This spell is new, but 'tis mighty. They'll not be able to use any witch-power they own, the whiles I hold them with my mind. Yet be sure thou dost keep the lads in check, when we loose them in their dungeon."

"I'll answer for the two larger ones," Phebe said, with certainty. "Yet the smallest . . . I ken not. Even babes have never been proof against me, so long as they were male—yet this one scarcely doth notice."

"Well, between us three, I warrant we can contain them all," Lontar chortled. "'Tis well we chanced upon one another. What we could not do singly, we may surely do together."

"I would we had done more with that horned horse," Phebe said bitterly. "She hath gored mine hand to the bone! Aid me in winding this bandage, Lontar . . . Ow! Pest upon her, that she would not let me approach!"

"Having certain powers doth preclude others," Lontar creaked. "Yet I will be pleased with those I do own, for they have brought mine enemies into my grasp. Now these meddling babes shall be forever made still!"

A chill ran down Magnus's back.

'Tis the peasant wench, the sorcerer, and the giant, combined against us, Cordelia thought, terrified. *Is't true what he doth say? Have we no powers left?*

We still can hear thoughts, at the least. Even Geoffrey was on the verge of panic. *Yet for the rest of it ... I do seek, even now, to catch and hold this giant's foot with my mind—yet naught doth occur!*

And I essay to disappear—most heartily, I assure thee! Gregory thought. *Yet 'tis even as thou dost say; I bide!*

Our thoughts do not move. Magnus fought hard against a rising panic.

Magnus—what shall we do? Cordelia's thoughts wailed.

Bide, and hope. And Magnus did—he hoped he sounded more confident than he felt. *We've faced worse.* It was a lie, but no one called him on it. Then inspiration struck, and he thought, *Be mindful—the Puck is yet free!*

By the time they came out of the trees, Gregory had wormed a hole in the side of the bag. "I see a tower," he reported.

"What is its aspect?" Magnus called.

"'Tis overgrown with mosses and ivy, and is hung with rusty chains. Old horseshoes are secured over the doorways and windows, and there's a deal of rusty nails and broken sickles and such hung about it."

"Cold Iron." Magnus's heart sank. "'Tis proof 'gainst the Wee Folk; even Puck may not enter there."

"What will they do with us?" Cordelia moaned.

"This sack is heavy, even for a giant, when 'tis carried so far," Groghat grunted. "Wherefore do we take them to thine home, Lontar? Why not slay them where we found them?"

"What—only slay them, and leave them?" Lontar giggled. "Nay, foolish giant! Wherefore ought we to waste them?"

"Waste them?" Phebe sounded uncertain suddenly. "Why, for what wouldst thou have them at home?"

"Why, for dinner!" Lontar's voice had a gloating sound that made the children shiver. "Hast thou never noticed, Phebe, that the youngest are the most tender? Nay, 'tis rarely that one hath opportunity for such! ... Ahhh!" He shrieked. "Eh-h-h-h, the pain! Yet my revenge upon them is worth it!"

Magnus felt his stomach sink. *I never thought the old man so enjoyed hurting folk, that he would be willing to suffer such pain,* he thought.

With the stab of pain past, Lontar began to boast. "Why, I mind me that I once cast a curse upon a wench who spurned me, so that, henceforth, she would seek to feed upon any who did thereafter seek to befriend her!"

'Tis even as we thought—'tis he did enchant old Phagia! Cordelia thought, horrified.

Then he hath the blood of many upon his head, already. Geoffrey felt anger rising. It helped hide the growing fear; he felt better. *We need have no qualm at seeking our freedom by whatever means we may!*

But Lontar heard their thoughts. "Indeed," he crowed. "And how shalt thou accomplish it?"

The dim light filtering through the sides of the hot, stuffy bag faded and was gone. "We have come into thy fortress," Groghat boomed. "Where shall we bind them?"

"Yonder," Lontar said.

Groghat muttered, and the children heard his feet gritting on stone, felt the bag jounce as he climbed stairs—and climbed, and climbed, and climbed . . .

Finally, rusty hinges groaned, and the bag shifted topsy-turvy. Howling in fright, the children tumbled out. They remembered Papa's lessons and tucked in their chins, so that their heads were at least a little protected as they slammed into the stone floor. The sudden light seemed horribly bright after the darkness of the bag, and they squinted, looking about—to see the old wizard standing in the doorway cackling, with Phebe beside him, looking very somber now, and unsure. Groghat was there behind them, stooping to peer into the room.

Lontar had put on his wizard's robe—dark blue, soiled and greasy, but with the gold of the embroidered signs of the zodiac still gleaming through. His tall, pointed cap, with golden stars and crescent moons upon it, came up to Groghat's chest.

"I'll come for thee anon," Lontar crooned, "when I've heated my cauldron. Enjoy what little time is left to thee whilst thou may. I have given thee my proudest room." He elbowed Phebe aside with a crow of triumph and slammed the door. A rusty bolt ground home.

The children turned to look at the "proudest room," and shuddered. The floor was carpeted in dust, the corners festooned with old cobwebs. The narrow windows let in only a little light, but enough to show piles of rotted cloth here and there. Cordelia took a stick and poked at one of the piles, then pulled back with a shudder. " 'Tis rotted cloth—but in garments!"

"Grown-up's garments?" Gregory asked hopefully.

Cordelia shook her head. "Nay. Small garments—children's."

Magnus felt anger growing. He glared at the pitiful pile, then frowned at the thin rod in Cordelia's hand. "What manner of stick is that? . . . Why, 'tis a switch!"

Cordelia dropped it with a sound of disgust, and wiped her hand on her skirt.

"We should not have restored his heart," Geoffrey said darkly. "He deserved death."

"For once, I fear I must own that thou didst have the right of it," Magnus admitted. "Yet that's past and gone; what remains is our lives. How shall we break free from here, brother?"

His siblings looked up at him, startled at the notion of hope. Then they came alive. Geoffrey sprang to his feet and ran to the window. He jumped up, levering himself onto the sill. " 'Tis a clear drop down, Magnus—naught to support a climb. Eh, if we could fly, 'twould be easily done!" Experimentally, he thought of floating, pushing away against the floor—but he didn't even feel lighter.

Magnus shook his head. "Whatever manner of binding Lontar hath done on our powers, 'tis thorough. Can any of thee do aught?"

Cordelia cast about, and dashed over to a corner with a glad cry. She caught up an old stick, sweeping the cobwebs off it with distaste, and held it out flat in her hands. The straws had almost completely rotted away, but it was a broomstick. She closed her eyes, concentrating furiously—but the stick stayed obstinately still. She threw it from her in frustration. "It doth naught!"

"Nor can any of us," Magnus said glumly. "Alas! What shall we do?" He slumped down, sitting cross-legged, head bowed, dejected.

Geoffrey dashed to him, clasping his arm. "Do not dare to despair! Fight, brother! There must be a way to life!"

Gregory sniffled and burst into tears. Cordelia dashed to him and hugged him against her. He buried his head in her skirts, crying.

"Do thou *not!*" Geoffrey insisted. "Weeping avails us naught! Gregory, *think!*"

"If only Vidor were here!" Gregory wailed. "He would know what to do! His magic's not like ours—it hath not our limits! It doth work by words and by symbols, not by thought only! Assuredly, Vidor would know how to defeat this vile sorcerer!"

Magnus's head came up. "What dost thou say?"

"He said Vidor would know!" Cordelia snapped, glaring at Magnus.

"Aye, I did hear him!" Magnus ran to his little brother, whirling him about and grasping his shoulders. "Gregory, think! Our other powers have been bound, but not our thought-hearing! Canst thou make thy Vidor to hear thee?"

Gregory looked up, wide-eyed, sniffling. "Why, mayhap I can—yet what good . . ." Then his face lit; he smiled. "Aye, certes! He may be able to tell us what magic will defeat this vile Lontar!"

Cordelia beamed at Magnus—but for cheering up Gregory, not for saving them.

Gregory plumped down cross-legged, back ramrod-straight, and closed his eyes.

His brothers and sister watched him in silence. Geoffrey looked fair to bursting, but he kept silent.

Finally Gregory opened his eyes. "Vidor saith that he is too little to attempt any such battle—and that his Papa cannot aid, because he can only reach our world through our Papa's mind."

"And he is not here." Magnus scowled in fury. "Confound! How *may* they aid?"

"Vidor," Gregory said, "hath an older brother."

They were all silent, staring.

"How much older?" Magnus asked finally.

"Seven years. He's of an age with thee, Magnus."

Big brother knelt there, staring at him.

"'Tis our one chance, my sib," Geoffrey said, his voice low. "Thou must needs open thy mind to this . . ." He turned to Gregory. "What is his name?"

"Albertus," Gregory answered.

". . . this Albertus." Geoffrey turned back to Magnus. "Hast thou the courage?"

Magnus swung about at him, glaring. "Mind thy manners, bairn! Still thyself, and behold!" He dropped down beside Gregory, cross-legged, back straight, imitating his little brother. "Is it thus?"

"Aye," Gregory agreed eagerly. "Now close thine eyes..." He closed his own. "Wait.... I've told Vidor; he doth summon Albertus ... Attend ..."

They waited—and waited. Cordelia bit back the urge to scream with impatience.

"Albertus comes," Gregory said finally. "Vidor doth summon his father, also ... Ah, we've good fortune! His father's not far distant! Lord Kern comes ... Albertus is nearly here! Now, Magnus, close thine eyes!"

"I have already," Big Brother said impatiently. "What now, lad?"

"Open thy mind ... widely.... Let all thy body and mind go loose.... Nay, Magnus, I know 'tis most difficult, but thou must needs forget what doth hap, and let thy mind drift.... Now ... follow me. Let thy mind blow where mine doth ..."

They were silent, eyes closed. Cordelia and Geoffrey held their breaths.

They heard footsteps on the stairs.

Cordelia opened her mouth to scream, but Geoffrey clapped a hand over it. She clenched her fists, fighting hard to keep silent, to keep from breaking her brothers' concentration.

"Now, 'tis time!" Lontar called from the other side of the door.

"I like this not," said Phebe's voice.

"Thou wilt be party to it, or thou shalt join with them! Groghat, seize her! ... Aieee! Mine head! The pain ... Nay! Mind me not—but seize her! Yiiii!"

There were sounds of a struggle; Phebe screamed.

"Ah, now," Lontar panted, "thou'rt decided. 'Tis well. One way or another, lass, thou shalt join us for dinner...."

The key groaned in the lock.

Geoffrey whirled, catching up the broomstick and leaping to his feet, stick raised to guard, jumping in front of his sister.

"I have him, Father," Magnus said suddenly. His voice sounded different, somehow—a little deeper, a little more resonant. "His mind doth meld with mine."

The door groaned open. Lontar stepped into the room, giggling; spittle drooled from his lip, and his eyes were wild.

Gregory opened his eyes, turned to look, and grasped Magnus's hand. "Lend him thine eyes, brother!"

"What! Wilt thou fight me, then?" Lontar pointed at Geoffrey, cackling. "Good, good! Exercise doth make a good appetite! Yet I think thou art too tough and stringy—I'll start with another!" He stepped forward, cackling and reaching out toward Cordelia. "Aieee!" His head whipsnapped at the sudden pain, but he squinted against it and came on toward her in spite of it.

Magnus turned slowly, opening his eyes and frowning. He saw Lontar and stretched out his arm, forefinger pointing.

"Ah! The biggest doth see me, then!" Lontar crowed. "Art ready to bathe, lad? The water is hot, and oiled with onions and carrots! Yet thou, too, art like to be tough; we'll start with the smallest! Yi-eeee!" He winced at the pain, but turned toward Gregory anyway.

A bolt of pure energy spat from Magnus's finger with a sound like a gunshot. It struck Lontar square in the chest. The old sorcerer screamed once, falling backward. His whole body heaved; then he lay still.

Phebe and Groghat stared, horrified.

Geoffrey disappeared with a thunder-crack.

Groghat came to his senses, knocked Phebe aside, and charged into the room, roaring.

Cordelia narrowed her eyes, glaring at him. A horde of old nails and scrap iron shot in through the window and crashed into Groghat's face. He howled, batting the stuff aside—but thunder cracked, and Geoffrey appeared on his shoulders. He jammed the brookstick across Groghat's throat and hauled back.

The giant made a gargling sound, eyes bulging, and grasped at the stick—but as he did, his feet shot out from under him, and he slammed down onto the floor with a crash that shook the whole chamber. A lump of old iron slammed into his temple, and he collapsed, unconscious.

Geoffrey turned on Phebe, his eyes narrowed.

She shrank back against the wall, horrified—then remembered herself. She managed a tremulous smile, and stepped away from the wall, eyelids drooping. "Nay, then! Hast thou come for me, young man?"

A wave of attraction seemed to roll out from her, fascinating, binding.

Geoffrey hesitated.

"Have at thee, hag!" Cordelia screamed, and a length of old chain lashed Phebe, wrapping itself around her throat. She gave a horrified scream that choked off into a gurgle—and the broomstick wrenched itself out of Geoffrey's hands to crash into her skull. Her eyes rolled up, and she folded.

Geoffrey drew a long, shuddering breath. "Sister—I thank thee! Remember it well, for I'll say it but rarely."

"'Tis wondrous as 'tis," she returned, and stepped over to Groghat. "Doth he truly sleep?"

Geoffrey stepped over with her, peering down. "Aye, well and soundly. Aid me, sister—roll him over."

Together, frowning, they stared at the giant. His body shook, heaved—and pitched over. "One apiece," Cordelia said tightly, and the giant's hands yanked up behind his back. A length of old chain shot out and whipped about his wrists; then Cordelia glared at two links. They glowed cherry-red, then yellow—then darkened again.

"Well welded," Geoffrey approved. "'Twas on the outside links, and 'twas so quickly done that he's not even burned."

"More's the pity," Magnus grunted.

They spun about, surprised. "Eh!" Geoffrey said. "Thou art come back to us, art thou?"

"Aye," his brother said, "and I gave Lord Kern great thanks for the power he lent us, and Albertus thanks for conducting it to me."

"And great thanks to Vidor," Gregory piped, "for bethinking him that his elder brother might be able to blend his mind with thine, and for summoning him."

"Aye. I thanked him, too." Magnus looked down at Gregory. "If ever they need our aid, lad, we must turn to them instantly."

"Aye, without fail," Gregory agreed. "Yet, Magnus, their Papa did say he was glad of the chance to repay our Papa for his good aid."

"'Tis not a balance of good deeds, but a chain," Magnus averred. He turned to his brother and sister, saw the unconscious bodies, and grunted, "Thou hast worked well, here."

"We had need to find summat with which to pass the time, while certain parties were abstracted," Geoffrey said, trying for nonchalance.

"Whiles we, of course, did play," Magnus responded. He rose, with difficulty. "Eh! But my joints ache!" He stepped over to Lontar and knelt beside him, placing a hand on the vein in his neck.

"Thou'lt not start his heart again!" Geoffrey protested.

"Nay." Magnus drew back his hand in disgust. "There's no need."

"He yet *lives?*" Geoffrey cried in dismay.

"And he called *thee* tough and stringy," Cordelia snorted.

Geoffrey looked about at the three, at a loss for once. "What . . . what are we to *do* with them?"

The brothers and sister exchanged a blank look.

"We cannot leave them to take up their evil again," Cordelia said.

"Aye, but 'tis not for us to say they must die, neither," Magnus answered.

They stared at one another in silence.

Then Geoffrey crowed, "I have it! We shall let Mama and Papa decide!"

"Oh, excellent, brother," Magnus scoffed, "most excellent! Aye, we'll bid Mama and Papa come here in judgment—as soon as we find them!"

"Oh, nay! We know they'll come home, soon or late—so we'll take these vile villains there, to await them!"

Cordelia and Magnus stared at him, floored by the sheer audacity of the plan.

Then Cordelia giggled.

Magnus grinned. "Wherefore not? 'Twill serve them well for going adventuring without us! Come, brother, let's bind them!"

"Aye," Geoffrey agreed, picking up another length of rusty chain. "And who knows? Mayhap Lontar will die on the way!"

Puck and Kelly stared, unbelieving, as the children came out of the doorway at the base of the tower. Then Puck turned to Summer. "To the King, straight away! Tell him they are safe, that he need not come! Scat!"

Summer flew off, casting an indignant look backward at him.

It was wasted; Puck and Kelly were already shooting over the floor of the clearing, straight toward the children.

"Magnus! Cordelia! Geoffrey! Gregory! By Oak, Ash and Thorn! Ye are safe!"

Cordelia managed a smile. "Aye, praise all saints!"

"We could not come to thine aid, for there was so great a deal of Cold Iron hung about that tower!"

"That foul, fell felon," Kelly howled, "who's so craven that he must needs drape his house in all that we dread! 'Tis naught but what ye should look for, from such vile fellows as . . ."

He broke off, staring at the procession of unconscious bodies that floated out of the tower behind the children.

"Eh!" Puck gasped. "How hast thou taken *these* trussed-up fowls?"

"With great difficulty," Magnus assured him, "and only with the aid of some folk who were not there."

"Not there? How is this?" Puck's gaze sharpened with keen suspicion as he looked up at Magnus. Then he stared. "Lad! Thine hair!"

"What of it?" Magnus put a hand to his head, suddenly self-conscious. "'Tis yet there!"

But his brothers and Cordelia were staring, too. "We had not noticed, in all the turmoil," she said, "yet now..."

"What *is* it?"

"I ha' known thee since before thou wast born," Puck avowed, "and ever was thine hair as golden as the crown of a king!"

"Wilt thou not *tell* me?" Magnus exploded.

"Gregory," Cordelia said, "thy friend Vidor—what color is the hair of his older brother?"

Magnus's eyes widened as he began to suspect.

Gregory looked up and blinked. "Black is the color of Albertus's hair, 'Delia."

"And of what hue is mine?" Magnus asked into the sudden silence.

"Black as jet," Cordelia whispered.

"Like the wings of a raven," Puck agreed.

18

It was an oddly-assorted parade that threaded its way through the dappled shadows of the late-afternoon forest—three Gallowglass boys of diminishing sizes, followed by Fess with a witch and a sorcerer slung over his back, and an improvised horse collar around his neck and shoulders, from which two ropes stretched back to Groghat's ankles. Cordelia rode behind the giant on her unicorn, frowning at Groghat as she concentrated on keeping his huge mass just high enough so that he didn't drag on the ground. She didn't worry too much about brambles, though.

The shadows were lengthening as they came out of the forest and saw their home, serene and warm with late afternoon sun, nestling under the huge oak against the hillside.

"'Tis yet there!" Cordelia breathed.

"Praise Heaven," Magnus agreed.

But Kelly suddenly struck his forehead with the heel of his hand. *"Oy vay!* How could I have forgotten?"

"How couldst thou indeed?" Puck asked. "Nay, elf, an thou hast any cause at all to be from us . . ."

"What is it, then?" Cordelia turned to him.

"The fairies' shoes! I had promised two flower-folk to have new slippers for them, for treading of the elfin ring this night! Nay, I must be off to my bench and last!"

"Do not dare!" Puck said, but Kelly was already darting off through the greenwood, crying, "Farewell!"

"He could not, after all, disappoint the two fairies." Cordelia scowled at Puck. "Thou art but mean, Robin!"

"I mean a great deal indeed." Puck glared after the fleeing elf. "Nay, an I catch that son of Erin and Israel again . . ."

"Thou must not injure one who hath shared our trials," Gregory protested.

"Aye, all but the final one."

"What dost thou speak of?" Magnus questioned.

" 'Tis my concern, not thine—and mine alone, now." Puck set his face toward the children's house, looking grim. "Come, children. At last, I believe I have some chance of bringing thee safe to home."

The boys yelped with joy and darted off across the meadow. Fess and Cordelia followed a bit more slowly with the captives, Groghat floating between them, bumping in breezes.

As they came near the door, Geoffrey looked back to check on his spoils of war and frowned. "They do begin to struggle again, Magnus."

Groghat and Phebe were thrashing about against their ropes, and Lontar had opened his eyes, squinting against the pain in his chest.

" 'Twill be merciful to restore them to sleep," Cordelia pointed out.

"Aye, and more safe." Magnus stepped up beside Lontar, glaring down at him. Cordelia let Groghat settle to the ground and rode over to stare at Phebe, and Geoffrey and Gregory took her place near Groghat. They all concentrated, staring at their captives. The thrashing dwindled, then stilled, and the prisoners' eyes closed again.

The Gallowglasses breathed a sigh of relief and turned back to the door.

Cordelia paused. "Where may we put them?"

"Only the parlor is large enough." Magnus rubbed his chin.

Geoffrey clapped his hands. "What could be easier? We'll but clear the table and chairs aside!"

"Mayhap 'tis not the best . . ." Puck began, but the children had already darted in. He sighed and followed, hearing the clatter of furniture moving.

They floated them in by size—Phebe first, then Lontar. Fess lifted his head as the sorcerer's weight came off his back, saying, "Children, your parents might not wish . . ."

"What else might we do with them?" Cordelia called over her shoulder as the old man's feet disappeared into the parlor.

"We might build a shelter," Fess suggested as they came back out.

Magnus shook his head as he untied Groghat's tow-ropes from the jury-rigged collar. " 'Twould have to be a complete cabin to protect them enough from wind, rain, and chill, Fess. Thou wouldst not have us let them catch their deaths, wouldst thou?"

"'Tis a consummation devoutly to be wished," Puck answered, eyes flashing as he watched the giant float into the house.

"Thou art still thirsty for blood, Robin," Cordelia sighed as she passed through the door.

"And what if I am?" the elf growled to himself. "Better their blood than thine, sweet chucks! Sayest thou not so, Walking Iron?"

"In some measure," Fess agreed. "But I must admit, I'm glad to see so much of compassion in them."

Magnus and Cordelia came back out. The boy caught Fess's bridle and led him away toward his stable at the back of the house. "Come now, faithful one! It hath been a long journey. Warm housen and oil for thee now."

"The rest will be appreciated," Fess sighed. "I have much new data to integrate . . ."

They disappeared around the corner of the house. Cordelia turned to her unicorn, and Puck suddenly found something very interesting to study in the patterns of the milkweed that had sprouted by the front door.

"I must bid thee farewell for now, Beauteous One," Cordelia explained, "for my mother would be even more wroth, did she find thee within doors! And thy quest is done now, is't not?"

The unicorn nodded, pawing the turf.

"But oh! Thou wilt not leave me forever, wilt thou?" Cordelia caught the unicorn's head between her palms, gazing up into her eyes. "I shall be so lonely without thee—and shall be forlorn, an I thought thou wert never to see me more! Thou wilt not leave me lorn, wilt thou?"

The unicorn shook her head, and stepped forward to nuzzle her face and butt her velvet nose against Cordelia's chest.

"Aye, thou art still my dear one," Cordelia breathed. "Fare-thee-well, then, till I do see thee again!"

The unicorn stepped back and tossed her head as she turned, cantering away toward the woodland. Just short of the verge, she reared, turning back, and pawed the air, looking directly into Cordelia's eyes; then she turned toward the woodland, her forehooves struck the carpet of dry leaves, and she trotted in among the trees, glimmering in the twilight, and faded from view.

Cordelia stood gazing after the unicorn with tears in her eyes. "She will not forsake me, will she?"

"Not so long as thou dost not wish her to," Puck said softly.

"Oh! How could I ever wish her to!"

"Thou wouldst not," Puck agreed. "Yet the day may come when thou dost crave some other being with greater yearning."

Cordelia shook her head with passion. "Nay, never!"

"Mayhap," Puck sighed, "yet mayhap also . . . Well! 'Mayhap,' and 'mayhap!' Thy world could drown in so many 'mayhaps,' could it not? And thou wouldst not haply be happy thereby. Nay, come away, child! Thou wilt see thy unicorn many times again, I trow, for a span of years more, belike! Nay, come away—I doubt me not an thy brothers have need of thine aid."

He turned away toward the doorway, looking up at her expectantly.

Cordelia smiled down at him through her tears, dried her eyes, and went in.

She found the three captives laid out on the floor by the fireplace and her brothers staring at one another blankly.

"Why dost thou stand idle?" Cordelia demanded. "Has the forest taken thy wits, that thou no longer knowest what to do within doors?"

"'Tis not even that," Magnus protested. "Nay, rather—'tis the management of captives that doth concern me. We dare not chance their awakening."

"There's truth in that," Cordelia admitted, "and who doth know how long 'twill be ere Mama and Papa return?"

"The more reason to be sure of them, then." Geoffrey darted over to the corner, caught up Papa's walking stick, and stalked over to Groghat, standing beside his head, glowering down. "If he doth flutter an eyelid . . ."

"Thou'lt use thy 'sleep spell,' not thy cudgel," Magnus directed. "'Tis safer, and more sure. And I will stand guard over the sorcerer; he might yet give us a bad turn or two." He stepped over beside Lontar.

"Thou must needs sleep, soon or late," Gregory pointed out.

Magnus frowned. "'Tis true. Let us bind them more securely. Geoffrey, dost thou know that coil of rope Papa doth keep in the shed?"

Geoffrey nodded and disappeared with a bang. Air boomed out a moment later, and he was back, a huge coil of rope over his shoulder. He dumped it on the floor and straightened, ex-haling. "'Tis *heavy!*"

"Aye," Magnus replied. "Thy pardon; I should have gone."

"Oh, nay!" Geoffrey said, irked. "Dost thou think me a baby?"

"Never, brother," Magnus assured him. "Now, then—let us do the giant first, whilst we're fresh. Gregory, thou must bind the knots. Geoffrey and Cordelia, now—UP!"

They all scowled in fierce concentration. Slowly, Groghat rose three feet off the floor. The top end of the rope darted toward him like a striking snake, whipped about his body, and tied itself in a square knot.

"Turn, now," Magnus grated.

All three older children tensed.

Slowly, Groghat began to turn, then faster and faster, like a table leg on a lathe.

Gregory frowned at the rope, guiding it as it laid itself in a neat coil all along Groghat's body. When it reached his ankles, he stopped turning, and the rope whipped itself into another knot.

"Now, down," Magnus directed.

The giant's body lowered itself to the floor again.

Cordelia, Geoffrey, and Magnus all heaved a sigh of relief. Geoffrey stepped in to cut the rope with his knife, and stepped back. Then Magnus said, "Now the sorcerer."

They didn't even scowl; Lontar's scrawny body floated up off the floor easily; the rope tied itself; Lontar began to re-volve.

When all three lay cocooned neatly side by side, Magnus and Geoffrey took up their stations again.

"Thou still must needs sleep," Gregory repeated.

"When we do, elves may stand guard; there will be time for us to waken, now that these three are so securely bound," Magnus explained. "They shall call us at the slightest sign of wakefulness. Will they not, Robin?"

"What . . . ?" Puck looked up from chewing his fingernails. "Oh, aye! Be assured, the Wee Folk will be most eager to aid thee in keeping these three from waking in the High Warlock's house! 'Tis bad enough as 'tis," he muttered, turning back to gaze into the cold hearth, chafing his hands.

Cordelia frowned. "What doth trouble thee, Robin?"

"Naught that need worry thee," the elf answered. "'Tis for myself to answer, children. Do thou not be concerned."

Cordelia still frowned but, unable to figure out what Puck was talking about, shrugged and went to the shelves to take up her embroidery. "Well then, sin that it may be some hours or, nay, even days yet, I will seek to pass the time." And she went to sit down by Phebe's feet, keeping an eye on the milkmaid and plying her needle, singing happily.

For himself, Gregory drifted up to the mantelpiece and sat there cross-legged, tailor-fashion, back straight, hands in his lap, gazing down at his brothers and sister fondly, smiling.

Puck looked up at him with a grimace, knowing Gregory's mother had forbidden the mantelpiece, claiming that if it had been intended for sitting on, his father would have carved a chair in it. The High Warlock had instantly volunteered to start whittling, but his wife had vetoed it with a glare and a remark about soot on boys' clothes. Her husband had pointed out that a little soot probably wouldn't make much difference, but mother had been firm, and the mantel had remained a forbidden zone. Puck remembered that now, and started to say something, but caught himself and heaved a sigh. What was one peccadillo more or less? He went back to a glum contemplation of his fate.

Around them, the room darkened into evening. Finally, with an impatient snap of the fingers, Puck summoned some brownies who skipped to light the fire and a few lamps, then disappeared back into their crannies.

Magnus and Geoffrey each sent their prisoners back into sleep again. Phebe began to twitch, and Cordelia looked up at her, briefly. The woman went back to sleep.

Which is how matters stood when the door opened and the High Warlock and his wife came in, with glad cries upon their lips.

The glad cries froze as they saw the scene before them.

Puck took one look at their faces, moaned, and shot up the chimney with a wail of despair.

The children looked at one another wide-eyed, suddenly aware that their behavior might have been a little less than ideal.

Then Mama closed her mouth, and took a deep breath.

But Papa beat her to it. "And just what do you think *you've* been doing?"

Gregory's chin began to quiver. "We . . . we are sorry . . ."

"We will not do it again," Cordelia promised with tears in her eyes.

"We did not *mean* to . . ." Magnus explained, with trepidation.

But Geoffrey squared his shoulders in defiance and stated, "Thou didst not say we *couldn't!*"